Athena's Ordeal

 HABERDASHERS
BOOK TWO

SUE LONDON

Athena's Ordeal: Book Two of the Haberdashers
by Sue London
bysuelondon.com

Amazon Edition
Graythorn Publishing
Copyright © 2013 Sue London
All rights reserved
Cover by Kim Killion, Hot Damn Designs

ISBN: 0991066316
ISBN-13: 9780991066315

For my mom, who made me a Haberdasher at heart.
Strong women raise strong girls.

Acknowledgements

*T*remendous thanks to my editors Kris Silva (@gravewriter71 on Twitter) and Jen Driver-Sylvia (www.thinkjenthink.com). The Haberdashers wouldn't be nearly as engaging (or well-written) without your influence. You went above and beyond.

Thanks to all of the people in the romance writing circle who have made me feel welcome. Especially thanks to Courtney Milan and Rose Gordon for their advice and support. You guys are awesome.

Thank you to my husband who helped to make sure that Quince and Sabre made their debut with love, support, nagging, taking on extra chores, and all those other things that authors need when they hear deadlines whooshing by.

And a huge thanks to the fans of the Haberdashers! Oh my gosh, you guys, my heart has grown at least three sizes from how much you have enjoyed Jack and Giddy's story. Back in the spring I was just a girl with a dream and now you've made that dream come true. Thank you so much for your support! I hope that you find Quince and Sabre's story to be as much fun.

And thanks again to all the people I mentioned in Trials of Artemis — my "friends and family" both in person and online. You guys are awesome and help me make it through every day.

"The hardest thing of all for a soldier is to retreat." ~ *Duke of Wellington*

"The essence of fencing is to give, but by no means to receive." ~ *Moliere*

"A day can press down all human things, and a day can raise them up. But the gods embrace men of sense and abhor the evil." ~ *Athena to Odysseus*

$\mathcal{O}ne$

May 1815, London

Quincy Telford, Duke of Beloin, knew the importance of discretion. Even a duke's power wasn't absolute and at such delicate times as these, a man of discretion was invaluable. That was why, if anyone *had* been attentive enough to notice, the duke would have been found on the doorstep of Robert Bittlesworth this fine spring morning, knocking lightly but politely, without a servant in sight. Even the best servants might not be trusted to be circumspect and on this occasion he could not risk any talk of what he was about. The door was opened promptly by a manservant too young and burly to be a proper English butler. Since Quince didn't want to present a card he simply drew himself up in his best ducal stance and said, "I am here to see Mr. Bittlesworth."

The manservant, noting the overall look of refinement that the duke cultivated, bowed him into the hallway and asked him to wait a moment while it was seen whether Mr. Bittlesworth might, indeed, be in to receive him. As the hallway was better than the street Quince was content to cool his heels looking at the paintings on display. Hearing footsteps on the stairs he turned, expecting to see Bittlesworth, but instead saw a vision that made him catch his breath. A young woman was just at the landing, perfectly highlighted in a beam of light from the second story window. Her hair was the deep, warm sable of a mink and had been gathered at the crown to cascade in a riot of curls down her back. She was petite in stature, her figure a perfect hourglass emphasized by the low cut red dress that hugged her curves. The dress was Italian in design if he wasn't mistaken. Expensive, no doubt, but worth every penny to any man who was fortunate enough to look upon her. Bittlesworth was a lucky man indeed, and brazen to have given his Cyprian free access to his home. As he stared up at her she glanced down and saw him, stopping with a startled "Oh!" She took the remaining steps slowly, and watching those hips coming toward him he had to admit that he would probably give her free rein of his home, as well.

"Good morning," she said after a moment, obviously entertained that they stood in the front hall staring at one another longer than was considered appropriate in polite company.

He had to admit that he was well pleased that this wasn't entirely polite company. Taking her hand to bow over he kissed her finger tips and, looking up, enjoyed another quite spectacular angle of her cleavage. For such a tiny thing she had simply acres of creamy white skin to admire, from her barely covered breasts to her shoulders, teasingly exposed by the drop sleeves of the gown.

"Good morning," he responded in as silky a tone as he could muster. As he straightened he saw that it had the desired effect, as she seemed to preen under his attentions. Her eyes were the color of bright sapphires and light danced in them from her good humor.

"You have me at a disadvantage, sir," she said, "as Bobbins has been derelict in his duties again and not announced you."

Still holding her hand and staring down into her beautiful face he came to an impulsive decision. He would have her, at any price. He had never wanted a woman, or really anything, quite like this. As though leaving without her was impossible, unconscionable. He rushed to claim her before his own fear, his inexperience in bargaining for such a woman, could stop him.

"Whatever Bittlesworth is paying you, I'll double it. Triple it. You'll never want for anything again in your life."

The change in her expression was so sudden it was almost shocking. The humor was gone and she was so expressionless as to be carved from stone.

"Pardon me?" she asked.

As Quince searched his mind for what to say to bring back the delightful fairy queen she had been and, better yet, to convince her to leave with him, his thoughts were interrupted.

"Your grace, I didn't realize it was you."

The Duke of Beloin released the young woman's hand and turned to see Robert Bittlesworth, who had apparently emerged from some room here on the first floor while Quince hadn't been paying attention. "That's rather the idea, old boy," his normal hauteur having returned to his tone.

Bittlesworth paused and then said, "Quite." He looked from the young woman and then back to the duke. "I trust my sister hasn't been too tiresome?"

The last time Quince remembered being this lightheaded was when he let his friend Giddy talk him into going three rounds with Gentleman Jackson. Apparently a sharp uppercut from a man nearly twice your size had exactly the same effect as deeply insulting the younger sister of a gentleman that you had hoped could save you. But just as he had borne up under Jackson's pounding as best he could, the duke barely faltered in his response now. "She has been delightful." Quince's eyes swung back to the dark-haired beauty who remained expressionless. Holding her gaze he said, "And I trust she can be discreet as well?"

The young woman raised her chin a notch as though accepting his challenge while her brother said, "Of course. Perhaps you would be more comfortable in my study?"

"Indeed," Quince said. Nodding to the young woman he said, "Miss Bittlesworth."

Bowing into a low curtsy she said, "Your grace."

Quince doubted that he had escaped so easily after such an insult, but beggars couldn't be choosers so he let Robert Bittlesworth lead the way to a small but well-appointed study so that he could explain his issue to the Hero of the Home Office.

Sabre, or as she was more formally known Sabrina Bittlesworth, stood quite still in the hallway for a few moments after Robert and his guest had left. She had heard of having your blood run cold before but had never experienced it herself. Until today. Until this supposed duke had mistaken her for some sort of…some trollop. When Bobbins returned to the front hall she proceeded with her original plan to call on her friend Jack, who, as of earlier this spring, was now Jacqueline Wolfe, Countess of Harrington. As she rather precisely put on her gloves, bonnet, and pelisse, she thought that's what one's oldest and dearest friends were for, someone to take comfort in when the day wasn't going quite as planned, and Jack would certainly be comforting. Looking down the hallway toward Robert's study, Sabre wondered when her other oldest, dearest friend Georgiana would come home from Scotland. Rather than comfort, George would just sneak down the hallway and poison the dratted duke's tea. Or at least threaten to, and that would be heartening. With a final tug to tighten her bonnet strings Sabre sailed out the front door of her brother's house and into the waiting carriage.

Having shut the study door, Bittlesworth wasted no time on pleasantries. "How can I help you, sir?"

"You've gathered this isn't a social call?"

Bittlesworth remained silent at that, waiting politely.

Quince realized he was glancing around the room and being in general more awkward than was his usual mien. Taking a deep breath he consciously forced himself to relax. "I'm being blackmailed."

"I see," Bittlesworth said, pausing. "Brandy?"

"That would be lovely," Quince agreed. Bittlesworth indicated a comfortable set of matching leather chairs near the fireplace and Quince sat while the drinks were prepared. Shortly, Bittlesworth sat next to him, handing him the glass of sweet liquor.

"Sir, you can tell me as much or as little as you're comfortable saying and I will help you in any way that I can."

It was then that Quince became clear on why Bittlesworth was so valued in his position. Bittlesworth was seated there, polite, attentive, and giving the impression that no matter the trouble that he was the man to solve it. That combined with the fact that he was set to inherit a viscountancy, and therefore implicitly trustworthy to any lord of the empire, was enough to give anyone in Quince's position a profound sense of relief. Perhaps he really had found someone who could help him with this most delicate of problems. He found himself relaxing more naturally into the chair. "Well, as you might imagine, it started with my father..."

Sabre marched on the front door of the Harrington town-house but was deprived of giving the door a solid, satisfying rap by the butler, Dibbs, opening it before she had even gained the last step. The austere butler bowed her in, gathered her bonnet, gloves, and pelisse, and then silently led her to Jack's morning room. With Jack in the morning room that meant her husband Gideon was already at his office. The Harringtons had only been in Town for just over a week and it seemed to Sabre that Gideon was always at the office, sunrise to long after dark. The fact that her best friend was still misty-eyed over the new husband that was obviously ignoring her struck Sabre as ridiculous.

"Miss Bittlesworth," Dibbs announced in a quiet tone, then withdrew from the room. Jack rose from her settle with a delighted smile that faded rapidly. The countess was gowned in a pale green muslin that set off her dark golden hair well, and the empire waist served to make her appear even taller than she was. Since she towered over Sabre by better than a head, it wasn't an effect that the darker-haired girl appreciated.

"Oh my," the countess said. "Who did what, and what are we going to do with them?"

Sabre held the sides of her skirt out, like a fashion plate. "How do you like my dress?"

Jack smiled carefully, "I like it quite a lot. Just as much as I did when we looked at all your new dresses the day after I came to London."

Sabre turned once and then settled the skirts again, twitching them into place. "Then you wouldn't look at me and perhaps offer to make me your private whore?"

"Oh." Jack's expression sobered considerably. "Well, now we have the what, I assume what we are going to do with them will be horrible indeed. So who was it?"

Sabre stalked over to a tiny damask chair and sat. She fingered the red silk of her skirts as she smoothed them out. "I don't know."

"Well that's certainly-"

Jack's voice was interrupted by the door clicking open again as the countess's young companion Emmy Hobbes stepped in. No more than eleven, the young Miss Hobbes was Jack's current project. "Miss Bittlesworth," the girl said, dropping a passable curtsy.

"Emmy," Sabre said with a polite nod.

Jack sighed. "Emmy, I'm afraid that today is not a social call. Sabre and I will need some privacy."

"Oh!" the young girl said, backing away. "My apologies, I didn't mean to intrude."

"Not at all," Sabre said, relenting her bad humor over the girl's apparent concern. "You know I adore you. Who couldn't love a child that takes to the sword so quickly? But this is...family business, and likely to be quite boring to you."

Jack nodded. "It's all right. Take a free morning. Perhaps practice your French?"

As Emmy nodded and pulled the door closed behind her Sabre leaned back in the chair. "Luds, Jack, do you even know what a free morning is?"

Jack's brow furrowed. "That's what I would do on my free mornings as a child."

Sabre laughed. "You were never a child. You were once smaller and you knew less, thank God, but a child? No."

"Tea?"

"You don't have anything stronger?"

Her friend raised a questioning brow and Sabre blew out her breath in a huff. "Yes, tea would be lovely."

11

Jack pulled the bell and then seated herself on the small couch that faced toward the chair Sabre was in. "And?" she prompted.

Sabre sat up straight again. "I need your promise, your vow as a Haberdasher, that you will not share this information with anyone."

"Except George, I assume."

"Yes, you may share it among the Haberdashers. If George should finally get herself back from Scotland you can certainly discuss it with her."

"But not with Gideon." Jack said it more as a statement than a question.

"No, not with Gideon." Sabre agreed.

Jack grimaced but nodded. "You have my pledge."

Sabre nodded just as a discreet knock announced a maid. The girls didn't speak again until the tea had been settled and Jack was prepared to pour.

"I assume three sugars today?" the countess asked.

Sabre smiled again. This was the comfort that she knew old friends could provide. Someone who knew that stress made her want sweets. Sweets that she regularly avoided since so much as an extra lump of sugar seemed to go straight to her hips. With her tiny stature it took diligence to maintain her figure. "Yes, three sugars today. And that tart if you don't mind."

Jack smiled sardonically. "I wouldn't think you would want to be seen consorting with tarts."

Sabre merely snorted. That was the other thing about old friends. They had absolutely no respect.

"So," Jack ventured, after handing Sabre the cup and saucer. "Where did you meet this man? In the street?"

Sabre nibbled at the tart. "I'd rather not say."

"Well, how are we supposed to find him?"

"He's a duke," Sabre ventured.

"Oh. Well. That certainly cuts the list down substantially. Are you sure he's a duke?"

"I have it on the utmost authority."

Jack narrowed her eyes, obviously wanting to question her friend further in a direction that Sabre didn't want to go.

Sabre sipped her tea and said, "Let's start with what we do know. He's a duke, about your height I would say."

"Many men are," Jack noted drily.

"Robert's age or a little bit older. Fair haired, almost as light as Charlie's," Sabre said, referring to her second oldest brother, the ever affable and horse-mad Charles Bittlesworth. "Cut in that fashionably tousled style. And his eyes are green. A very light green, a spring green George would probably call them. You would expect such innocently colored eyes to house a more wholesome soul." Sabre realized Jack had become suspiciously quiet and looked over at her friend. The countess had one hand clasped over her mouth, eyes wide with horror.

"You know who it is," Sabre accused.

Jack closed her eyes and let the hand fall away. "Oh Quince, what did you do?"

Sabre slammed down her teacup with a crack and jumped to her feet. "You're telling me the obnoxious toad that propositioned me this morning is the Duke of Beloin?"

Jack nodded, "I think so, yes."

"The same Duke of Beloin you have been raving about since I came back from Italy? That you have been bragging I will meet at your ball?"

Jack shrugged helplessly, "Are you sure you didn't misinterpret what he said?"

Sabre loomed over her seated friend and hissed, "Do you want to know what he said? It was, 'Whatever he's paying you, I'll double it. Triple it. You'll never want for anything again in your life.' Do you think I misinterpreted that Jack? Really?"

Her friend gasped in shock. "That's terrible! I can't believe he would say that."

Sabre stalked off to stare out the window. "Either it was the Duke of Beloin or he has a twin. Who is also a duke."

"And who was the 'he' that the duke was referring to? I'm confused, Sabre. Did this happen this morning? Where?"

Sabre turned back to her friend. "I've said all I'm going to say on that matter. Thank you for providing the information I needed."

Jack launched to her feet as well. "Sabre, I don't like that look. What are you planning to do?"

Sabre tilted her chin up. "I'm planning to defend my honor."

Two

Quince felt surprisingly good after sharing his burden with Robert Bittlesworth. Enough so that his step was lighter as he headed toward the front door to exit the house, but then the scene of his meeting with Bittlesworth's sister stopped him short. Gods, how could he have been so stupid? With one impulsive offer he had insulted a young lady and perhaps, if she decided to confide in her brother, ruined the chance that Bittlesworth would help him with this issue. Yet, glancing up the stairs to the landing where he first saw her, he had to admit that the vision of her in that dress would be with him for the rest of his life. Knowing that simply seeing him again would probably cause more offense to the lady, he accepted his coat from the doorman and departed.

"Oh Sabre..." Jack said. "Surely you don't mean to challenge Quince to a duel?"

Sabre nodded. "Of course I do. It's his just desserts. And didn't you say that he believes in women's rights? Why shouldn't it be my right to defend my own honor?"

Jack sighed. "There is a sad symmetry to it."

"You'll be my second?"

Jack scowled but nodded. "Of course."

Sabre nodded again. "Good, that's settled. I shall send a message to the duke informing him that his second can meet mine." Sabre searched her mind for an appropriate location that wasn't a men's club. "At the private room in the back of the George and Vulture?"

"The George and Vulture?" Jack asked. "Are you sure you can stand the idea of me wearing breeches and having Welsh rarebit without you?"

Sabre pouted. "You have a point. Perhaps I could come with you?"

"Don't be ridiculous, you know that's not how it's done. Perhaps Twinings would be a better option?"

"The tea and coffee house? Now who's being ridiculous? The duke's second would laugh all the way home." Sabre looked up at her friend with a bit of disgust. "Stop thinking like such a girl."

Jack just laughed and shook her head. "Considering there's more than a fair chance that the person I'll be meeting is my husband I am simply trying to head off his complaints."

Sabre knew she was frowning as she felt a shudder of disapproval run through her. She had been at first delighted that her prudish, intellectual friend had married Lord Lucifer. Based on the stories from Robert and Charlie she had expected the earl to help Jack loosen up a bit. Instead it seemed the lord was even more reserved than Jack herself. Meanwhile, the freedom-loving and headstrong woman Sabre thought she had known was now content to submit to her overbearing husband. It was enough to make Sabre swear off the idea of marriage forever. "No," she said, "I think the George and Vulture. I don't wish to tip our hand too early."

"Tip our hand?"

"He has to believe the challenge comes from my brother or he won't even show up to the field."

"Won't the game be up when Giddy sees that I'm the second?"

"Not if you convince him to help us."

"Sabre, that's not very likely."

"I have every faith in you."

A full day had passed since Quince had visited Bittlesworth. He hadn't expected immediate results, of course, but now that he had initiated a solution he found himself impatient to get on with it. Instead, he was spending his mid-morning reviewing correspondence. One of his least favorite activities. None of the duties of a duke were particularly appealing to him, but reading all these invitations and solicitations ranked lower than low. And these were only the remaining letters after his secretary had already parsed through the majority. Blessedly it seemed the torture was coming to the end for today. There was only one, small missive left on the tray. Cream colored heavy stock. When he turned it over he saw "Duke of Beloin" in a heavy, flowing script and a blank seal that had been broken, he assumed, by his secretary. Something about the letter made him uneasy and he regretted that his man had opened it first. Unfolding the paper he saw the dark script inside.

Your proposition yesterday was unconscionable. I will have satis-faction. Your second shall meet mine this evening before nine at a private room of the George and Vulture. — Bittlesworth

Quince felt his body go cold. Not only would Bittlesworth not aid him, the insult to his sister had driven the man to challenge a duke to duel. Apparently even a man with a reputation for reserve could be pushed too far. Numbly pulling out a blank sheet of paper the duke considered how to best phrase the request to his second.

Sabre had been pacing in the front hall much of the morning, waiting for Jack. Finally hearing a familiar knock on the front door she schooled her expression and opened it. Jack stood on the steps, eyeing her friend critically.

"I don't like that look," the countess finally announced.

"What do you mean?" Sabre countered, but she could feel the grin beginning to tease at the side of her mouth.

"You did it. You sent the challenge."

At that, Sabre's eyebrows drew down. "Shh!" she admonished. She pulled her friend into the front hall and looked around to see if any servants were present to have overheard them. Not seeing anyone she hustled Jack up the steps to the sitting room.

"Sabre!" Jack admonished in a fierce whisper. "If we can't talk here then perhaps we should go elsewhere?"

"We've had a predictable pattern since you've been back to Town," Sabre responded, also in a whisper, "changing it now could be disastrous."

Jack settled herself onto a love seat and smoothed her skirts. "Your definition of a disaster might be quite different from mine," she said, but still kept her voice low.

"No, I'm sure that inspiring my brother's suspicion rates fairly high on your list of disasters."

Jack raised a brow but remained silent.

Sabre sat in the chair opposite her friend and spent some time fussing with her own skirts.

"And?" Jack finally prompted.

"And what?" Sabre asked calmly.

"And what? And everything. What did you send? Did he send anything back? What is the plan?"

Sabre could feel the frown tugging at her lips. "I sent a short letter this morning. Of course he hasn't sent anything back. The plan continues with you at the George and Vulture tonight, as we already discussed."

"Then why am I here?"

"Because every other morning you and I have a mid-morning chat in this sitting room."

Jack threw her hands up in the air in exasperation. "So you're going to leave it all to me to explain this to my husband?"

Sabre knew a true frown was marring her expression now. "Do I need to be concerned? You act like you're afraid of him. You've never been afraid of anything."

A poignant stillness enveloped the room as the two young women eyed one another. Jack finally set her jaw in a mulish expression that Sabre recognized and quite honestly, it was a welcome relief.

"Of course I'm not afraid of him," the countess said vehemently. She looked down and traced the pattern on the arm of the love seat and after a pause added more softly, "Some things are just not worth the trouble of arguing about."

Sabre felt a rush of blood that made her head swim. She stood up abruptly. "Well, if my honor isn't worth the trouble then I can certainly look elsewhere for a second."

Jack looked stricken. "Oh, Sabre, no! That's not what I meant! Not at all. It's just, well…" Her friend looked up at her with tears in her green eyes. Jack was never scared and she never, ever cried. Now Sabre didn't know whether to be angry or frightened herself.

"It's just what?" she prompted.

After a moment Jack bit her lip and gave a watery chuckle. "Oh, never mind," she said, shaking her head. "You'll find out for yourself one day. Or you won't. I'm not sure you're the type who will marry for love."

"You didn't marry for love."

"Yet I found it all the same. Funny that." Jack shrugged. "And I must apologize once again for letting my pregnancy get the best of me. My moods of late have been quite abominable. Of course I will be your second. I will handle Giddy."

Sabre didn't know whether it was the pregnancy or the husband that was having the worse effect on her friend. All she knew was that she wanted neither affliction for herself.

Quince heard heavy boots in the hallway and knew the earl had arrived. He hadn't asked Giddy to come in his letter. Had asked him quite specifically to appear at the G&V at the appointed hour, in fact. But that was Giddy for you. Managing. Had to come see everything for himself.

"The Earl of Harrington," Larkins intoned from the door.

Harrington strode across the room with his usual air of purpose and then stood looming over the duke's chair as though a question had already been asked and he was impatiently waiting for the answer. Unlike the duke's own impeccable appearance, the earl looked as though he had been out riding in a stiff wind.

"Hullo, Giddy," Quince said softly, swirling wine in the bottom of the glass he was holding. "Feel free to make yourself a drink. Not too many, though. We must be sharp in the morning."

"What on God's green earth have you gotten yourself into, Quince? Your letter said to expect Charlie Bittlesworth as a second?"

Quince nodded. "That seems most likely."

"So you and Robert are at crossed swords? What on earth do you have to duel about?"

"He perceives that I insulted his sister."

At that Gideon looked thoughtful, then did turn to the side-bar to fix himself a drink. "Little Sabre?" he mused. "Doubtful. She would have run you through herself if you had."

Quince gave his friend a questioning look. "Little Sabre?"

Gideon sat in the chair opposite his friend. "Certainly I've told you that Miss Sabrina Bittlesworth is my wife's best friend."

"No, I don't remember it coming up."

"What did you say about her?"

"Say about her?" Quince asked.

"That she or Robert took as an insult."

"I haven't said anything about her."

"Then what was the nature of this supposed insult?"

"I may have, inadvertently... asked her to be my mistress."

Gideon choked a bit on his swallow of wine. "I'm sorry, you may have what?"

"Asked her to be my mistress."

"I don't know who it was you asked to be your mistress, but as you are devoid of wounds I have to guess that it wasn't actually Sabrina Bittlesworth."

"I'm quite certain it was."

"How do you know?"

"Robert referred to her as his sister mere moments later."

"You made this proposition in front of him?"

"No, shortly before he entered the room. I assume she told him about it later."

Gideon set his glass down and sat back, crossing his arms. "Well. Aren't you a piece of work?"

"Whatever do you mean?"

"You still look as saintly as ever, yet there you were. Propositioning a young lady of Quality. Even I never did that."

"In my oh-so-slender defense, I did think she was Robert's mistress at the time."

"What? Why on earth would you think that?"

"If you'd seen the dress she was wearing you'd think it, too."

Gideon merely raised a brow in that way he had that made you know he was questioning your sanity.

Quince frowned into his glass. "The particulars of the matter don't really signify now, do they? Tonight you meet his second and in the morning there will be a duel."

"Tonight Charlie and I commiserate over what half-wits you both are, and in the morning we get to watch you *be* idiots. Shall I advocate for swords?"

"The choice is Robert's, of course."

"Yes, but if he chooses pistols and if he's angry... Well, you might not make it through the morning."

"There are any number of reasons we might not make it through the morning, Robert Bittlesworth's pistols notwithstanding. If he wants pistols, then pistols it shall be."

"There's likely another way to solve this, you know."

"Don't say it, Giddy."

"Offer for her."

"No."

"Why does everyone say no when I propose marriage? You know the idea is valid. Expected even."

"No. I shall not marry a Bittlesworth."

"The current viscount can't live forever, and Robert is a good enough sort."

"This isn't a topic open for discussion, Giddy."

"You would rather die than marry her?"

"If need be."

Gideon sighed. "Well, old boy, I propose that in the future you be more careful about whom you invite to be your mistress."

Three

$\mathcal{A}$t precisely half past eight Gideon was informed that his horse was ready. The earl considered going up to check on his wife before leaving. She had been quiet and distracted at supper, not quite her usual self, and had retired early. But if trouble was brewing in her mind it might be best to get this foolish duel out of the way first. He paused at the door and looked up the steps. He had promised himself that he wouldn't avoid confrontations with her but certainly this was a special case. And, he thought to himself with the beginnings of a smile, if he told her what he was off to do then she would undoubtedly want to come along.

Jack kept her head down with the brim of her cap low, sipping at a bitter beer. It was ridiculously easy to pass for a young man in her loose-fitting trousers and vest. The barman had been busy and rushed when she came in and hadn't looked twice at her. He had taken coin at her mumbled request to hold a private room for her master, leaving her here with the door open for the supposed master's imminent arrival. Now she just had to wait for what she still assumed would be Gideon. If not, he would soon find her missing at home and she could just imagine what sort of trouble that could cause. Lara, her maid, was sworn to secrecy... unless the earl started forming a search party or some other silly, overwrought thing. There was no reason to upset the entire household for what was essentially a short ride and meeting a friend at an alehouse. Not that women in her station were allowed to do such things. She ran her finger over the grain in the heavy wooden table and grinned.

The tiny room she had secured held only a table and four chairs, but it did have the advantage of a small fireplace and a lantern. There was enough light to read, if she had only thought to bring a book.

She heard the heavy stomp of boots approaching and schooled her features into the discontented scowl that was as much a part of her disguise as the ratty old cap that she wore. Keeping her chin low she looked over as the boots stopped in the doorway. Black Hessians. She recognized those boots.

"Boy, who else is here?" The earl's voice was brusque, impatient. "I'm expecting Charlie Bittlesworth."

"You can expect him," Jack replied, "but I haven't seen him since we've been back to Town."

After a deathly still pause the earl said, "Jacqueline?"

She looked up at him and smiled. "Hullo, Giddy. Fancy meeting you here."

Shock gave way to irritation as he saw that it truly was his wife. He closed the door to the room with a thump and strode over to the table. "Bloody hell, what are you doing here?"

"The same thing you're doing here, unless I miss my guess."

He sighed and pinched the bridge of his nose. "Then it is Sabre who took exception to Quince's misstatement."

"Misstatement? Is that how he put it? And of course Sabre took exception to it. I believe we have some terms to discuss."

"Why didn't you tell me about this? Why the subterfuge? We could have discussed this at home."

"I couldn't be entirely sure that Quince would choose you as his second. Why didn't you tell *me* that you were to be involved in a duel in the morning?"

Gideon crossed his arms and stared down at her. She could tell that he desperately wanted to demand that she leave off this pursuit. He changed tacks instead.

"There's no point in this since Quince would never fight her."

"We choose swords. Sabres, in fact."

"Again, he won't fight her. And the last thing you want to do with Quince is choose swords."

Jack arched a brow. "The last thing you want to do with Sabre is choose swords. But she wants swords."

"I'm sure she's quite accomplished for a woman."

"She's quite accomplished for anyone. Our terms are to the blood."

"There's no point in arguing about this because there will be no duel!"

"Sabre and I assumed you would have that perspective," Jack said primly.

"Well, that was bloody brilliant of you."

"I have one point for you to consider."

"And that is?"

"Your friend Quincy Telford, Duke of Beloin, has been plaguing you for years about rights for women. Isn't it time that you make him pay up by proving he's capable of treating a woman as though she has equal rights to a man?"

Gideon slowly uncrossed his arms and put them on the table to lean toward her. Once he was scant inches away he finally spoke. "You, my love, are diabolical."

She grinned. "I thought you might find that line of thinking appealing."

"Irresistible. Quince will have to admit that he does see differences between men and women. That actually is quite brilliant. Can we go home now?"

"Silly man, you haven't even had a drink yet and you want to go home to your wife and cozy bed at the unfashionably early hour of ten o'clock? What will your friends think?"

"Lucky man? Although perhaps not if they saw how you were currently dressed."

She lifted her nose in the air haughtily. "I'll have you know that this is the *stare* of fashion among street rats."

"Undoubtedly. Can it be hoped that you rode a horse here this evening?"

"Of course. And," she added in a conspiratorial whisper, "I had a groom ride with me."

"Really?"

"Yes. If I don't bring a groom on my rides my husband gets very upset with me."

"He sounds like an ogre."

"You have no idea. Overbearing doesn't begin to describe him."

"I don't know how you stand it."

She fluttered her lashes at him. "He only worries about me because he loves me."

He pinched her chin. "We'd best go before someone comes in and finds me kissing what appears to be a stable boy."

"Indeed. That might be the only way to darken the reputation of Lord Lucifer."

Four

*A*s the carriage rolled through the streets before dawn Sabre had to admit to herself that she was nervous. Jack sat to her right, quiet in the gloom. They had hardly spoken this morning, just confirming the timing and weapons as Sabre had boarded. Jack had been waiting with the carriage a few blocks from Robert's house so that he would be none the wiser about their plans, provided Sabre had slipped away as silently as she thought she had. It wasn't uncommon for her to sleep until noon, so she should be able to sneak back into the household before anyone noted her absence.

She gave herself the satisfaction of a small smile. It reminded her of the shenanigans from their childhood. Sneaking out to hold mock duels at dawn. But this wasn't a game and Jack had shared the warning that the duke was quite proficient with a sword. Instead of the exhilaration that she had always felt when meeting her friends on the dueling fields, Sabre was overcome with a sense of dread. A sense of foreboding. Just nerves, she reassured herself. It wasn't often she faced an unknown opponent. She hadn't had an opportunity to study him, to see what his strengths and weaknesses were. She would be coming into a high-stakes combat essentially blind.

"What are you thinking?" Jack had spoken quietly into the velvety silence and the words hung there, almost tangible.

"About how I will humiliate the duke, of course," Sabre answered with a grin.

Jack laughed. "That's our Sabre. Sometimes I think Napoleon has only half your confidence."

"He should be so lucky."

Quince realized he was staring at Gideon's profile as the earl gazed out the carriage window into the darkness from the seat opposite. Gideon was far too pleased with himself this morning, making Quince wonder what he and Charlie had discussed the night before. Not that Gideon had said much as yet. But Quince knew the earl. Something was afoot.

"You say they asked for swords?" Quince said, breaking the silence.

Gideon returned his attention to the duke. "Indeed. I could not have been more surprised."

"And how did you influence that?"

"I guarantee you that it was not my suggestion."

"That isn't the question that I asked."

Gideon grinned. "You're splitting hairs, Quince. Does this duel have you nervous?"

Quince shifted his gaze to the dim light outside the carriage. Nervous? Not precisely. But he could think of no name for what he was feeling.

Now that he had begun talking the earl didn't seem inclined to stop. "You know no one can equal you at swords and it's only to the blood. It should be short work and an early breakfast." As the duke maintained his silence Gideon continued. "Come now, Quince. If you were any more dour

I would put you up for abbot. Is something else amiss? Not just this duel?"

His gaze flicked back to the earl. Gideon usually wasn't one to notice things. At least not about people. Thank God the man had married a forthright woman, any other creature would have been doomed to a lifetime of misery. "Nothing to speak of, Giddy," he finally replied.

The earl's brow furrowed, indicating that he didn't quite believe the duke, but the carriage was pulling to a halt. They had arrived at the dueling field.

As Quince stepped out of the carriage he saw that they were the first ones at the clearing. Perhaps Robert and Charlie wouldn't arrive and this could all become an unpleasant memory. Certainly it couldn't be too hard to avoid one family among all those in the *ton*? He would just spend more time at his country estates and wait for tempers to settle. Then he heard the rattle of carriage wheels approaching and had to admit that this duel was going forward. His eyes narrowed at the conveyance. "Gideon, isn't that one of your carriages?"

"Gracious, old boy, even I don't recognize all of my equipage, but I suppose it is."

The carriage rolled to a stop and a small figure jumped out almost immediately. Too small to be Robert or Charlie. Why would they bring a boy with them? Then the boy turned to accept a package handed down from inside the carriage and Quince realized it was no boy. Even in the dim light of dawn he could tell it was a woman. Sabrina Bittlesworth. He turned his glare on Gideon.

"You knew about this."

Gideon shrugged. "Of course I did. I met with the second last night, remember?"

"You knew about this and didn't tell me? What happened to you being *my* second?"

"You don't think she should have a chance to defend her honor? That was quite an insult, after all."

"You let me stew all morning about whether Robert would try to kill me."

Gideon's brows drew down. "You said you weren't worried about that."

"And Napoleon said he would stay at Elba. Gods, man, even you can't be so thick."

Now Gideon was truly scowling. "Why would you even think that Robert would try to kill you?"

Quince snorted. "It's obvious that you don't have sisters."

"Neither do you."

Quince let the comment pass and went back to watching the women ready themselves. It was apparent that Miss Bittlesworth's second was Gideon's own wife, Jacqueline. Even if Gideon was perverse enough to play this game it shocked the duke that *Jack* hadn't told him what was afoot. He turned back to the earl. "As my second, it is your duty to go tell them that this sham of a duel is off."

"I'm sorry, come again?"

Quince looked over to where the young Miss Bittlesworth was warming up her arm with a light sabre. "It's off. And please note that I don't appreciate being played the fool."

"Well, *my* reaction was of course that it was ridiculous that the lady fight you. But my wife was insistent that you would want to grant her the same rights than any man would have."

Quince looked at his friend. The earl was downright gloating. "Gideon, this is petty and vindictive. Honestly, I expected better of you."

The earl cocked his head to the side. "So you're admitting that a woman shouldn't have the same rights as a man?"

"That's not what I'm saying at all! It just doesn't make sense to partake of a contest against a smaller, less trained opponent. It would be cruel."

"Odd. If Robert had arrived with his pistols that description would have fit you. Yet you were more than willing to do it. Considered it a point of honor, I think, with all that broody talk of dying rather than marrying the girl. Well, she's here to claim the same right."

"And if I refuse?"

"Then as your second it falls to me to fight for you." The thought seemed to sober the earl. "If Sabre steps aside as well and makes me fight my pregnant wife I can assure you I will take that debt out of your hide."

Quince frowned again. Then he heard the dratted woman's voice come across the field. "If we could get started, your grace, I have appointments to keep."

Gideon held out the duke's sword, obviously fighting the desire to smile over what he no doubt considered to be a fabulous joke.

Five

Quince withdrew his sword from its scabbard and turned to stomp across the field toward the small woman who had duped him with a forged note. This morning she was garbed in a loose white shirt overlaid with a tailored vest that showed off her curves. The buff colored trousers did nothing to disguise her gender either, highlighting the flare of her hips. This at least made it clear that it wasn't just the dress that had attracted him. She saluted with her sword as he approached but he kept his own sword low. Stopping a few feet away from her he gave a small bow. "My deepest apologies for the insult to you, my lady. It was not my intention to upset you or to besmirch your honor." With that he brought his sword up high enough to slash across his left palm. Holding the hand up to her he said, "First blood. The terms of our agreement are met."

He turned to walk away, but her voice flowed over him again. "That is not acceptable to me, your grace."

He turned back. "Deception was not acceptable to me."

"In which way did I deceive you?"

"Impersonating your brother in order to draw me out to this duel?"

"I in no way impersonated my brother. I did not use his seal, I did not disguise my handwriting, and my name is, in fact, Bittlesworth. It is unfortunate that you mistook the information you had to assume the letter was from my brother."

"That you can enumerate those items so quickly indicates that you knew exactly what you were up to, and exactly what my assumptions would be. It is intention that underlies deception, my lady. Arguing the facts of the case will in no way alleviate you from the responsibility of intending to deceive."

"Is that how you justify your insult to me as well? By dressing a certain way it was my intention to seduce you, and therefore you bear no responsibility for asking me to be your mistress?"

"Don't be ridiculous. I had no idea Robert had a sister. But I do know Robert, and it takes no stretch of the imagination to assume a beautiful woman wandering his house to be his mistress."

"Now you insult my brother as well?"

"I doubt that he would consider it an insult. Perhaps even a compliment."

"Well, I do not take your walking off this field of honor as a compliment, I take it as an insult. But I suppose we can just add it to the insults you have already done me."

"I do not mean to insult you."

"First you dishonor me by calling me a Cyprian and now you disrespect me by not allowing me to defend that honor. In what way are you not insulting me?"

Quince set his jaw. "This has all been entertaining, I'm sure, but I will not be dueling you this morning."

"Oh, wait," she said, her eyes widening. "Are you… are you afraid that I might best you?"

"Of course not."

34

She looked contemplative. "No, that makes sense. My reputation is very good among certain circles. The Little Dervish and all."

"You're the Little Dervish?"

"You've heard of me?" She looked pleased.

Quince narrowed his eyes. He had indeed heard of the Little Dervish from some of his fencing partners but none had indicated that it was a woman. They had, in fact, said boy and there was nothing boyish about Miss Bittlesworth in these clothes. "Are you deceiving me again, my lady? So soon?"

"No deception here, your grace," she said, offended.

He walked around her, looking her up and down. "You aren't built for fencing. Too many curves and no length."

She sneered at him. "And now you plan to dismiss me out of hand, justifying your decision with yet more insults?"

"Well, then show me what you can do."

"Salute and fight me."

"No, show me your practice drills." He stood back, watching her keenly.

"I will not dance for you like a pet monkey. Fight me or the Little Dervish will spread word of how the Duke of Beloin was afraid to take up the sword."

Quince glowered. "That's ridiculous. And no one would believe you. Provided you are the Little Dervish after all, which I highly doubt."

"I am, and I refuse to fight a man who won't defend himself."

"You assume I won't defend myself?"

"You're still holding your sword behind your back."

He smiled at her. "And?"

She paused for a moment, then nodded. "I see. As you wish." She saluted again and slid into prime position for attack so quickly that he barely had time to step back and raise his own sword in parry. Within seconds it was clear that she had trained. Quickly thereafter it was clear she was among the best he had faced. After that he was absorbed in the dance. Footwork. The flash of the swords. The sound of steel on steel. What the Little Dervish lacked in reach or strength she more than made up for in speed.

Sabre could see the moment when the duke transitioned from arrogance to concentrating on the duel. Knowing that he was fully engaged she pressed harder, faster. Attack, parry, counter-attack. While the duke's attention narrowed into the focus of a master, Sabre found it difficult to concentrate. His form was flawless. She wished she could be watching this match, could behold the beauty of it. She knew that her own style was frenetic, capitalizing on her speed and energy. The duke, in comparison, was grace personified. He was slower but anticipated every move she made well in advance. She did a flurry of attacks that always conquered her opponent's guard and he parried her as though they had practiced this particular exchange a thousand times.

She misjudged his coupé and was open on the left side for mere moments. But those moments were all the time he needed to get past her guard with a simple extension. She felt the steel bite into her arm with the gentleness of a mere brush. But she knew that an injury from a sharpened edge could be deceptively painless. It was clear that the duke's blade had scored true because of his reaction. As she drew back into salute position again he threw his own blade down and stepped forward to inspect her arm.

"I'm sorry. I'm so sorry."

She looked up and saw the concern in his eyes as he gently peeled back the edges of her rent shirtsleeve to evaluate the wound. "I'm not," she said. "'Tis not but a flesh wound."

"Gideon!" he called out in a demanding tone. "Why do we not have a doctor in attendance?"

The earl had bent to retrieve the duke's sword as he approached them. "I wasn't expecting anyone to get hurt."

Sabre laughed. "That was rather dense of you."

The earl looked affronted but the duke chuckled, unexpected amusement crinkling his eyes at the corners. "She has you there, Giddy."

Jack had joined them, unwinding a bandage. "Don't worry, Quince. She's had worse."

Six

*A*lthough the cut to Sabre's arm was shallow, Jack thought her friend seemed to be in shock. As such, she bundled her into the carriage to take her to the Harrington townhouse.

"This certainly won't look good with your new gowns," the countess commented.

Sabre was looking out the window as the carriage set into motion. "I can wear shawls," she murmured.

Jack wasn't quite sure what to think about her friend's distracted behavior, but as the carriage rolled forward, Sabre knelt on the carriage seat to look out the back window. Jack joined her to see that the only thing she could be looking at were Quince and Giddy, still standing in the field and apparently arguing.

"Isn't he wondrous?" Sabre whispered.

Jack looked at her friend and realized that what she had thought to be shock might actually be the rapt absorption that Sabre rarely displayed, but usually signaled the beginning of a grand obsession. Fortunately her obsessions were usually confined to objects and experiences, such as shoes and being allowed to do a tour of the continent. The idea of her developing an obsession over a person worried Jack immediately.

"Who are we talking about?" the countess asked cautiously.

"The duke, of course. You saw the duel. He was magnificent."

"He's certainly among the best you've fought."

As they had lost sight of the men Sabre turned and flopped onto the bench and Jack seated herself opposite.

"Not among the best, he *is* the best. I'm going to marry him."

"What?" Jack felt her heart still in her chest.

"I shall marry him. Then I will be a duchess. And I will be able to watch him any time that I want. Duel him any time I want."

"Sabre, these don't sound like reasons to marry," Jack cautioned.

Her friend gave her a speaking look. "Says the woman who married for no reasons whatsoever."

"My reputation! You know what could have happened to Sam and my mother if it had turned into a true scandal."

"Of course I do. I'm just saying that other than that you had no reason to marry the earl. You didn't admire him. Quite the opposite. And you had never shown any interest in marrying for a title."

"That's true," Jack said carefully.

"At least I have reasons."

Jack recognized the look in her friend's eyes. Sabre would have the duke at any cost. God save Quince.

Sabre pinned Jack with a shrewd look. "I assume that I can count on your assistance with this?"

"Well, what do you need?"

Her dark haired friend looked out the window again. "This isn't a war, it's a hunt." She smiled. "That's your providence, Artemis."

Jack thought she had best tread carefully. "When Gideon and I met he suggested seeing seduction as a war. That's your expertise, Athena."

Sabre returned her attention to Jack. "Really? Well, I suppose who would know more about seduction than Lord Lucifer?"

Quince and the earl faced off in the middle of the field after the ladies left. The duke didn't know the last time he had been so angry. Wait, yes he did. And Gideon Wolfe had been the cause of that, as well. He couldn't decide if this was better or worse than the earl undermining the first bill Quince had tried to raise in Parliament. "Gideon, what on earth were you thinking, allowing this to happen?"

Gideon, wiping down the duke's sword as part of his duties as second, asked, "What do you mean allowing?"

"I asked you to stand for me here because I trust you. I can see that is yet again a mistake."

"About that, I've been meaning to tell you that you were right."

"I..." Quince realized what Gideon had actually said and it pulled him up short. "What do you mean I was right? About what?"

"If you calm down a bit perhaps I will tell you."

Quince stopped and focused on his breathing. He could feel the tension throughout his body, irritation prickling under his skin. But what was done couldn't be undone. And short of wresting the sword from Giddy, who seemed intent on polishing it to death, in order to run his irritating friend through with it, there wasn't much he could think of that would satisfy his unease.

"Feeling better?" the earl ventured.

"Just a moment," Quince said, closing his eyes. He could hear the horses shifting in their gear as they and his coachman patiently waited. Birds were singing in the nearby trees, content with the early morning Spring sunshine. The scent of blooming flowers carried on the light breeze. Bluebells, if he wasn't mistaken. That made Quince smile. He had sent Gideon's wife a bouquet of bluebells once, as a sign of gratitude when she had made him laugh. Few people were capable of that anymore, it seemed. Feeling calmer he opened his eyes and saw that he had been correct. A blanket of bluebells bloomed under the trees that bordered the clearing.

Gideon cleared his throat and Quince glanced over to see that the earl had finally finished polishing the sword, having sheathed it to hold loosely in his off hand.

"Would you like to go?" Gideon asked.

"I recall there being a mention of an early breakfast," Quince looked up at the sky. "Perhaps not so early, but there is certain to be plenty at my sideboard if you care to join me."

Gideon grinned at him. "Angry as you were, I thought you would shake me loose at the earliest opportunity."

Quince grabbed the sword from Gideon and started toward the carriage. "Then you started telling me how right I am about everything."

"I didn't say everything."

"Hmm. I definitely heard everything."

"Yes, I've noticed you tend to hear what you want."

"Better than you and never hearing anything at all."

"I'm sorry, what was that, old boy? I didn't hear you."

Quince grinned to himself as they boarded. Perhaps everything would turn out all right after all. But his grin faded as he thought about the blood on young Miss Bittlesworth's sleeve.

Seven

$\mathcal{G}$ ideon looked across the breakfast table at the duke and could tell that although Quince was attempting to behave normally, something was still a bit off. His motions were stiff, his reactions delayed as though his mind were elsewhere. Although Gideon preferred to deal with things straight on, he knew Quince was quite different. The duke had been his friend for twenty years, since long before either of them had ascended to their titles. In all that time he had only seen Quince truly upset three times. The day they had met, again when Quince's father died, and today. As much as Quince liked to tease that Gideon was dense and unobservant, and Gideon would admit that there were many vagaries of daily life that he considered beneath notice, no one knew Quincy Telford, Duke of Beloin, like Gideon did. And based on what he knew, Quince's behavior had him worried.

"So," Gideon asked with a grin, "did you still think Sabrina Bittlesworth was mistress material after seeing her in breeches with a sword?"

That sufficed to rouse Quince from his distraction. "Seeing her in that clothing was... intriguing. She filled it out in a most fascinating way."

Having Quince actually talk about a woman was intriguing. The duke was usually more pious than a vicar on the subject of women. This one he had propositioned to be his mistress and now thought she looked well in men's clothing. "But," Gideon said, "with a figure like that she's like as not to run to fat."

Quince shrugged. "I can't see any danger of that, considering her interest in fencing."

"Jack is very strict about what can and cannot be served with tea when Sabre is in attendance."

"I notice you speak of Miss Bittlesworth very familiarly."

"She stayed with us for almost a fortnight at Kellington. As she and my wife are always in each other's pockets, if I wanted to spend any time with Jack it was a surety that Miss Bittlesworth would be there. Well, unless we were in the bedroom, of course."

Quince stopped buttering his toast. "You're not going to use this as an opportunity to tell me about your bed sport, are you? This *is* the breakfast table."

"Worry not that I will spoil your digestion, Quince. I don't want you thinking of my wife in that way."

The table lapsed into an awkward silence again and Gideon began to wonder if he should press his friend to find out what was wrong. Although Quince was obviously upset over hurting the girl, it seemed a bit much to be this put out over it. But if it was something else then Gideon didn't know what it could be. There had been some rough times getting the duchy put to rights after the elder duke had died, but things seemed to be going well now. Gideon himself reviewed the books at least quarterly to make sure of that. Quince had no vices to speak of. If it wasn't money then Gideon didn't know what the issue might be.

The one thing he did know was that Quince had to be handled very carefully or he would withdraw into himself, refusing to talk about what was bothering him. Gideon found himself wishing Jack were here. Jack, who had a finer sense of people, and who seemed to have a bit of a talent for drawing Quince out. They shared a quick wit, something he laid no claim to for himself. Quince stared vacantly at his plate, pushing food around with a fork and distracted by his own thoughts, as Gideon contemplated what to say. If Gideon couldn't ask directly and couldn't cajole an answer out of the duke, then he wasn't quite sure what to do.

Quince finally said, "I plan to go out to the country for a few weeks."

"Do you need company?"

The duke looked up in surprise. "You would leave London while Parliament is in session? Surely you jest."

Gideon shrugged in what he hoped was a casual manner. "We spent the better part of March at Kellington."

"The countess spent March at Kellington. I happen to remember you were in London a good bit of that time."

"How was I to know that coming into Town for the vote on the Corn Laws would trap me here? I certainly couldn't anticipate Napoleon's escape."

Quince looked as though he were going to say something and thought better of it. Gideon felt his worry edge into mild panic. Where was the sarcasm, where was the arrogance? Even at eight years old, Quincy Telford had always had a way of looking down his nose at everyone. It was, in a roundabout way, how they had met. But at the moment the duke was lacking his usual pomp. He seemed sad, hollow. Quince was probably right, he needed time out in the country to clear his head. Gideon would just wait until the duke mentioned something that could be done. The earl knew himself to be at his best when he could *do* something.

Not knowing what else to say, Gideon ventured, "If you do want company, just send us an invitation, old boy."

"You would die of boredom within a day."

"That's not true."

"When is the last time you spent a whole day doing absolutely nothing?"

Gideon smiled and Quince held up his hand. "Spending all day in bed with a woman doesn't count."

"True enough, probably not."

"The answer, which you are trying to avoid giving me, is never. You have *never* done so. But that is precisely what I'm going to be doing. Nothing. Most likely for an extended period. So no, you are not invited. I do not wish to interrupt my nothing in order to entertain you."

Not sarcasm or wit, but a harsh and direct set down. If anyone else had taken such a tone with him, Gideon would have laid him out on the floor, duke or no. But this was Quince. And more importantly, this was Quince not acting like Quince at all.

The men finished their meal in silence.

Eight

Quince stared out the window as his carriage sped toward his estate closest to London, Belle Fleur. When he had gone into his bedroom at the townhouse there had been another letter. On his bed, as though perhaps he himself had tossed it aside earlier in the day. Innocent eggshell colored paper. Folded over and unsealed. But he had recognized it immediately because the first letter had been delivered in just such a way. It inferred that someone in his household was delivering them, which was both disheartening and vaguely threatening. Rather than read it he had tucked it into his coat pocket and set his staff to packing for the country. Now he could hear the paper crinkle in his pocket whenever he shifted in his seat. It didn't really matter what the latest letter said, did it? He could still recall the first missive, word for word.

My dearest duke,

I hope that this letter finds you well. It has come to my attention that you are in possession of papers from your father that you have been discussing with others. If you surrender those papers to me then I will not find it necessary to share some interesting facts that I have discovered about your mother. I will give you a fortnight to gather them. Await instructions in my next letter.

Sincerely,

Your father's friend

That first letter had gone into the fire the night he had received it. No need for the information to get into the wrong hands. Now he had the second letter. Part of his reluctance to open it was that whatever instructions were contained, he could not follow them. He had no idea what papers from his father he supposedly had in his possession. He, of course, had many papers from his father. But nothing incriminating. Nothing that would inspire this veiled but menacing threat. Everything he did have was related to the running of the estates, so unless something was in code it was hard to believe that any of it was causing this reaction. It was beyond low to be threatening his mother, but he knew the former duke had run with an unsavory crowd, men who would not hesitate to threaten even the most innocent and unprotected. The stories that his father would tell over the supper table had made Quince cringe. Honestly, if his father had documented his group's exploits half as well as the forty years of grain reports, then it was no wonder why someone would want to ensure that those papers never saw the light of day. But he had never seen evidence that such was the case. Not one note, one letter, one piece of paper hinted that his father had written down the salacious tales he had enjoyed telling. Even in the stories the elder duke had told names had never been used. Quince had very few clues about the identities of the men his father had run consorted with, save for one whose identity he had learned by accident. For the rest he only knew that they were of an age with his father, were lords, and seemed capable of almost anything.

Perhaps he should send a note to his mother, warning her of the potential outcome of this threat. Not that he was entirely sure what the anonymous blackmailer thought they had to exploit. Certainly his mother had her eccentricities, but it was hard to see where any of them would be earthshaking if revealed. She was a bluestocking, a freethinker, but she was hardly shy about it. On the other hand, attacks to one's reputation were rarely pleasant and often had long-reaching effects. Even Harrington had kept a relatively low profile since the scandal that had led to his marriage.

But regardless of how many times he turned it over in his mind, Quince came to the same conclusion. At present there was nothing he could do. Nothing but wait to see what Robert Bittlesworth came up with. If he had any faith that there was some cache of documents as yet uncovered he would look for them, but he had little hope of that. Most of the non-entailed estates had been sold years ago, with all relevant papers reviewed by his stewards. It was possible, of course, that one of his staff had found the papers and was currently attempting to use them to their own benefit. But the letter had clearly indicated that the person talking about the papers had been Quince himself. Had he made some offhand comment that had been misinterpreted? That certainly bore looking into. But that would be more Robert's talent than Quince's.

Quince sighed and moved, the paper in his pocket crinkling again. If there was a solution he wasn't seeing it yet.

Once he reached the estate he tossed the letter into a bed-side drawer and prepared for bed. It was not yet four in the afternoon but he could think of no better alternative than to escape into sleep.

Three nights passed in relative quiet while Quince stayed ensconced in his rooms. The ducal suite at Belle Fleur was one of the few that he had gone to the expense to update, and it was by far his favorite. Maple furnishings, swaths of dark gold fabric, and all of it offset by jewel-colored flowers, painted and embroidered, to echo the gardens outside. He had some of his favorite artwork displayed here and could spend hours staring at a particular piece and letting his mind wander. Works from Goya, Friedrich, and Turner were all visible from where he lay on the bed. Selling artwork had been among the hardest decisions when setting the estate to rights, but he had been determined not to accept Gideon's insistent offers to bolster the duchy's coffers until the books were balanced. His friend had done enough as it was. The only time he had considered countering that decision was when he had unwisely, and without thought, made an outrageous offer for a mistress.

On the third morning, however, the door to his bedchamber was opened with a good deal more force than usual. Still half-asleep, he roused himself to look at the doorway, anticipating that Giddy had decided to insert himself into affairs. As usual. But instead of the overbearing earl, Miss Bittlesworth glided into the room as though entering a ball. Her smile was sweet and dimpled while her words slashed as quick and true as her sword.

"I wouldn't have expected you to be a slugabed, your grace. Yet I see your butler was correct. Have you really been in here for days?"

Quince cleared his throat. "My former butler."

Miss Bittlesworth went to the window and wrenched back the curtains, allowing a stream of sunlight in. Although horribly bright, it also served to highlight her figure under the flowing muslin gown. "I'm sorry, your grace?" she asked.

"My *former* butler. If my man can't stop one tiny woman from disturbing me then he shall have to find employment elsewhere."

She turned and sailed toward him with that pleasant smile firmly in place, stopping mere inches from the edge of the bed. "Don't blame him for meeting a woman who always gets what she wants."

"Do you?" Quince asked. He could tell his voice was still husky from sleep. He had obstinately not pulled the coverings up since she had chosen to intrude, and remained bare to the waist. "Do you always get what you want?"

She looked at him appraisingly. "You seem skeptical, but I can assure you that I do."

"What do you want right now?"

That seemed to make her reflective and she sat down on the edge of the bed and worried the edges of her shawl where they fell across her lap. "To help you."

"To help me? What sort of help do you fancy I need?"

She gave him a lopsided grin. "I'm not sure. Robert wouldn't tell me."

"Yet you assume that I do need help?"

"Why else would you come to see my brother? Early in the morning, unannounced, with not so much as a footman or coach in sight? It doesn't take a great deal of deductive reasoning to arrive at that conclusion. You need help with something."

"I'm sure your brother has whatever I need well in hand."

She frowned. "While I'm sure my brother has the best of intentions, his energies are spread across any number of issues. I, on the other hand," she said, replacing the frown with a smile again, "can provide you with my undivided attentions."

Her emphasis on the word *attentions* gave Quince all manner of unreasonable ideas. He had never recovered from their first meeting and thought often of what it would be like to touch her. Would her skin be as soft, her hair as fine, as he thought? Sitting there in the sunshine from the window, with her cream colored gown, she was the brightest spot in the room. He realized he was staring at her as he often did at his paintings. Barely breathing, trying to absorb every detail. Her skin was a flawless cream and her eyes sparkled again with the amusement that had drawn him into that most unwise proposition in the first place. Ringlets of dark hair brushed over her shoulders and fell down her back. He wanted to feel those curls, tangle his fingers in them. If she didn't leave the room soon he would do something untoward. Something that actually would deserve to have Robert fetch his pistols.

His extended silence drained away her smile until she was looking at him curiously. While she had spoken she had set one of her hands on the coverlet to lean closer to him. Now he couldn't resist running a finger over the skin on the back of her hand. Yes, it was soft. Soft and warm like a rose petal in the sunlight. She didn't resist or pull away, just looked at where their hands met with a ghost of her smile returning.

"Would you like to hear a secret?" she asked softly.

"Of course," he replied.

She leaned forward until her lips neared his ear, her cheek warm against his own. A curl of her hair tickled his nose, ripe with an exotic floral scent he didn't recognize. "What I really want?" Her breath fanned hot against his neck as she whispered. "Is you."

Her heart beat erratically from a boldness that even Sabre hadn't realized she possessed. She tried to draw back but the duke had tightened a hand on her upper arm, holding her in place against him. Her cheek and temple were heated from contact with his skin. He smelled, she thought, as a duke should. Like lemongrass soap and sunshine. How anyone could lounge about for three days and smell so compelling was beyond her. Nor had he looked lazy and dissolute, lying here in this bed. She had, in her time, seen any number of men without their shirts on. She had grown up in the country with brothers, after all. But the duke seemed different somehow. He was no taller nor more muscular than her own brothers, but he had a sense of presence that drew her. If she weren't afraid of the consequences, she would touch all that warm skin he had so casually left revealed even after she entered the room. What would his chest feel like? His arms? His stomach? She began to feel lightheaded from the shallow, gasping breaths she was taking and knew that she had edged toward panic. Taking a deep breath to steady her nerves meant that her senses were flooded in the duke's scent. She felt trapped between panic and surrender, and the better part of her just wanted to sink against him. To bury her nose in his hair, to feel the heat of his skin against every inch of her own. She felt him shudder against her, a moan low in his throat, as though he were considering the same things. She struggled to sit up and he released her. They stared at one another for a moment. His fair skin was flushed as she was sure her own was, and his eyes dark with intensity.

He closed his eyes and said tightly, "You must leave this room."

She hesitated, "I…"

His eyes snapped open again and the gaze he gave her was both intense and tortured. "You must leave this room. Now."

With that Sabre did something she had never done before, had not known she was capable of doing. She quit the field. The door to the room closed with a very quiet click behind her.

Nine

As she had expected, Sabre found servants haunting the hallway waiting to find out how their master would treat this interloper in his home. She took a deep breath to settle herself before trying to address them. Most of them melted away as soon as she gained the hallway but she caught one of the slower ones.

"Girl. Show me the duchess's quarters."

"Oh Miss," the young woman said, holding her apron up to her face. "I'm sure I shouldn't."

"Where is the housekeeper?"

"I'm here, Miss," came a voice from the stairwell. Sabre saw an older woman, tall and severe. She wore a dark gray, unadorned dress. "Mrs. Caldwell, if you please. Havers warned me about you."

Sabre watched as the housekeeper drew near. Controlled, no-nonsense. A slight limp on the right side, which Sabre found intriguing. With her height, plainness, and dour disposition Mrs. Caldwell could easily dress to pass as a man. Sabre wondered if she ever had. The butler Havers had been more feminine with his snowy white hair and delicate pink skin. What a fascinating household the duke had. She wondered if he noticed or simply spent all of his time locked in his rooms while he was here. Whereas Havers had been easy enough to run roughshod over it was clear that Mrs. Caldwell would resist such an approach.

Dropping into as deep a curtsy as was appropriate to give one's housekeeper, Sabre dimpled into a smile. "Miss Bittlesworth, if you please. Daughter of the Viscount Bittlesworth. Now that I have ensured that the duke is as well as can be expected, I could use some help settling into a room and would be oh, so grateful for the hospitality of a light repast. And a maid."

Mrs. Caldwell narrowed her eyes suspiciously at Sabre's apparent friendliness. "And why do you ask after the duchess's chambers?"

Sabre followed the unintentional shift of the housekeeper's gaze to the door across the hall from the duke's own rooms. People always betrayed themselves if you watched for it. She had found the duke's room in the first place by testing which door Havers absolutely didn't want her to go through. Being equipped with significantly less steel than the housekeeper seemed to possess, the butler had fled at that point. Sabre shrugged. "It seemed logical to stay as close to the duke as possible while helping him." With that she turned and went through the door the housekeeper had accidentally betrayed.

All of the drapes in this room were closed tightly against the sunshine outside, the air stale and heavy. Within two steps Sabre had sneezed from the dust kicked up from the carpets.

Mrs. Caldwell's voice was heavy with reproach, "This wouldn't be the best room for you to stay in, my lady."

Sabre held the end of her shawl over the nose and went to the window to wrest back the draperies. More dust motes danced in the air, falling on her hair and dress. With the light from the window she could see the truth of the room. It had remained untouched for years upon years. A thick coating of dust lay over everything.

Sabre coughed and looked to where the housekeeper and maid hovered at the doorway. "Why on earth has this room not been cleaned?"

The housekeeper raised her chin. "At his grace's insistence, of course."

"Some of this dust is older than him. Why would he care?"

"Not the present duke, his father," Mrs. Caldwell corrected.

Sabre scanned the contents of the room. A dainty four-poster bed was across from a bank of windows that, if Sabre didn't miss her guess, faced east for a lovely view of the sunrise. The style of the furnishings seemed years out of date. If Jack were here she would know what style this was. Tiny bottles were still on the vanity. What looked to be a robe was cast over the foot of the bed. It was as though someone had walked out of the room expecting to return many years ago and had never come back.

"How long has the duke's mother been dead?" she asked the housekeeper.

Mrs. Caldwell responded in a neutral tone. "I have never met the duchess, but she is not dead."

Sabre frowned. "Then whose room was this?"

"The duke's first wife. She passed without issue."

"When?"

"Nigh on forty years ago now."

"Forty years is more than long enough for a room to be a mausoleum." Sabre wrenched the window casing open and turned back to where the servants still stood in the doorway. "Well? Are you going to help me? Or do I need to clean this room by myself?"

After hesitating in the doorway a moment longer, Mrs. Caldwell turned to the maid. "Fetch Molly and Sarah. And Owen and Hugh as well. We'll be needing to take all these fabrics outside for a good beating."

Sabre was wrestling open the third window, most likely marring her gown beyond repair with dirt and grime.

"I thought you were hungry," Mrs. Caldwell said.

"Yes, but I can't rest while there is work to be done."

That appeared to be the right thing to say because the housekeeper helped Sabre open the remaining windows without comment.

While bathing and dressing Quince noted that his household was alive with more noise than usual. Heavy footsteps up and down the steps. Banging and rattling in some room nearby. He couldn't decide if he wanted to demand that all the uncharacteristic noise stop, or just be happy that, while entertained with whatever she was doing, the estimable Miss Bittlesworth wasn't personally torturing him. When she had leaned down and whispered in his ear... And what she has whispered. Gods, a woman had never affected him like this before! But, he cautioned himself, her actions seemed far too practiced. Far too smooth and clever. He hadn't been far wrong, he didn't think, to suppose she was some man's mistress. Perhaps she was. Or had been. The Viscount Bittlesworth was a man of low morals and his two sons had run wild through London for years. Why wouldn't the youngest of the Bittlesworths have a similar character? Well, the Bittlesworth bastard Justin Miller, whom Gideon had taken on as a clerk recently, seemed of a solid character. But that was more likely due to his common blood than any association with the Bittlesworths.

Now dressed, Quince went downstairs for his meal, barely dodging a footman with an armload of fabrics that had been coming up. The man, whose vision had been blocked by the stack, dropped them when he realized he had almost plowed through his grace, bowing and apologizing so many times that Quince almost ran in retreat. Gaining the dining room Quince saw his staff scrambling to fill the sideboard for his breakfast. It seemed quite possible that Miss Bittlesworth had disturbed the entire household, not just himself. Once he was settled he waved over a footman. "Tell my guest that I would be pleased for her to join me."

He had only just buttered his toast when the footman returned. The man bowed and said hesitantly, "She respectfully submits, your grace, that she is busy."

Quince narrowed his eyes. He wasn't one to enjoy contests of wills. But he wasn't going to let one tiny, pushy woman to run over his household. "Please inform Miss Bittlesworth that it was not an invitation. It is an order."

The footman looked stricken but bowed again before retreating. "Yes, your grace."

Moments later the girl herself appeared at the doorway, but not as he had been expecting her. He rose to acknowledge her presence, as a gentleman should, his action slowed by his confusion. "Miss Bittlesworth?"

She gave the most cursory of curtsies. "You needed me, your grace?"

Her hair was tied back under a kerchief now, her gown covered in a large apron. Every inch of her, garbed or bare, was coated in some variety of dirt. If he didn't know better he would assume she had been wrestling someone in the yard. "What on earth have you been doing?"

"Cleaning, your grace."

"You feared we didn't have a sufficient number of maids?"

She smiled. "On the contrary. I feared you had far too many without enough to do."

"What did you find for them to do?"

"We've started with cleaning the unused bedrooms."

"I don't know what to say."

"I'm sorry that I'm not dressed to join you in your repast. I'm famished."

He looked down at his plate full of food. "I could wait until you're available."

She sauntered closer. "No need. Although a piece of ham would be heavenly."

She had come close enough to be within reach and opened her mouth. Quince found himself placing a morsel of ham on her tongue, her lips closing over his fingers before he withdrew them. She closed her eyes as she chewed and gave a tiny sigh of appreciation. No, it hadn't been the dress that first time he had seen her. It was *her*. Here she stood dirty, tired, and hungry, yet all he wanted was to push the food out of the way and take her on this very table. He was shocked by his own thoughts and gripped the back of his chair to keep himself from reaching for her. Then he noticed the red marks under the grime on her left arm.

"You needed stitches?"

The young woman turned her arm to look at where his sword has scarred her. "Probably not, but Jack can be overly cautious. And she has a fine stitch so it wasn't a bother."

Quince cradled her arm and ran a finger over the puckered flesh. "I'm sorry. It was never my intention to hurt you."

"Well, I did goad you into it."

"That's no excuse for my behavior."

59

"Come now, your grace. I wanted you to fight me and I've told you that I always get what I want."

That only served to remind him of what she had most recently said she wanted. Would she let him pull her down onto this table as he wanted to? Would she raise her skirts for him?

She must have sensed his desire because she blushed and drew back. "If I may be excused, your grace?"

"Of course," he said thickly.

He sat back at the table and picked at his breakfast while the household continued to buzz with activity around him.

Ten

S abre was sure that her plan would work with the duke. Twice now he had looked at her in a way that made her heart race, as though he had found her naked. Any gentleman would offer for a lady after he had Compromised her. That was how mama had always made it sound, as though it should be capitalized. Compromised. It was exactly how Jack and Gideon had ended up married. They had barely kissed in the library before Lord and Lady Wynders had found them. Gideon had covered the awkward discovery by announcing their engagement. And Gideon was hardly a prime example of an English gentleman. His nickname was Lord Lucifer, for the love of goodness. Sabre wondered if the Duke of Beloin had a nickname. If so, she had never heard it. She was tempted to call him Lord Primandproper. But there was another side to him, too. The side that was succumbing to her flirtation.

After spending most of the day at it, she and the maids had set the bedroom to rights. The fabrics were freshened, the wood polished, and all of the glass glistening. Having investigated the layout she found that the suite had its own dressing and bathing rooms, and adjoined the duke's bedroom through a sitting room that also had its own double-doors into the hall. The staff had apparently stopped questioning her place in the household and seemed content to let her decide where she should be and what she should be doing. She had her luggage brought up to the newly freshened room and ordered a bath so she could be presentable for supper. While waiting for the bathwater to be brought up, she checked to ensure her coachman was being treated properly and went over the evening menu with Mrs. Caldwell, an activity that the housekeeper seemed surprised that anyone would be interested in. It made Sabre wonder if the duke was often in residence at this estate at all.

Finally, after hours of dirty, grueling labor, she was able to sink into hot water scented with her special oils. She started thinking of the things that would need to be done tomorrow, not the least of which was to express her gratitude again to the servants who had helped with this suite. It had ultimately been four maids, three footmen, and Mrs. Caldwell herself. They had all swept, dusted, polished, mopped, and straightened until the room was habitable. She had left the drapes down for now, the tall windows with their view of the gardens that circled the house were too beautiful to cover again just yet. In the morning, when the sunrise brightened and woke her up early she might regret it. But the room needed the light and air.

She heard a bump in the next room, followed by a knock at the door.

"I'm not ready yet," she called out.

The door pushed open, revealing the duke. "Then that is poor planning on your part," he said.

With a gasp she crossed her arms over her bosom. "Your grace!" she exclaimed.

He ignored her at first, intent on inspecting the bathing room. "I've never been in here before," he finally commented.

She huddled down into the tub as best she could to avoid the gaze that he periodically passed over her.

At last he seemed to have completed his review of the room and stood over her, hand clasped behind his back. "When I inquired after what rooms were being cleaned, Mrs. Caldwell informed me that you were having the duchess's suite cleaned for your own use. That seems presumptuous, don't you think?"

"I assumed you would want me to feel comfortable."

He laughed and looked up at the ceiling for a moment. "Miss Bittlesworth, whatever am I to do with you?"

"Let me finish my bath in peace would be my suggestion."

"I will be as clear as I possibly can. It is unseemly for you to reside in the duchess's quarters as they adjoin my own. If you have only the slightest care for your reputation certainly you understand that."

"You lecture me as though I don't have a mother."

"Your actions indicate you have a neglectful one. You arrived here without so much as the protection of a maid, tried to seduce a man in his own bed, and have now taken up residence in a room that adjoins his. Were you my daughter I would lock you away until you started to show some sense."

"How fortunate for me that you're not my father."

"Indeed, I am not. However, I am your host and with such authority shall be moving you to the south wing. Before you think to argue with me, do know that it could be my preference to have you board your carriage and return to London this evening instead."

"As you wish, your grace."

The duke paused, looking at her shrewdly. "I do not trust your acquiescence."

"I'm likely to say anything to get you to leave the room," she admitted.

At that he nodded and left without further comment.

Sabre sighed. The water had gone cold during her exchange with the duke. No matter, it was time to dress for supper. And prepare her items to be taken to the south wing.

Quince only made it to the shared sitting room before he needed to sit down. Gods, what had possessed him to do that? Yes, he had been angry when he had heard of her presumption. She seemed bent on being intrusive, bossy, and managing. But to intrude on the girl's bath was beyond the pale. Not only was it untoward, it had been very dangerous. If she had been bold enough to stand up when he had entered, he would even now be making love to her on the floor of that room. It had been distracting enough to see her bared shoulders, the globes of her breasts barely covered by her small hands, the hint of dark hair at the juncture of her thighs beneath the soapy water. That was why they absolutely could not share this suite. Tonight he would be thinking about what he had seen, what she might yet let him see. To know that she was barely a room away would drive him to distraction. If she were any other woman he would consider it. But Bittlesworth's daughter? Never. No matter her attraction. No matter her willingness. That she was the only woman he had ever felt this attracted to seemed a petty and cruel joke by a vindictive god.

Eleven

S abre set herself to being the ideal guest after settling into the south wing. She was always timely to meals, always pleasant, always smiling. The duke did not require much in the way of entertainment and she ended up with a great deal of time on her hands. As it seemed the duke primarily ignored his staff, she began to see to their needs. Nothing significant, of course. Nothing, heaven forbid, *presumptuous*. But it was apparent that it had been some time since anyone of the Quality had taken an interest in their welfare. She listened with interest to their stories and helped them with their chores as was appropriate, such as washing and slicing fruit in the kitchen. She insisted that Mrs. Caldwell take an afternoon off since it was something the older woman did with such infrequency that no one on the staff could remember the last time she had done so. By the end of the third day, acting as the de facto housekeeper while Mrs. Caldwell was in the village, Sabre felt she had made sufficient progress with the staff. Having always looked forward to running a household, she was relieved to know that the servants here were as likeable as the ones at home, if perhaps a bit more peculiar. But she had made a place with them where they looked to her as both lady of the manor and friend.

If only it were so easy to sway the duke.

After three days of observing him in close quarters it was clear to her that Quincy Telford, Duke of Beloin, was not one to share much of himself with others. He was a loner, preferring to spend long stretches of time in solitude. Although he did possess the wit that her friend Jack had complimented him on, it was apparent that he primarily used it to push others away rather than to entertain or commiserate as some do. Perhaps that was because he wished to rid himself of his current company, but she didn't believe so. Honestly, she was surprised that he had not yet insisted that she pack up her carriage and leave his home. It made her think that although he seemed to prefer solitude, he was lonely. Even an unwelcome guest could be better than no guest at all.

But she did not see where she was making progress engaging his affections. She could go that most direct route to her goal by depositing herself naked in his bed. She didn't think he would resist such an advance. However, her lesson from the first day here was that even her boldness had its limits. Merely considering such a thought had her heartbeat racing again painfully in her chest.

She was also surprised that for a man who used the sword so proficiently he did not seem to practice. On the third day she asked if he would like to practice together and received a scowl and polite refusal. His eyes had strayed to her injured arm shortly after that and she knew that he was still bothered by the fact that he had hurt her.

Plagued by all these thoughts, on the morning of her fourth day at Belle Fleur, she decided to go for a ride and clear her head.

As breakfast wasn't a formal affair, Quince didn't feel that he needed to wait for Miss Bittlesworth to arrive before eating.

But when she still hadn't arrived thirty minutes later he found himself concerned. She seemed to be an earlier riser than himself, not that it was difficult to be, but for the last two mornings had taken breakfast with him. She had seemed bent on being an affable guest, though why she thought he would believe her to be anything other than the domineering harridan she had exposed herself to be on the first day, he had no idea. He waved over a footman. "Did our guest already eat earlier this morning?"

"No, your grace. She left for a ride earlier this morning and has not yet returned."

Although happy to have his question answered so quickly and completely, he wondered why the dining room footman already had that information. Belle Fleur was far from his largest estate but it had a fairly large complement of staff. At least fifty, he thought, though he wasn't quite sure. Had the staff already been talking among themselves about her absence?

At luncheon she still hadn't arrived and Quince found himself a bit perturbed, but refused to worry about it overly. He allowed her to stay here because in his opinion people ought to be able to do as they liked. Surely he had to allow her the latitude to do as she wished with her time. In the afternoon as he sat in the library staring at a book but not reading a single page, Havers came to him.

"Your grace, the lady has still not returned from her ride."

"I see." Quince had known that the Bittlesworth girl hadn't returned yet due to the deathly silence of the house. What had seemed a peaceful quiet before her arrival now seemed dull. As though the entire household awaited her return to breathe life back into it again.

"The men would like to search for her. With your permission, of course."

"Of course. It would not be seemly to lose a viscount's daughter. Have them search."

"Very good, your grace," the butler responded, withdrawing quietly from the room. Quince returned to staring at a book he had yet to read a word in.

Sabre reared back from the sharp scent that assaulted her nose. As she shook her head to clear it she heard scuffing on a wooden floor and the creak of someone sitting in a chair. She was sitting as well. Tied to a chair, in fact. She struggled with the ropes on her wrists while tossing the hair out of her eyes to identify her captor. Who she saw made her stop struggling immediately.

"Robert, what is this meaning of this?" She looked around the room, which appeared to be a cellar in a run-down house.

"Hullo, little sister. Shouldn't I be asking you that? I thought you were going to Jack's house."

Her brother had seated himself on a wooden chair a yard away. Just far enough away to avoid any kicks if she should manage to get her foot free. His chair was turned around and he rested his folded hands and chin on the chair-back as he studied her. She began to struggle against the ropes again and he held up a finger.

"Ah-ah. How will you explain rope burns to your lover?"

Sabre blew out a frustrated breath. "He's *not* my lover."

"Really? Then why have you been at his house for three nights? The house where his father planned all his trysts?"

"Trysts? I find that hard to believe. There was a veritable shrine to the former duchess there."

"Be that as it may, why were you there? If you hadn't come out soon I was going to come in after you."

"I wanted to…to help him. How did you figure out where I was?"

"I always know where you are, Sabrina."

Sabre felt her eyes widen. "You knew about the duel?"

After a short pause, one too brief for anyone who didn't know him to notice, he said, "Of course." She knew her brother well enough to know that his pause and lack of reaction was an indication that in fact he hadn't known, but had decided to gamble on appearing omniscient. She was glad that her riding habit hid the healing scar she still carried from where the duke's sword had sliced her arm.

Knowing that she had gone down a path that needed a story before he decided to dig and find the real one she said, "I know it was foolish of Jack and me to duel, especially while in London, but she had made me so angry. And, well, once a challenge is issued…"

"It cannot be withdrawn," he answered.

She nodded.

"However, you still haven't answered my question."

"Yes, I did. I want to help him."

Robert sighed. "Don't play games with me, Sabrina, I know you're not obtuse. *Why* do you want to help him?"

"Perhaps I like him."

"Not good enough."

"Fine," she said, tossing her chin up in the air. "I plan to marry him."

Her brother stared at her and she could tell that his mind had engaged the possibilities. "Does he plan to marry you?"

She smiled. "He's made no mention of it as of yet, but you know I can be very convincing."

He sat up and continued staring at her. "There are complications," he finally said.

"Like what?" she asked, narrowing her eyes.

"We won't discuss them as yet. How do you rate your chances?"

"Good." She mused a bit and smiled. "Very good."

Now it was Robert's turn to narrow his eyes. "This is a dangerous game you're playing, Sabrina. What makes you think you will win?"

"I always win."

That made him smile in return. "Always?"

"Almost always," she corrected.

He shook his head. "Sabre, although I know you would adore being a duchess, I'm not sure I can recommend that you marry the first duke you can talk into the idea. You will need more challenge than that."

Putting her nose in the air she said, "Once I'm a duchess I will outrank you and you won't be able to say such hateful things to me."

Robert laughed. "In your dreams."

Sabre chuckled as well. After a moment she sobered and said, "Robert, I really do care for him quite a bit."

"You mean you care for Quincy Telford, not just the fact that he's the Duke of Beloin?"

She looked down at the floor, furrowing her brow, and nodded.

"Well," her brother finally said. "Will wonders never cease?"

She looked back up at him with a questioning look.

He shook his head. "Never mind. If I let you go back to Beloin-"

"Let?" she asked acidly.

"Indeed, if I let you. Note that I ensured you were well secured before we had this conversation. If I let you then you must promise me two things."

"Perhaps."

"First, if anything seems dangerous you will leave."

"Why would things be dangerous?"

"Just promise me."

Sabre blew out a frustrated breath. "Very well."

"Second, if anything interesting happens you will tell me about it."

She looked at her brother for a long moment and realized that although the Duke of Beloin thought that he had engaged Robert's help, there was something else afoot entirely. "Of course," she finally said.

In her own mind she reassured herself that she was to determine what rated as dangerous or interesting. It might not be the things that Robert would hope for.

Twelve

*L*ate in the afternoon the house began to buzz again. Quince set aside the correspondence he was essentially ignoring anyway and went out to the front hall. Miss Bittlesworth was there, surrounded by well-meaning staff who fluttered around her like butterflies over a flowering bush. The young miss was a bit the worse for wear. Tired, dirty, and disheveled. When she saw him she dropped a curtsy and his staff followed her lead.

"Your grace," she said.

"You have been returned to us at last."

She nodded. "I'm very sorry to have caused trouble, your grace. My horse had a stone in his shoe and I needed to walk him. I assumed he would know his way but I think we ended up walking in circles for hours. We would most likely still be out there if John hadn't found us and brought us home."

Quince nodded his understanding, although he had no idea who John was. Perhaps a footman or stable boy. It was also a bit troubling to have Miss Bittlesworth referring to Belle Fleur as home, but after a long, hot day walking in a velvet riding habit she would probably be content to call a dirt-floored hovel home. She seemed close to tears. "Perhaps after a bath you would like to take supper in your room to rest?"

"If it wouldn't be too much trouble, your grace."

"Think nothing of it," he reassured.

She turned to ascend the steps, her bevy of maids still around her, and then turned back to him. At first it looked as though she was going to say something, then she simply dashed forward and burrowed against his chest, wrapping her arms at his waist. He hadn't been expecting that and his arms reflexively came around her. She didn't sob, just gave a shuddering sigh as she clung to him. After a few moments she backed away, damp-eyed and miserable. They stood there, hands joined and staring at one another for a moment. Then she turned and slowly trudged up the steps.

Quince finally admitted to himself that he was, in fact, relieved that she was home.

Sabre sent all of the maids away and sank down into the warm water, wrapping her arms around herself and leaning her forehead on her drawn-up knees. Robert had blindfolded her before leading her out of the house she had been held in. Then he and his men, men she hadn't recognized, had left her in the woods after ensuring her horse did, in fact, have a stone in his shoe. That last part was a bit cruel, she thought. She had tried to dig it out with her hatpin but was afraid of causing the animal more pain than good and had given up. With the stone in the gelding's shoe she had only walked a bit, not nearly as far as she had pretended in order to account for her absence. While walking she had practiced in her mind what she would say when arriving back to Belle Fleur. It had to be believable and she needed to seem distraught enough that they wouldn't question her too closely.

Then he had walked into the foyer and she actually *had* felt distraught. Terribly so. Until that moment she hadn't even realized that her confrontation with Robert bothered her. Robert was just being Robert. Controlling and manipulative. She loved her brother, but as she had grown older she had come to know his flaws. She worried that she shared many of them. But if she was honest with herself, Robert had scared her this time. Her abductor had pulled her from her horse and covered her head with a black sack. She had struggled and fought, but with the close air inside the bag she had passed out after a few minutes. Then to awaken tied to a chair in a cellar? Under those circumstances finding her brother there had only added to her unease. She might try to talk her way around a common cutthroat, try to trick or beguile a thug, but Robert? No, her brother was more than her match.

She believed Robert cared about her, and it seemed obvious to her that he was as, or even more, interested in keeping her away from the duke rather than the reverse. It made her wonder what sort of trouble the duke might be in and how, exactly, it had occurred to Robert to use her to advance his own aims. Or what those aims might be.

But those few moments in the hallway, when she hadn't been able to control herself and had flung herself into the duke's arms? She had felt uncharacteristically comforted. Safe. In a way that perhaps she never had before. Her friends had certainly always been a comfort to her. And her brother Charlie. But something always made her push them away. To insist she could do everything on her own. But the duke...he didn't seem bent on telling her what she should do. He wasn't patronizing or judgmental. At least he hadn't been with her. She sniffled. Perhaps she was just being maudlin and reading more into the situation than it warranted. Perhaps the duke didn't care about her at all, making it quite easy to keep from telling her what to do. It seemed a bit more likely that she was just a lonely girl crying in a bathtub, wishing someone cared about her.

She finally pulled herself together and finished her bath. Returning to her room she found a note that made her heart leap.

If you would care for company we could dine in the north sitting room.
- Q

Smiling, she rang for her maid and sent a reply for him to read while she dressed.

That sounds lovely, but wouldn't it have been easier if I were still in the adjoining room?
- S

She was, she thought, even closer to being a duchess than she had realized.

Quince drummed his fingers on the small, round table in the sitting room that would serve as their dining room table this evening. He wasn't usually an impatient man but he could feel that he was on edge now. Too many pressures building up, both large and small. And he imagined Miss Bittlesworth was taking her sweet time arriving just to put a point upon the idea that if she had still been in the duchess's quarters she could have arrived sooner.

The light outside had gone to dusk but the sitting room was lit up with enough candles to hold a ball. The double doors to the hallway were wide open, the hallway lit as well. When he first saw her she was hurrying, almost running in her haste. Then she saw him and slowed her gait. He felt his heart race at the sight of her. What he thought had been general impatience was clearly just a need to see her, as his attention focused almost acutely. He rose to wait for her.

For a moment he thought she was wearing that dress again. The red one that had so distracted him when they met. But this one was darker, more modestly cut. If the previous gown had made her look a courtesan, this one made her look, he conceded, like a duchess. And he supposed that was exactly what she wanted it to convey. Women were transparent in their desire to marry up and he couldn't blame her for that. If she weren't Bittlesworth's daughter he would consider it. He might more than consider it.

As she entered the room she smiled and held her hands out to him. "Thank you, your grace, for understanding that I would like some company, if not the formality of a meal in the dining room."

He bowed over her hand and kissed it. "You've had a tiring day."

She seemed loathe to release his hands and as he enjoyed the feel of her fingers clasped in his own, he did not pull away either.

Havers' voice gently intruded. "Would you like for me to serve, your grace?"

"Yes," Quince answered automatically, still not taking his eyes off her. The butler and footmen organized the table and pulled out chairs for the duke and his guest. Quince finally released her after seeing that she was properly seated. He watched her as she settled into her seat, smoothing her skirts and fidgeting with the silverware.

"What?" she asked, smiling and looking at him from under her lashes.

"Nothing," he answered, but still didn't look away. She riveted him. Like a living, breathing painting that he couldn't get enough of studying. This evening she had pinned her hair up, highlighting the delicate curve of her neck and jaw. The curls were not in evidence so they must be more artifice than natural. The candle-light softened her features, lending her a gentleness that he hadn't previously noticed. She seemed more reticent than usual, but he supposed it was her tiring day of hiking around the countryside.

After the wine was poured he asked, "Are your rooms comfortable?"

She nodded. "Indeed. It's a beautiful estate."

"Thank you. Keeping Belle Fleur was one of my few vanities."

She gave him a confused look. "What does that mean, your grace?"

"For all that you lived in Giddy's pockets for a fortnight he didn't speak of me?"

At that she rolled her eyes. "Oh yes, they spoke of you."

Quince couldn't help the burst of laughter. "Then what did they say that earned your disdain?"

"They made you sound boring and saintly."

"Boring and saintly?" he mused. "When you add poor to that list it does make me sound rather like a vicar."

"Poor?" she asked, looking around the room.

"Perhaps not compared to most, but for a duke? I am veritably in the poor house."

"But…" she trailed off, obviously at a loss.

"Worry not. Gideon has taken it on as his mission to ensure that all is straightened out."

"I thought…I thought that you and earl had been at odds for some time."

Quince smiled. "If you think something like a political feud would keep Gideon Wolfe from helping his friends then I submit that you don't know him."

"That's very odd."

"There are some weeks where we spend all Monday shouting at each other across the House, but on Friday he still pesters my man of business to review the books. Perhaps some weeks he won't talk to me, but he will always talk to my man of business."

"Why do you even let him have such access to your accounts?"

"Why wouldn't I? I detest paperwork. Gideon loves it."

She looked puzzled.

"I've disappointed you now, haven't I?"

"I'm just confused over why you wouldn't want to have control over your own interests."

He shrugged. "Ultimately I do."

"If I were you, I wouldn't be satisfied with that."

He tapped his finger on his wineglass. "Yes, I think we may not be much alike, you and I.'"

"How boring would the world be if everyone were alike?"

Quince smiled, finding himself amused by her observation.

"Do you need me to look at your papers?" she pressed.

He cocked a brow at her. "What would you do with them?"

"That depends on what I find in them. But certainly some attention to the goings-on of your estates is better than none."

Quince waved a hand. "I have men for that."

"And the earl is their only oversight?"

"Why does this bother you so?"

"I'm hopeful that it bothers you."

"Not in the least."

She frowned. "You want to complain that you're poor, but you don't want to do anything about it?"

"Why do you think I'm not doing anything about it?"

"It seems evident. Do you have any idea how much the candles burning in this room cost?"

"Do you?"

She scanned the room, turning in her chair to see all of the candles that were burning. "Four pounds, provided that you burn them all down tonight."

"Your talents run to pricing candles?"

"I was raised to run a household. Awareness of household expenses is a key component of that."

"Somehow I doubt that a viscount's daughter will need to run a household that scrimps on candlewax."

She gave him a speaking look. "Well, I suppose one never knows."

"I share these insights about my financial condition so that you may know how unsuitable a match that I am."

"As though I couldn't figure that out for myself?"'

"You seem a bit slow on the subject, yes."

"You think that's why I'm still here, to convince you of the suitability of our match?"

"I know that's why you're still here."

"Really? It couldn't be, as I originally said, to help you?"

"There has been nothing said on that front for three full days. Certainly you would have tired of waiting and taken yourself elsewhere by now if that were your only goal."

"I thought you needed time to decide if you trusted me before you would share your issue with me."

"And why should I trust you?"

"Why shouldn't you?"

That was the question. She was Bittlesworth's daughter, but seemed to have no particular affinity for her sire. And she was

Jack's best friend. Perhaps he could trust her. But she was still holding something back of herself. He could sense it.

She fidgeted. "You're staring at me again."

"My apologies."

"Where do you go when you look like that?"

"Go?"

"You're obviously not fully here, but somewhere in your mind."

"I was just thinking about why I shouldn't trust you."

"It was a rhetorical question."

He smiled and took another sip of wine. "Even rhetorical questions should be entertained for their potential truth."

"And what potential truth might that be?"

"I shouldn't trust you because you're keeping something from me."

Thirteen

abre set her wine down. "What makes you say that?"

The duke shrugged. "Just a feeling I have."

"Is that how you run your duchy, then? On feelings?"

"Primarily."

"That's ridiculous."

He shrugged again. "Be that as it may, I feel we are at an impasse."

"Do you want me to tell you my entire life history in hopes of uncovering what is giving you this feeling?"

"No. Whatever it is, it's bothering you. Otherwise I wouldn't be aware of it."

Sabre paused. Was the duke as keen an observer as she knew herself to be? It was hard to feature since he was often not paying any attention at all. But he seemed quite confident in his assertion. She quickly thought through her options. "Well," she said, "it is true that my goal is to be your duchess."

He was quiet for a long time, absently swirling the wine in his glass as he looked at her. "That's unfortunate," he finally said.

His choice of words made her choke out a laugh. "Unfortunate? In what way is that unfortunate?"

"You're a lovely woman of many fine qualities. But I will never marry Blaise Bittlesworth's daughter."

The duke used such a tone of finality that for just a moment Sabre faltered. But, she reminded herself, she always persevered and won out in the end. This would be no different. "Well," she said. "I suppose we will see about that."

He smiled at that, gazing at her as though he was considering something. "I suppose we will," he said.

He turned his attention to cutting his roast and the conversation flagged for a moment. Sabre was contemplating what general topic to converse on when he spoke again.

"I went to see your brother because I'm being blackmailed."

She was surprised, both at his revelation and the fact that he'd shared it, but tried not so show it. "I see I'm not the only one uninformed about your poverty."

"Not over money. Over papers they believe I have."

"That you do not?"

At that he paused to stare at the dark windows. "No," he said quietly. "I don't believe that I do."

"Based on your interest in paperwork I have a hard time believing you know that conclusively."

Her acerbic comment brought his attention back to her. His habit of looking at her intently was becoming unsettling. "Here is a thing I wonder," he said.

"What?"

"How did you and Giddy spend a fortnight together without killing each other?"

Sabre flashed a knowing smile. "My incredible forbearance."

"Yes, I'm quite sure that was it," the duke said drily.

"What papers do they believe you have?"

"Something of my father's. Unfortunately they were not specific enough for me to be sure what the papers might be about."

"Was this threat in a letter then?"

"Yes."

"Let me see it."

"That's not possible."

"Why?"

"I burned it."

"You... Why did you burn it?"

"It is one thing for a duke to be blackmailed. It is quite another for it to be known that a duke is being blackmailed."

"Well, what did it say?"

The duke stared at her again for a bit. Finally he said, "It simply said 'It has come to my attention that you are in possession of papers from your father that you have been discussing with others. I will give you a fortnight to gather them.'"

"What did he threaten?"

"I would rather not discuss it."

"How am I supposed to help you if you won't share the details with me? Did you tell Robert all the details?"

"I did share the full text with Robert. He has a bit more of a reputation with this sort of issue than you do."

"You have no idea about my reputation."

He raised one golden brow. "Since you don't balk at eating alone with a man in his quarters I can only imagine."

"Not with just any man. With a duke."

"I see. So at least you have standards."

She sniffed. "I was far more impressed with your fighting skill than your title, if you must know."

"Your skill was impressive as well."

"Thank you very much. I will admit to being confused that you do not appear to be practicing. Certainly you don't go more than a few days in order to maintain your proficiency."

He smiled. "Sometimes more than a few days. But yes, I do practice often."

"As do I. Perhaps, as I said before, we could practice together."

"Perhaps."

Perhaps was better than no. Sabre realized that with the wine, food, and company that she was finally recovering from her confrontation with Robert. What would the duke do, she wondered, if she told him about her morning? Would he remain as placid as he typically seemed to be? Would he demand that she leave because there was obviously more afoot with her brother? She had yet to fully deduce what motivated the duke. He did not appear to fit the mold of anyone she had known before.

His voice called her back from her distraction. "Shall we snuff some of the candles and save the duchy's coffers for another extravagance?"

Thinking that it was a gently placed ducal command, Sabre rose to do his bidding. However, the duke rose as well.

"I could ring for a servant, your grace," Sabre said.

"No need." The duke shook his head. "It becomes tiresome having someone hover over you."

Once they had both located snuffers they began dousing the lights in the room

"How long has it been since you received that letter, your grace?"

"Almost a fortnight."

"Oh!" Sabre said, pausing in her work. "You could receive the second letter any day."

"I already have."

"What does it say?"

Now the duke paused. "I don't know."

"What do you mean you don't know?"

"I haven't read it."

Sabre was fairly sure she stood there with her mouth open for a full minute. "How could you not have read it?"

"How will reading it help me? I don't have the papers. I have no clue as to what the papers are or where they would be."

"But...if you don't read it then you have no additional clues whatsoever!"

The look the duke directed at her was nothing short of obstinate. Well, she knew how to deal with that. She walked over and put a hand on his arm, schooled her mouth into a sympathetic moue, and said in her most compassionate tone, "I'm only concerned that you be able to navigate this, your grace."

Rather than look mollified he seemed intrigued. The last time she had seen such a keen eye turned on a subject was the summer George had become enamored of bugs. The entire hot, disgusting summer every time they came across a fallen log her friend had turned it over and dug around, investigating every crawling, rolling, flying insect she could find. It had been disturbing. But far more disturbing was the intense silence as the duke stared at her.

He finally broke the silence by murmuring, "Aren't you an interesting little chameleon?"

She drew back a bit. "What do you mean?"

"Most people... How can I explain this?" He looked off towards the dark windows for a moment, and then brought his attention back to her. "Most people are consistent. Predictable.

Enslaved to the habits of their own minds. The only thing predictable about you is that you will change your tactics."

"I. . ." Sabre didn't really know what to say to that.

"Don't worry," he said with a glimmer of a genuine smile. "It's something of a compliment."

Her expression must have amused him because the small smile broke into a grin. All of the reserve and hauteur cleared away like clouds parting to let the sun shine down. As she gazed up into his spring green eyes she felt an odd sensation, like a tiny bubble bursting in her chest. Part of her wanted to reach toward him. To trace the dimple revealed in his cheek. Another part, perhaps even a greater part, wanted to run away. It was a moment of indecision and near-panic like she had never experienced before.

"Your grace, I-"

He interrupted. "Do you like the stars?"

Her mind was surprisingly slow to track his change in topic. "I suppose?"

He took her hand and began leading her to French doors that opened to the balcony. "When I dine here, which I do often, if the night is clear I spend part of the evening stargazing."

Stepping outside she discovered that the evening had cooled off nicely. Of course, she thought, being left to walk home in a heavy velvet riding habit in the afternoon had altered her perception of the heat of the day. The balcony was stone with a semi-circle overlook to the garden. He led her to the balustrade and released her hand to grip the railing, breathing deeply of the fragrant air from the gardens below. It was indeed quite lovely here, with the stars sparkling above them and the warm glow of the candlelight in the room behind. It was charming. Intimate.

"Thank you for a lovely evening, your grace."

That turned his attention to her again. After a pause he said, "Quince."

She couldn't help the smile that bloomed on her face. "Thank you for a lovely evening, Quince."

Fourteen

When she smiled up at him, said his name in her light, musical voice, Quince felt himself physically sway toward her. As though his body refused to follow the orders issued by his mind. She was, to put it simply, trouble that he didn't need in his life right now. But every time he told himself to send her on her way, to have her carriage packed and ordered off his estate, he found himself hesitating. Found himself wanting to hear her voice one more time. To see her. To watch how her facile mind leapt from topic to topic. She perpetually intrigued him. Endlessly attracted him. Just now he was almost dizzy with his desire to kiss her. She would let him, he knew, still convinced that she was to be his duchess. Every moment she spent alone at his estate with him she risked her reputation. With his position and power he could undoubtedly ruin her, in fact, without fear of repercussion. It frightened him to know what he could do to this girl. What she seemed bent on inviting him to do. He broke eye contact before his instinct to lean down and cover her lips with his own overwhelmed him.

"Which is your favorite constellation?" he asked. The huskiness of his own voice surprised him.

She looked out across the horizon. "A favorite? I'm not sure I have one." She wrapped her arm around his, leaning into him. "Which is your favorite?"

Even though he knew that everything she did was calculated, she was having what was undoubtedly her desired affect on him. His thoughts were evaporating faster than he could form them, his being focused instead on the warmth of her twined against him, her soft breast pressing against his arm. He cleared his throat. "I suppose your education didn't run to astronomy." Although he regretted saying it almost immediately, he knew that most likely nothing would push her from him as quickly as questioning her intelligence. And right now pushing her away seemed imminently wise.

She surprised him by laughing. "My education runs to anything that Jack could get her hands on when we were children. The only thing that she enjoys more than learning something new is explaining it to someone else. Sadly, much of it has remained resident up here." She tapped her forehead with her free hand.

He chuckled. "So that included astronomy?"

"And associated mythology lessons in Greek." She looked out at the blanket of stars. "Jack teases me by calling me Athena, so she says I should understand all the poor souls I cast into the sky."

"It sounds as though you were enthralled."

Sabre shrugged. "Some of it was interesting. Like Auriga there on the horizon, to symbolize the four-wheeled chariot that Erichthonius used to become King of Athens."

"Why is that interesting?"

"Erichthonius used his lameness as a motivation to create a superior weapon and take over a kingdom. How many of us use our weaknesses in such a way?"

SUE LONDON

Quince looked down into her eyes again. She seemed so earnest in that moment. So pure.

"And," she said, smiling again, "now that I've identified a constellation, hopefully to your satisfaction, what is your favorite, your grace?"

"Quince."

"Quince," she said lightly enough that it was almost a whisper.

"Do you know Lynx?"

She shook her head, looking back out to the sky. "No, I don't believe so."

"It's very faint. Identified relatively recently. It wouldn't have been one that Jack could have lectured in Greek. It's a line there," he said, pointing, "between Ursa Major and Auriga."

"How many stars is it?"

"The line is drawn with eight stars." He traced it with his finger, showing her the pattern.

She shook her head and squinted. "I'm not sure I see it."

He shifted behind her, leaning down so that his face was near hers, and sighted down his arm. "From Ursa Major if you look to the left that is the brightest star of Lynx. Right now it cascades down over Auriga, toward Camelopardalis. I can show it to you on a star map in the library."

"You may have to because I'm still not sure I see it."

Leaning so close to her, he was enveloped in her scent and heat. Her hair smelled heavenly and was still damp from her bath. Noticing that only succeeded in making him think of that damnable tub in the duchess's rooms. He had interrupted her bath that day in order to discomfit her as she had already managed to discomfit him in his own home. Instead he had only fueled his attraction to her. He hadn't really seen much, but knowing that she was naked in the tub... It had led to him thinking often of how the exchange could have progressed far differently. How it would have progressed far differently if he were more like his friend Gideon. Lord Lucifer.

Quince straightened away from her but set his hands lightly on her shoulders, knowing it would keep her in place while he gathered himself. He was not, nor would he ever want to be, a man that others would feel inspired to call Lord Lucifer.

She looked over her shoulder at him. "Somehow this entertains you? Spending nights standing on the balcony studying the stars?"

Her tone was teasing but he could tell that she truly could not feature such an activity as entertainment. "Well," he said, "I usually lounge on the balcony rather than stand, but yes. Essentially."

She looked around and spotted the chaise lounge near the windows. "I see," she said, walking towards it. She settled onto the chair and stretched out. "What you really like to do is daydream while staring at the stars." She wriggled once to find a more comfortable position. "Yes, this has distinct possibilities."

His hands felt achingly empty so he folded them together as he leaned on the railing to watch her. She was beautiful. He could stare at her in that pose for hours. If only she weren't her father's daughter. But if she weren't Blaise Bittlesworth's daughter, then what would he do? He had felt no desire to marry before now. Would he change everything in order to bring her into his life? Make her his duchess to keep her by his side?

She sat up again. "It's not fair of me to monopolize the chair. Come," she said, patting the cushion next to her. "Show me how to daydream under the stars."

Quince was moving to do her bidding before he had a chance to think about it. Dangerous girl, he thought, made all the more dangerous by knowledge of her own power. She stood up as he approached and waved her hand to indicate that he should lie down in the chair. He did so while knowing it was among the riskier things he had ever done. She smiled down at him before turning and seating herself to lie along his front. Shortly she seemed to have everything arranged to her satisfaction although the two of them barely fit on the lounge together. Her head was tucked under his chin, her shoulders nestled into his chest, and she had wrapped his arms around her waist. Her bottom was pressed so intimately against him that he was afraid he wouldn't be able to breathe.

"So," she said quietly, as though she felt a more somber note was appropriate for entering into his pastime with him. "What do you see?"

At the moment his vision wasn't the sense he was most focused on. Scent, yes. Touch, God yes. And he craved tasting her like a man dying in the desert craves water. But she wanted to know what he saw. He cleared his throat and focused on the night sky above.

"One of the clues that I have is up there, if I can just figure it out."

"Really? How is that?"

"My father had a group he ran with when he was younger. He would tell me stories about them. They did some quite... inappropriate things in their time. And when he would talk about them it was never by name, he would refer to them with an animal. It took me a long time before I realized what I was seeing in the late spring. All four of them, lined up." He raised a hand to point at the stars above. "Leo, the Lion. That was my father. Ursa, the Bear. Draco, the Dragon. And Cygnus, the Swan. If someone has reason to be concerned about papers my father kept, it is probably one of them."

"If your father was the Lion, who are the rest of them?"

"I don't know." Quince paused for a moment, wondering how Miss Bittlesworth would take his next bit of insight. Or if she might already know. "I only know that one of them is your father. But not which one."

She was silent so long he feared he had indeed offended her. But she hadn't moved, not even an inch. They were both silent for long minutes, pressed together in a delicious intimacy of touch.

Finally Miss Bittlesworth spoke again, her tone remote. "Tell me some of the stories and I can tell you which one is my father."

Quince made a noise somewhere between a snort and a chuckle. "They are hardly stories fit for a young lady."

She curled her fingers around his hand and squeezed. "Yes," she said drily. "I'm obviously easily shocked."

Bold as she thought she was, he didn't want to give her the details of the group's sordid excursions. Instead he thought to sketch their characters. "Leo, the Lion, was their leader. At least that was how he told it. As I've never heard any of the stories from the others I don't know for certain they felt that way. But to hear my father, he was their inspiration and their organizer. If you had met him you would know it would be a role he would relish. He enjoyed control. In his final years he lost his iron grasp on affairs, but his pride kept him from admitting that. Something from which the duchy is still recovering." He pointed to the sky above. "Next is Ursa, the Bear. He sounded a brute of a man. Arrogant, entirely self-concerned. Then Draco. Cruel and vindictive. And lastly Cygnus. Vain and secretive."

They were quiet for awhile, staring up at the stars, and finally Miss Bittlesworth asked, "Is that all?"

"All that I want to say."

She gave an unladylike groan. "You've described over half the men at the George and Vulture on any particular night."

"What do you know about the men at the George and Vulture?"

"Society events get quite boring, but there is always a conversation of interest at the G and V."

"I find myself shocked at you, Miss Bittlesworth."

"Sabre," she corrected. "And if you find yourself shocked then you obviously haven't been paying attention."

"How often do you find yourself at the George and Vulture?"

"As often as I can slip away. Which has been not at all since my return from Italy. My only regret of staying with my brother is that he keeps a closer eye on me than my parents do."

"Yes, he's obviously been very diligent, seeing as how his sister has hied off to a man's house for a seduction."

She was quiet longer than he expected her to be. "He thinks I'm at Jack's."

"Well, at least you didn't try to convince me that you aren't here to seduce me."

She wriggled until she had turned over, propping herself up on an elbow to look down at him. The candlelight from their dining table cast a warm glow through the window and he could see the sincerity in her eyes. "You'll find I'm not one to be coy."

He stroked her cheek. Softer than rose petals. "I don't think that's true."

She gave him a guarded look. "What makes you say that?"

He smiled. "Because, my little chameleon, I think you would do, or say, whatever is needed to achieve your goals."

"You make me sound woefully untrustworthy."

"That depends on your motivation."

She gave him an angelic smile. "I have only the best of motivations, I assure you." She turned over again, nestling back into his embrace. "Now, really tell me about these men, if you please. I can't help you without facts, information."

"From that sketch you can't tell which one was your father?"

She was silent for a moment. "He could be any of them," she said solemnly.

Quince could sense the gravity of her statement. The viscount was as unpleasant a man to his daughter as he was to others. "I don't want to tell you about them," he said. "I don't like to think about them myself."

"Yes, you seem able to avoid most everything you don't want to think about."

"You don't approve."

"Not in the least. We'll open that letter before the night is out. But first, tell me some of these stories."

He laced his fingers through hers as he thought. He didn't want to tell her, but it was also true that he hadn't yet figured out the connection on his own. For years his father had regaled him with those tales at the supper table. Stories that Quince had never wanted to hear, and that he certainly had never thought would be significant. He had done his best not to listen, to forget. But now it was time to try to remember, if only to divine which of his father's friends would be the most alarmed at the idea of documents surfacing. Which one would not hesitate to use blackmail as a means to an end. The vindictive dragon? The self-centered bear? Or the secretive swan?

"Don't say I didn't warn you," he began. He paused for a moment to gather his thoughts, his fingers playing over the velvety softness of the back of her hand. "The stories that my father particularly liked to tell concerned the parties that he hosted for The Four. That's what they called themselves, The Four. He would load them up into a windowless carriage that he drove himself, never taking the same route, and bring them to a special cellar out in the woods. They would bring all the food and drink themselves because no servants were allowed to know the location. And they would bring women. Whores. Blindfolded and bound." He stopped stroking her hand for a moment, lost in the disgust of the memory. "That was his favorite part, I think. That the women were bound. He liked it if they fought of if they begged, so long as they were bound and unable to...unable to stop him."

Miss Bittlesworth's voice was subdued but steady as she asked, "What of the other lords?"

"Draco...Once he started drinking he would beat the girls. He enjoyed making them scream. Choking them." He sighed. Remembering the stories was painful. And he certainly couldn't tell Miss Bittlesworth the sort of details that his father had thought nothing of sharing. "Cygnus was... probably the least offensive of The Four. He only liked to... engage multiple women at once. Ursa, the Bear, was brutal and enjoyed some very distasteful acts. Often with women but also boys and young girls. He sounded beastly." Quince tried to repress the details that flitted through his mind, far worse than anything he had hinted at. "Are there any you would rule out as your father?"

Miss Bittlesworth was silent for a long moment and finally said, "No. And it sounds like a Hellfire Club."

Quince was disquieted that she found none of the descriptions to be out of character for her own sire. What had she seen of the man? And her knowledge of these activities was also disturbing. "What do you know of Hellfire Clubs?"

"I go to the G and V to hear the soldiers talk of battles in the war. But I hear other things. Horrible things. It makes me wonder why men have one face they show ladies and another that they only show in a place like that."

"You would prefer that they consistently show their baser nature?"

"No, indeed. It's not even something I would expect to change. But it makes me curious. It also makes me wonder how difficult it might be for us to reconcile your stories with the men as we know them in Society."

"In Society, yes, but it's apparent they can't hope to step foot in the G and V without you knowing of it."

She giggled. "It's not quite that bad, I assure you."

"I feel certain that at any moment you will tell me you are the proprietor."

"No. But the man knows me. Or at least knows me as the little fat boy, Gaston."

Quince laughed. "Little fat boy?"

"Yes, if I wear enough padding to disguise myself I'm quite the chubby little boy. The loose clothes of the serving class don't help at all, may I add."

"You didn't seem particularly masculine at the duel."

"No, those are the clothes that I wear when we duel at home. Out in the country."

"Your parents truly do not pay attention to your whereabouts, do they?"

"So long as I arrive at supper on time there aren't any issues."

"Even I am starting to worry about how you spend your time."

"Fear not. I'm usually with the other Haberdashers and we look out for one another."

"Haberdashers?"

"Our club. Jack and George and myself."

Quince felt an unfamiliar and fierce twinge. "Who is George?"

"George Lockhart. We all grew up together in Staffordshire." Miss Bittlesworth sighed. "Now Jack is married and George is off to care for her ailing aunt in Scotland."

At the hint that George was a girl after all, he felt the pain in his chest subside. He hugged Miss Bittlesworth closer. "And now you're lonely?"

He felt her stiffen in reaction. "No, I'm not saying that. It's simply different." She sighed again, relaxing back into him. "I was gone for eight months and when I came back everything was just different." Her tone had become a bit forlorn at the end.

"It's the nature of growing up," he said.

"Don't patronize me," she warned.

Quince smiled to himself. "Like it or not, I have a few years on you. Perhaps I know what I'm talking about."

That made Miss Bittlesworth wriggle to turn around again. He was fairly sure that her skirt was becoming woefully tangled by this point.

"I'm not arguing whether you are correct," she said. "I'm saying that you're being patronizing."

"And you don't care for that?"

"Not at all."

A lock of her hair had come free from its pins and curled down along her jaw. He smoothed it back behind her ear. As he watched, her expression changed from mild irritation to specu-lation, and then to a wicked delight.

"What?" he asked.

"It just occurred to me that I have the high ground. A strategically superior position."

Quince ran his thumb over her jaw. "Really? And what do you plan to do with that?"

"Conquer," she whispered before lowering to cover his mouth with her own.

Fifteen

$\mathcal{S}$abre could feel her own heartbeat increase as she leaned down to kiss the duke. When she pressed her lips to his she felt him tense. He gripped her arms and for a moment she was afraid he was going to push her away. Then he succumbed and pulled her closer. Their lips slid and clung in a dance similar in tempo to their duel. Sabre's skin flushed and her breathing became uneven. She had been kissed many times, but never to this effect. She had made a study of kissing, actually. It had started when she was six years old and convinced one of the stable lads to teach her. He had been only eight and more than happy to comply. She had continued this tutelage with the local boys until she was ten and her mother had found out. It had led to the most severe punishments she had ever known in her life, followed by years of lectures about her Reputation. And how her Reputation could be Compromised. But Sabre was nothing if not determined and had resumed her education on kissing as soon as she began to attend dances. All of that effort had seemed for naught now. Here was the man she was meant to kiss. No one else had ever made her feel like this.

Lying on his chest she threaded her fingers into his tousled hair and heard him moan low in his throat. His arms circled her and his hand fastened at the nape of her neck, holding her close. They deepened the kiss, mouths open and searching. Even this didn't seem enough and she found herself overwhelmed with a desperate hunger. He moved his hands to the sides of her face and gently held her still while pulling his own mouth away. She heard herself huff in protest.

His breathing was as labored as her own. "A moment, please," he said between gasps.

She nodded and, once he released her, nuzzled her face into his neck. His pulse was speeding in his veins, further testament that she wasn't the only one affected. He put his arms around her again, stroking her back. Lower, she could feel his manhood jutting against her thigh. Some of the serving girls back home had been willing to tell her about what happened between a man and a woman. Opinions seemed to vary on how enjoyable the act was, and before now Sabre had wondered how it could be quite as transcendent as some girls as had described it. But that had been before his kiss. Before being pressed up against him in an intimate embrace. The only thing she wanted was to be closer to him. To feel his skin under her hands. She started to unbutton his shirt but by the second button he had captured her hand.

"Sabrina," he said in a chiding tone. But he moved her captured hand to his mouth and kissed her fingertips, her palm, her wrist.

"Quince," she responded in a whisper, kissing his throat where his pulse still beat fast and steady.

"This is—" he paused to kiss her palm again, sending shivers through her. "Unwise."

"Is it?" she asked.

"Most unwise," he assured her before gripping her arms and pulling her up for another kiss.

The friction of sliding against him made her skin tingle. And then his kiss. Where their first kiss had quickly led to a driving hunger, this time it was sweet. Sacred. She felt she could go on kissing him like this for hours. Forever. Finally, her lips swollen and tingling, she gave a small sigh and rested her head on his shoulder. Her heart felt whole. Nothing existed outside the sweet cocoon of his touch. Weary from her day, she slept.

Quince awoke with a hot, heavy blanket on him. Shortly before he was going to toss it to the floor he realized it wasn't a blanket but Miss Bittlesworth. Sabrina. Sabre. They had slept the whole night on a silly chaise lounge on his balcony. He felt foolish. And delighted. And rather intensely wanted to take her into his bedroom to finish what they had started. She was so warm and soft. Rounded in all the perfect places that a lady should be. He caressed his hands over her hips and derriere. Were that she could be his mistress, he would feel no need to leave his chambers for the foreseeable future. He had never felt that way about any woman before, but she seemed to incite all of his carnal desires. She had from the first moment he saw her.

She stirred and he moved his hands from their intimate wanderings back up to her shoulders. She raised her head and smiled at him. "Good morning."

His fairy queen was rumpled, hair fallen from pins. Her voice was scratchy from sleep. He had never seen anything more beautiful. "Good morning," he whispered, cupping her cheek. She leaned into his touch, closing her eyes. He couldn't stop himself from kissing her again. She giggled in surprise but enthusiastically returned his kiss. She twined her fingers into his hair. Shortly, what had started as a morning greeting changed to exploration. Changed to seduction. He moved his hands to her hips, anchoring her against himself. Wanting so desperately to remove the clothes that separated them. He felt something that was beyond desire. Beyond seduction. He wanted to push her down on the floor and raise her skirts. Wanted to drive into her relentlessly and hear her screaming his name.

If asked, he wouldn't have thought himself capable of rising from the chaise that quickly and setting her bodily aside. She looked confused and swayed a bit on her feet.

"I..." Quince stopped, unable to say anything. He couldn't even meet her eyes. He had always prided himself on being better than his father. Better than Gideon. They had given in to their desires, used women as nothing more than objects for satisfaction. Now he found that with the right temptation his willpower was no stronger than theirs.

Her voice subdued, she said, "If you could excuse me, your grace, I need to refresh myself."

Now he did look at her to see that she gave him a brilliant smile, her eyes sparkling. "Quince," he reminded softly.

"Quince," she agreed, her tone that of someone sharing a secret. She curtsied and left the room as though everything were perfectly normal. As though she woke up every morning lying on top of a duke. What did he know, perhaps she did. He tapped his fist against his thigh, not sure where to put his conflicted feelings. A large part of him wanted to pursue her. While they were kissing he had been afraid he would demand her favors. Now he was afraid he would beg for them. She was a complication he didn't need.

Once she was out of sight of the duke, Sabre put a hand to the wall of the hallway and took a moment to balance herself. For all that she had followed her curiosity over the years to discover what there was to know about kissing and lovemaking, everything from last night and this morning was outside of her experience. She had never *felt* like this before. In fact, *feelings* weren't something that she equated with any of her previous encounters. Unless curiosity, discovery, and, at times, disgust counted as feelings. But this had been different. The duke had been different. Quince. Just thinking his name she found her skin burning. When he had gripped her and held her tight against his manhood, her body had responded with a searing ache low in her belly and a wetness that she could still feel. Then he had set her aside. It was like being cast down from heaven.

But she had seen the panic in his eyes, the tension in his body where only moments before there had been a languid pleasure. Regardless of her own desire to protest, to argue, to seduce, she could see that he was very much on the edge of ordering her away. And thus she had used the only strategy that occurred to her to set things to rights. Pretended nothing was wrong. Pretended everything was normal. But leaning here on the wall she knew nothing was normal at all.

And drat the man, she had forgotten to badger him until he produced that letter. What had she been thinking? Nothing at all, was the answer. After he had started kissing her she didn't remember having any thoughts of substance. Well, she would march back in there and make him show the letter to her. In a moment. Perhaps after she had an opportunity to straighten herself and change into fresh clothing. Pushing away from the wall she made her way back to her room.

Not sure what else to do with himself and too restless to sit still, Quince had repaired to the ballroom to practice his fencing forms. He had no fencing master in residence, something he would consider changing since he found himself at Belle Fleur more often. For today he certainly didn't want to invite Miss Bittlesworth to partner him as a good deal of what he needed to do was get *away* from her to think. Or not to think. He wasn't really certain anymore. But now he was tired, slick with sweat, and looking forward to some repose before luncheon.

What he didn't want was to find his intrusive guest up to her elbows in the bottom drawer of his bureau.

"Is there something I can help you find, Miss Bittlesworth?"

She startled a bit but then addressed him over her shoulder while reaching even deeper into the drawer. "I'm trying to find that bloody letter."

"You won't find it there."

"So I've noticed." She slid the drawer shut and turned to face him while still on her knees. "Well?" she asked.

"Well what?"

"Where is it?"

"What makes you think I'll tell you?"

She shook her head, sighed gustily, and folded her hands together like a forbearing governess. "I'm only trying to help you, your grace."

He couldn't help but to laugh at her overly dramatic mien. She rewarded him with a smile and held out her hands to be helped up from the floor.

At sight of the duke Sabre had felt a little lurch in her heart. He had obviously been doing something vigorous, seeing as his white shirt was damp and clung to his form. His hair, usually artfully tousled in keeping with the modern style, was instead slicked back from his face. She had wondered how he kept his physique since the last creature she had known as apparently lazy had been an old cow on the Bittlesworth estate. But evidently he was willing to engage in physical activity from time to time.

As he walked toward her his posture was more relaxed, looser, than she had seen before. Best of all, he was smiling down at her as he grasped her hands to raise her to her feet. She realized, with a small *frisson* of worry, that she would do a lot to see that smile. Part of her heart was clamoring '*look at me, smile at me, I will do anything.*' She tried not to let the worry over her own weakness be reflected in her eyes.

"Where is it?" she asked again, still smiling. But her heart was saying, '*touch me, kiss me.*' Treacherous thing, her heart. Best not to be trusted no matter how fast it beat or strongly it yearned.

He stared down at her a few moments, as though considering her request. Their hands were still joined and his thumb absently stroked over her fingers. She wanted to step into his embrace. To lift her lips for another kiss. But she didn't know what had disturbed him this morning. And not knowing she didn't want to risk his rejection.

He squeezed her fingers and turned to walk towards the bed. Her heart sped again, wondering his intentions. But he merely slid open the drawer of the bedside table and drew out a folded paper. Her startlement pushed aside the distracting intentions of her heart.

"You had it *there*? Anyone could have found it!"

He grinned. "You didn't."

"I obviously thought too highly of you! The next time I have to find your important papers I shall start by looking in the middle of the floor."

He shook his head in amusement, still smiling. Then looking down at the paper in his hands his smile slowly faded.

Sabre bustled across the room and held her hand out. "Unpleasant things are best dealt with quickly. Let me open it if you don't want to."

The duke frowned but handed the paper over to her. She inspected it closely. Fine, heavy paper. Unsealed and a bit crumpled. Sabre couldn't imagine resisting simply unfolding the paper to discover what it said. She glanced at the duke and saw that his attention was focused on the paper in her hand, the frown still on his face. She opened the letter and the first line after the salutation chilled her heart through.

My dearest duke,

Your mother is doing quite well. I'm sure she would send her love if she knew I was writing to you. Sadly I must leave her soon for my rendezvous with you in London. I say rendezvous but it is best if we don't meet. Leave the papers on the sideboard of the anteroom at White's at precisely eleven o'clock in the evening on the eleventh. Leave the building and don't look back.

Sincerely,
Your father's friend

Sixteen

"He's threatening your mother?" Sabre asked, shocked.

The duke turned and walked towards the window, hands clasped behind his back. "So it seemed from the first letter. What does he say now?"

Sabre knew she would have been able to read the text upside down from where he had been standing, but perhaps his talents didn't lie in the same direction hers did. Or he didn't want to read it.

When she read off the first sentence he spun to face her again, his expression frighteningly remote. As she continued reading he walked back to where she stood, his attention still on the paper. She was beginning to think it quite probable that he had burned the first letter with his gaze alone. Between the cold threat of the blackmailer's words and the banked fury she sensed from the duke she felt, for the first time in her life, out of her depth.

He pulled the letter from her fingers. "Thank you, that will be all."

Being dismissed like a common servant brought her chin up. "I beg your pardon?"

"You may leave."

"I will not. I came here to help you and I will."

She realized her mistake when his icy demeanor cracked a bit and rage poured out. "Really? You know where the papers are that this madman wants? You can protect my mother? You need to stop offering things that you cannot supply!"

But she wasn't one to be easily cowed. "You might not be in this bind if you'd done more than lounge about for the past week! In case it had escaped your notice, tomorrow is the eleventh!"

"Of course I know that!" Crumpling the letter in his fist he strode back to the window. He braced his hands on the casing and stared out at the gardens. After a few moments he hung his head and said more quietly, "What is it you would have me do? There are no papers. To the best of my knowledge there never were."

Sabre joined him at the window. "He believes there are papers? Give him some."

Quince looked at her, tension clear in his expression. "Forgeries?"

Sabre shrugged. "Forgeries, or better yet some of your father's papers that, with a stretch of the imagination, could be misconstrued to be damning. Can you think of anything like that?"

He shook his head but had a distracted look as though he were running through the options in his mind.

"Now may I look at your father's papers?" she asked.

He glared down at her. "Why?"

"It is only a hunch, but I believe I may be far more devious than you. There are probably things we could use that you just aren't seeing."

He considered it for a moment, jaw tensing, then finally nodded. "I'll take you downstairs shortly. You may spend the afternoon looking, but we will need to decide on something quickly." At that he strode to the fireplace and pulled out a match.

"No!" she cried, snatching the paper from him.

"There's no reason to keep it," he argued, reaching for the letter again.

"How can you say that?" she asked.

"We already know what it says."

"But we might forget or mix up the wording."

He recited the letter to her word for word as she reviewed the paper incredulously. She wasn't sure which was more disturbing, his precision or the detached monotone he used. This was his *mother*. He had obviously known she was at risk since the first letter, yet he had done nothing. But Sabre didn't resist when he took the paper away again. He set fire to it and dropped it in the fireplace. They watched it burn in silence. Once it was ash he broke it apart with the poker to ensure that no trace remained.

He looked at her again, still remote and tense. "I'll show you to the study and have luncheon sent in to you."

"Yes, your grace," she said quietly. He preceded her without looking back and she followed. She noted that he hadn't corrected her that time to use his name rather than his honorific.

Quince had conducted Miss Bittlesworth downstairs, had eaten, bathed, dressed, and now found himself staring down at the gardens again. Hours had passed and he found he was still furious. How dare that odious monster intimate an association with his mother? Was the swine courting her? Attending her salon? Now, since he had put off opening the letter, he didn't have the time to visit her and reassure himself that she was safe. Try to ascertain whether anyone new had joined her circles. Warn her that any such person might try to do her harm. He was, to put it bluntly, exactly the idiot that Miss Bittlesworth had accused him of being.

And as for Miss Bittlesworth, she was perhaps in a good deal more trouble than she realized. When she had insisted that she wanted to help, his first thought was that she could help by spreading her legs for him. He had never thought that rage and passion could be so closely intertwined, but the desire to lose himself in her, distract himself from the realities of these blackmail threats by burying himself in her scent and heat was almost too much to bear. Knowing she would let him, would be enthusiastic, made the temptation all that much more staggering. Even if she weren't a virgin, and he increasingly doubted that she was, it was beyond the pale to treat her like a doxy. She was still a woman of the Quality, no matter what seductions she attempted to use on him in pursuit of a title. It was best for both of them that he ensure she didn't remain here at Belle Fleur.

He heard a knock at his open door and, turning, he saw her, as though conjured up from his thoughts. Her gown today was a cream muslin decorated with subtle gold embroidery. Fetching, and certainly appropriate for a girl of her age and station. Nothing that should inflame his desire. She had left off with covering the scar on her arm with a shawl. All things he had noted earlier but filed away as facts. Now they seemed like something more. As he scanned his gaze down her body he saw that she was carrying a sheaf of papers. Sadly, she had not come with seduction on her mind. She seemed hesitant at the doorway.

Hesitancy was not something he had heretofore associated with her. He strolled toward her. Prowled, actually.

She still hadn't said anything so he supposed there was something in his demeanor that didn't invite conversation. He pulled the papers from her hand and set them on a nearby table. Circling her wrist with his fingers he pulled her into the room and closed the door. He backed her against the wall and nuzzled her throat.

"If you want to leave," he warned in a whisper, "you should run away now."

Her only response was to grip his arms and pull him closer.

He knew it was wrong, but he was tired of fighting this attraction. "I won't marry you," he said.

"We'll see about that," she replied.

He cupped her breast and heard her quick gasp of breath. As he met her lips he moaned low in his throat. This was all he wanted. She was all he wanted. Everything from the first moment he had seen her had been leading to this. His hand continued to stroke and fondle her breast. He couldn't wait to lay her down on his bed. To strip her clothes so that she laid nude before him, all softness and curves and needy desire. She surged against him, suckling his lips and tongue even more desperately. After a few moments he pulled away.

"Sabrina."

"Don't worry," she whispered, "I know what to do."

She pulled her skirts up her thighs. He thought his heart might burst from his chest it started galloping so fast. If she wanted their first time to be against the wall with their clothes on, who was he to argue? He unbuttoned the flap of his breeches with shaking fingers and she wrapped her leg around his hip. His first thrust slid along her wet folds and he groaned with the intimate contact, but it wasn't penetration. Gripping her hips he lifted her against the wall and adjusted the angle. With a shallow thrust he felt the entrance to her channel, so hot and wet and tight. Instinct made him buck into her. As his cock slid in he felt a momentary barrier and then he was buried to his root. The sheer pleasure of joining with her for the first time brought him to completion. It might have been the greatest moment of his life if she hadn't screamed.

Sabre had known that joining the first time could be painful but nothing had prepared her for this. In her time she had been shot, stabbed, and broken more than one bone. She had been thrown from horses and brawled with her friends more times than she could count. She had experienced pain but had never been particularly intimidated by it. Perhaps it was the surprise. Perhaps it was the intimacy of this particular pain. But it had shocked a scream from her and she could feel tears at the corners of her eyes.

The duke set her on her feet, cradling her face and tipping her chin up. She could see his concern and worry. "Sabre, I'm so sorry. I didn't know. You acted as though... I didn't think you were a virgin."

For some reason that made her want to cry all the more. She turned her face away and smoothed her skirts down. "If I may be excused, your grace," she said in a toneless voice.

"Quince," he corrected miserably.

She nodded and slipped through the door out into the hallway.

Seventeen

$\mathcal{Q}$ uince leaned his head on the wall. He felt like crying. This was like the duel, but worse. He had hurt her. Again. He had no excuse for allowing her to incite him. Again. If his intention were to marry her then he could at least feel that this was some challenge on the road to their happy union. But he could not ally himself with Blaise Bittlesworth any more than he could fly. Every fiber of his being rebelled at the thought. He had been clear with her that there would be no marriage and she had offered herself freely. But it would always be a weight on his soul now, knowing that he had ruined her. And hurt her while doing so. If she had experienced some pleasure in the joining it might have been a balm, but it was clear she had not. Standing straight again he set to putting himself to rights and buttoning his breeches. A sticky wetness made him look at his hand. The blood he saw made him dizzy.

"Sabrina," he choked out. He turned to the door to find her, to soothe her somehow, though he didn't know how. Then he realized that his first order of business was to clean himself so that he didn't terrorize her by being a bloody mess.

Sabre let herself into the sunny, rose-colored room she had been assigned at the estate and closed the door. The day seemed too bright and she went from window to window, drawing the curtains closed. Even with the dimmer light the room felt too open, too exposed. She went into the dressing room. It was better here. Darker. Quieter. She sat in the corner, pressing her forehead into her drawn up knees. She didn't cry or keen, even though she wanted to. She didn't even think. Just breathed and tried to let her body settle. She wasn't sure how long she had been there when she heard the duke's voice calling her name. She lifted her head to listen. It sounded as though he was opening all the doors in the hallway calling for her. She heard the door to the Rose Room open.

"Sabrina?"

He sounded worried. She wanted to call out to him, to go to him, but she found herself still immobilized and huddled into the corner. This wasn't like her. She didn't even have the energy to be angry with herself for being such a wilting flower. Something in the room must have hinted of her residence and she heard him walk inside.

"Sabrina?" he called more softly.

She whimpered. Quietly, involuntarily. But he heard it because his footsteps came towards her more quickly. He pushed the door to the dressing room the rest of the way open.

"Sabrina?" he said again, this time his voice choked with emotion. Something in his voice, his presence, broke the spell holding her trapped and, standing, she launched herself into his arms. He held her close.

"I'm so sorry," he said.

She shook her head. He had done no more than she had asked. She burrowed into his warmth. Even if she didn't enjoy joining with him, his touch did more to feed her soul than anything she had ever known. His scent gave her comfort. When she had come to his room to show him the papers he had been freshly shaved and perfect, from his artfully tousled hair to his brown top boots. She wasn't sure which she preferred, the perfectly turned out duke, the lazy man who could lounge in bed for all hours and make her want to join him, or the sword master who seemed made of concentration, talent, and sweat.

She pulled his face down for a kiss. She felt empty and she needed him to fill her. He was hesitant at first, but surrendered to her avid lips. She moved her hands down to curl in the silk of his vest, holding herself tight against him.

Quince had felt his heart break to find her huddled in the corner of what was essentially a closet. And now she was wrapped against him like a vine. It was a more extreme version of the hug she had given him yesterday after her horse had gone lame. He was unreasonably pleased that he could offer her comfort, even if dismayed that the comfort she needed was for his treatment of her. If what she wanted was his kiss, his touch, he would give them to her gladly. After some time her desperation eased and she laid her head against his shoulder. He caressed her back and waited to see if she had anything to say. She was silent so long that he felt sure the sun was setting.

"Shall I send up a bath?" he asked gently.

She gave a gusty sigh and nodded.

"Will you need help cleaning up?"

She looked up at him, confused. "Why?"

Quince found himself too embarrassed to speak of it. "I'll send up a maid. And supper."

"Will you stay?"

"I..."

"You've already seen me at my bath," she pressed. He found that she didn't seem inclined to let him go even though he was trying to extricate himself in order to ring for the maid. He finally gave up and instead pulled her to his side to walk across the room with him. After the maids came and the footmen carried up the bath he was finally able to convince her to let him leave to attend to some things before they ate. He managed to escape while a table and chairs were brought in. The servants fluttered around her, paying more attention to her than they ever had to him.

Sabre was still terribly sore. When she removed her dress she discovered why Quince had asked her if she needed help cleaning up. There was blood on her dress and on her thighs. She had supposed the wetness to be the same as the night before, a clear, slick liquid her body produced as part of her attraction to him, but it hadn't been. It was like having her menses. Women had told her that losing her virginity could make her bleed a bit, but this was far more blood than she had expected. She washed carefully and prepared for further bleeding just in case.

When she returned to her room she found that Quince was already seated at the impromptu table with a glass of red wine. He rose when he saw her, setting the wine aside.

"Miss Bittlesworth."

She raised up on her tiptoes to kiss him. "Sabre."

He smiled and kissed her again. "Sabre." He tasted of wine and lazy afternoons. She thought she could happily kiss him forever. Drawing back he ran a finger over her cheek and looked at her keenly. "Are you feeling better?"

She nodded. She could tell he wanted to apologize again and set her finger against his lips. "Shh. You only did what I asked. What I wanted."

That earned her one of his wry grins. "You did say that what you wanted was me." He leaned in to nuzzle at her ear. "And that you always get what you want."

She laughed. "It would do well for you to remember that."

"Then I can't say you didn't warn me."

"No you can't."

"Are you hungry?"

"I'm not sure."

"How can you not be sure?"

"My thinking gets muddled when you're touching me."

"Interesting. Noted. Then let me assure you that you are hungry."

"How can I argue with a duke?"

"Generally not recommended, but you seem quite good at it." He kissed the top of her head and pulled her chair out for her.

She seated herself gingerly and waited for him to settle in. He poured more wine for both of them and made sure that she had what she wanted on her plate. "You sent the staff away?" she asked.

"I thought that we might need to discuss tomorrow's meeting."

She nodded. "Did you look at the papers I brought upstairs?"

"I was otherwise occupied," he said drily. "Why don't you tell me about them?"

"There are three items. The first is from some investments that your father executed in 1810, which I think was shortly before he died."

Quince nodded, his eyes narrowed in thought. "Yes, he passed in early 'eleven. Why were those investments relevant?"

"I think they were false."

He sat back in surprise. "What makes you think that?"

She thought back to the quick assessment she had made as she flipped through the papers in the study. It had been evident that many of the older ducal papers were housed here at Belle Fleur, which she found odd. Why not at the London townhouse? Or at the ducal seat? Had the elder duke spent the majority of his time at Belle Fleur? "All of the other investments over the years had gone through a man of business in London, but there was a series of investments directly with a private company over five years. The first four years showed incredible returns, at least on paper. Rather than being paid out, those returns were being reinvested and your father was putting in even more funds. Then in the fifth year, when your father doubled his original investment in this company and it was almost his sole financial commitment, the company dissolved and he received a statement that all funds had been lost."

Quince gave her a startled look. "How did you find that in an afternoon? Gideon never mentioned anything like that."

Sabre felt herself smile smugly. "The papers were not well organized but I am excellent at seeing patterns. At any rate, the first item is that final statement. I made a copy of the information so that we still have documentation. But it occurred to me that one of his cronies might have recommended the investment, supposedly objectively, when in actuality it was a front for draining the ducal coffers. Perhaps one of The Four."

"I see," Quince said, somber while considering that the losses to the duchy might have been by design. "What is the second item?"

"The second item, also potentially damning, is a letter that mentioned 'ursine cuckoos' and suggested they might be useful. The letter was addressed to your father, dated in early 'eleven, and unsigned. He may never have seen it."

"Ursine cuckoos?"

"A suggestion that the Bear may have cuckolded someone, though why those children could be useful I have no idea."

"Perhaps for blackmail?"

"Perhaps. But it suggests that the letter writer was either Draco or Cygnus."

"What else did the letter say?"

"Everything else was pleasantry."

"And the handwriting didn't match the note that I received?"

"No, but I did recognize it. That letter is from my father."

Quince set down his wine. "So you strike your father from the list of suspects for this blackmail since my note is not in his handwriting?"

"Not necessarily. If the history of The Four is as unsavory as you suspect then it may be that more than one of them involved. Most likely all of them have something to lose."

The duke nodded and looked down at his folded hands. Sabre's heart ached to see him despondent. He had barely touched his supper. She reached a hand out to him across the table and waited until he stirred himself to join hands with her. "We'll get through this," she promised. "All will be well."

His grip was strong and the look he gave her was full of grief and pain. She felt an instinct to soothe him. Care for him. Not sure what else to do she stood to move towards him. Courtesy made the duke rise as well, though he looked confused. She put her hands on his shoulders and pushed gently, encouraging him to sit again. Once he had she seated herself on his lap, one arm curled around his shoulders. They began kissing as though it were something they did every night. A combination of desire and familiarity. His hand stroked down to her hip and anchored there. She felt a tension low in her belly, an ache. She regretted that joining was so painful and knew that it would be some time before she wanted to try it again. But if her heart was treacherous then her body was doubly so, yearning for a greater intimacy with this man. She pulled her lips away and tried to change her focus to the other reason she had come to sit in his lap. Picking up his fork she speared a bite of fish and offered it to him.

"Sabre," he said in a warning tone.

"Eat," she insisted.

After a few bites he relaxed back into the chair and seemed to enjoy her ministering to him. He was stroking over her hip, which she found terribly distracting, and the ache in her belly had progressed to a throb. She felt overheated and awkward.

"What are thinking?" he asked.

"Nothing, why?"

"You have a blush that has started here," he traced a finger in the valley between her breasts in the low décolletage of her dress, "and I assume travels to some interesting places." Sabre felt her cheeks heat and the duke chuckled. "Now it travels up as well as down."

She wasn't sure what to do. Her breasts felt tight and heavy. She wanted him to caress them, squeeze them. Better yet, to kiss the bare flesh. But if she encouraged him to do so it was tantamount to inviting another joining and that she could not do. Suddenly she remembered advice on what could be done when one didn't want to join. She slid off his lap to her knees on the floor.

The duke looked surprised. "I am beginning to wonder about your education."

Sabre smiled and began unbuttoning the front flap of his trousers. "I will warn you that I haven't done this before, either. Hopefully it will go better."

"Were you raised in a whore house?"

She laughed. "If you ever talked to your servants they would obviously shock you."

"You learned this here?"

She shook her head. "No, but I'm sure that there are one or two who have a great deal of knowledge. There always are."

Removing the last button, she revealed his manhood, the first time she had seen one erect or so close. Wrapping her hand at the base she heard him groan and smiled to herself. It felt like silk wrapped steel. She licked the tip and the duke hissed, his hips bucking slightly toward her. Encouraged, she closed her mouth over him and his fingers dug into her shoulders.

He called her name in a choked whisper, "Sabre."

After a few moments they found a rhythm with his shallow hip thrusts, her stroking hand, and her mouth. She felt his shaft grow even larger, thicker, as his breathing became harsher. She used her other hand to stroke under his sack as one serving girl had advised and heard him shout. Her mouth filled with his hot, salty seed as she had been warned and she swallowed as quickly as she could.

He pulled her back up into his lap and hugged her tightly, his face buried against her neck. She ran her fingers through his hair as she waited for him to settle.

By the gods, Quince thought, how had she managed that? It had been the most intense pleasure of his life. Yet he was already growing hard again, his cock wanting desperately to be inside her. He would need to wait a few days considering how badly she had bled with her first joining. But oh, how he wanted her. She was his Venus. His Helen of Troy. He would gladly fight a nation to lie with her. He ran a palm over her breast, the ripe curve and turgid tip, and heard her soft moan of pleasure. Needing no other encouragement he pulled her dress down to expose the globe and suckled on her velvet skin.

"Quince!" she cried, gasping and writhing. He lifted her in his arms, knocking the chair over in his haste. In a few short steps he laid her on the bed. She bit her lip and looked up at him. "Quince, I can't…"

"Shh, I know." He lay down half on top of her and set to laving her nipple again, his hand caressing her other breast still covered by muslin.

"Oh, Quince…" She ploughed her fingers into his hair, gripping handfuls as she gasped in pleasure. He thought he might spill his seed again just listening to her exclamations of passion. He would do anything to make her feel as he had felt with her mouth closed around him during his release.

Sabre ran her fingers lightly over the duke's shoulder. She had convinced him to shed his jacket, vest, and shirt to lie with her flesh to flesh. After a lifetime of excellent ideas she felt this had been one of her best. Feeling his skin against her own was both thrilling and comforting. He had wrapped his arms around her and after some time drifted off to sleep and now snored softly in her ear. The last candle in her room had almost burned down and flickered with the dancing light that often came before guttering. She took those remaining minutes of light to study his face. The curve of his jaw, the straight line of his nose. If she had to choose between time like this with him and being a duchess she thought she would choose him. But he needn't know that.

Eighteen

When Sabre awoke in the morning she was covered by a light blanket and found a note on the pillow next to her.

No, you are not going to London.
- Q

She laughed. He had expected her to argue about it but that had been the furthest thing from her mind. Running into her friends or family in London and having to explain herself would just be a complication. Hopefully he would return soon. But until then she could continue her mission to set Belle Fleur to rights. The staff did as well as they could, but certain things required decisions that no servant would feel comfortable taking upon themselves. And Sabre had never had any difficulty making decisions for others.

Quince hoped Robert would be in residence. Ten in the morning was something of an awkward time in the *ton*. Most of the *beau monde* wouldn't even be up yet, while others such as Robert, who had more productive lives, might already be downtown in their office. Having waited so long to open the second letter he had hardly given time for Robert to be involved in thinking through strategies. At last Robert's doorman opened to his knock and, seeing who it was, waved him in. "If you could wait in the study, please, sir. Mr. Bittlesworth is otherwise engaged for the moment but will want to see you."

The doorman led him to the study where he and Robert had met before, offered him a drink, which he declined, and left him to his own devices for the nonce. Although he was near vibrating with impatience no one who looked upon him would have guessed. He studied the hunting prints in Robert's office as though he had all the time in the world. Finally, at what he would guess was better than a quarter hour later, the door opened and Robert appeared.

"I received instructions," Quince said abruptly.

"I see. Drink?"

He didn't really want one but didn't want to alienate his host. "Whatever you're having."

Robert poured two tumblers of scotch and offered one to the duke. Quince was surprised at such strong spirits at this time in the morning but took the tumbler readily enough. Robert grinned as he sat down, indicating that Quince should take the chair opposite him. To treat a duke in such a casual way indicated either long-standing friendship or a great deal of disrespect. Quince wasn't sure which Robert thought he was exhibiting but they had never been particularly close.

"I suppose you know," Robert said without preamble, "the nickname we used for Gideon?"

"Of course. Lord Lucifer."

"Do you know the one we used for you?"

Quince frowned. He had hardly spent any time with the Bittlesworth boys and had a difficult time imagining he had earned a nickname with them. At his silence Robert continued.

"We called you Gideon's Angel." The younger man tossed back his scotch in one go. Then he leaned forward, resting his elbows on his knees, the empty tumbler dangling loosely in his fingers. Robert had dark eyes and sometimes, such as now, his gaze could be more intense than a hawk's. "You were so fucking self-righteous all the time. As if you were averse to fun and couldn't even stand anyone else having it. But every time Gideon had a problem you were right there. Always cleaning it up for him."

Quince was surprised Robert bore such anger for him. For the most part he had stayed out of the way while the three of them had run wild all those years. Yes, when push came to shove he had always been there for Gideon, as Gideon had always been there for him.

Not sure what Robert was getting at, Quince relied on the iciness and hauteur that had seen him through many other unpleasant encounters. "I don't see what this has to do with the case at hand."

Robert laughed. A world-weary laugh without humor, too aged for his actual years. "No, you wouldn't."

Indicating that there was, somehow, a connection. Quince felt himself become confused, knocked off his balance. He had enough to worry about without this. He looked at Robert, truly inspected him. The young man seemed tired, haggard. Were this four, even two, years ago he would have assumed that Robert had spent the night carousing. But he didn't have the look of a man who had spent his evening in dissolute pleasures. This was the look of a man with too many cares, a man who had either worked or worried all night, probably both. For a brief moment Quince felt guilty for adding more weight to Robert's concerns by thrusting his own problems into the mix. Perhaps Sabrina had the right of it. Robert had too much to worry about whereas she had made Quince's issue her sole concern. The packet of papers she had given him pressed against his ribcage where he had stowed it in an inner pocket of his coat. He could take his leave of Robert and proceed with the plan that Sabre had outlined for him.

Robert set aside his tumbler and rubbed a hand over his head. "What I'm attempting to say is that even annoying little angels can be useful sometimes."

Not sure how to respond, Quince waited.

"Useful because they can be trusted to do the right thing."

For a brief, panicked moment Quince wondered if Robert knew precisely where his sister was.

Apparently past whatever maudlin mood had struck him, Robert held out his hand. "Show me the note."

"I burned it."

Robert narrowed his eyes at the news and Quince was struck with how the expression was exactly like Sabre's.

"What do you mean you burned it?"

"I don't like the idea of someone finding out about it, so I store all of that information," Quince tapped his head, "in here."

"Fine. Recite it for me, then."

Robert closed his eyes as he listened, asking the duke to repeat it twice more. Finally satisfied, he nodded. "If you get another note, keep it. I would like to examine the handwriting."

Although uncomfortable with the suggestion, Quince nodded.

The younger man continued. "I don't like the idea that he has insinuated himself with your mother. I would like to dispatch two of my men to check on her."

Quince nodded again. "That would be something of a relief as I can't go to Bath immediately myself. And I can trust your discretion regarding my mother's household?"

"Of course," he confirmed. "My entire career is built on discretion. Now, as for the deadline for papers tonight..."

Quince pulled out the packet. "The plan is to provide him something, but also stall for time."

Robert nodded. "Good. What do you have?"

"A letter and three items." Quince tucked the single sheet with Sabre's instructions back in his coat pocket and handed the rest of the papers to Robert. The young man took them and looked through them. The letter was simple enough.

To my father's friend,

I find the most interesting things in my father's papers and thought you might like to see these. Perhaps if we meet at the Harrington ball we can discuss this topic further?

Your friend's son

Having looked at the items Robert said, "I understand why the invitation to the ball is in here, but what do the other items mean?"

"The first item is the last document in a trail of investments that smack of fraud which leads one to suspect that one of my father's friends may have duped him. The second indicates a mutual friend cuckolded someone and the children may be useful. In what way, I don't know, but suspect that the mere knowledge of it is somewhat incendiary."

Robert frowned at the second item and Quince knew he recognized the writing, just as Sabre had. "Were either of the notes in the same handwriting as these?"

"No."

He nodded and handed the packet back to the duke. "Unless you want us to deliver it?"

"I doubt that would go over well."

"Your plan seems a good one. We will watch White's."

"Is that wise?"

Robert gave him a wolfish grin. "It would only be unwise if we were caught."

"One other thing," Quince said. "How I have received the blackmail letters disturbs me."

After he described how the letters would appear Robert said, "We will investigate your townhouse staff."

At that, Robert stood up, indicating that the meeting was over. He picked up Quince's tumbler where it had sat untouched on the table and downed that one as well. "Be careful tonight," he said. "The language this man uses...I believe him to be truly dangerous."

Quince nodded and followed the younger man to the front door. Once outside he let himself contemplate two things. First, Robert asked far fewer questions than Sabre did about the circumstances of the case. He hadn't noticed the first time because he had still been overwhelmed, and relieved that someone could help him. Second, he had felt no desire to tell Robert about The Four. During their first meeting he had only vaguely mentioned that his father had a number of dissolute cronies whose names he wasn't sure about. Now, when he was more certain that The Four were involved, he was also more circumspect in the information he gave Robert. His instincts had held him in good stead before so he didn't wish to betray them now. But if he couldn't trust Robert then what would he do?

The thud of a door and light from a lantern woke Sabre up.

"I should have known you would be in here when I didn't find you in your room." The duke's voice sounded...odd. It had to be the middle of the night. She shoved aside the bedclothes to sit up in his bed.

"What happened?"

He set the lantern on the table next to her and pulled a paper from his greatcoat. After shoving the paper in her hand he walked to the window, his steps stiff, jerky. She studied his silhouette. Had he been drinking? Or was this the expression of some emotion? She unfolded the paper and tilted it toward the light.

If you think to toy with me you have made a grave mistake. If you anger me further then perhaps I will need to share that anger with a sweet little girl I have seen at Miss Filbert's School. Do you think she would spread her legs for me? Do you think she would scream for me? I accept your invitation to the Harrington Ball and if you do not surrender the papers at that time, just know what may happen.

Sabre folded the paper up again. This time she wanted to burn the letter herself.

"Your daughter?" she asked.

Quince turned and stared at her for long moments but she was unable to see his expression in the darkness. "My sister," he finally said. His voice rose as he continued. "She's twelve years old. What sort of monster threatens to do that to a twelve year old girl?"

"When did you receive this?"

"It was on my bed in London when I returned to the townhouse at midnight. I had planned to stay there tonight, but after I found this..." He ran his hands through his hair. "I just couldn't."

Sabre slipped from the bed and padded over to him. She pulled the greatcoat from his shoulders and laid it aside. Then she took off his jacket, cravat, and vest. He stood quietly, watching her but not interacting.

She indicated a side chair. "Sit."

He did so and she removed his brown top boots and stockings. Standing up again she offered her hand to him and he took it as he rose. She led him to his bed and lay down with him, pulling the covers up securely around them. Nothing more could be done tonight but she could offer him the comfort of her touch.

Quince jolted awake from a dream. He couldn't remember most of it, only that it had been disturbing. Shortly before he awoke, he had been running down an endless hallway. He didn't know why he was running, just recalled the abject panic and anxiety that fueled his flight. It was a deeper and more intense emotion than any he had ever experienced in his waking life.

But he was awake now and Sabrina Bittlesworth was lying half on top of him in sleep. Her arm was curled over his chest, her leg wrapped over one of his. Feeling her warm skin, smelling that delightful scent she wore that he still hadn't identified, his heart rate slowed to a normal pace. He wanted nothing more than to kiss her awake and make love to her. But the memory of the brutal pain she had experienced in their first encounter was more than enough to stop him. He could wait.

Running his fingers lightly over her arm he encountered the healing scar from his blade. At first he frowned, remembering the moment when he had slipped past her guard and followed his instincts to score the win. Then after a moment he smiled. There was more than one way to work off the energy of their passion. He rolled her onto her back and she made a protesting sound. He took her lips in a swift kiss, then moved to kissing her throat.

"Quince!" She managed to sound both grumpy and pleased at the same time.

Her nightgown tied in the front and he set to opening it, revealing her beautiful bosoms. He suckled first one, then the other as she squirmed beneath him.

"Quince!" Now she was breathless. How he loved thrilling her. Cupping her breast in his hand, he moved his lips back to hers. They settled into a comfortable but passionate mating of lips and tongues. He was so hard he feared he might burst from his breeches. What he had hoped to be a simple awakening for a lover had turned into something too heated. Perhaps she would join with him. Certainly they had to do it again in order for it to get better. He pulled up the hem of her nightgown and ran his hand underneath, stroking the outside of her bare thigh. He felt her tilt her hips beneath him and the motion made him want to couple with frenzied thrusts.

Gods, he had to stop this before he was hammering into her whether she wanted it or not. He tore his lips from hers.

"I thought today we could practice." His voice sounded breathless and hollow, even to himself.

She looked at him blankly, clearly not understanding. Then he saw the light dawn in her eyes. "Really? When? Now? I need to go get dressed."

She wriggled and bucked, no longer with sexual desire but in order to dislodge him and escape the bed. Quince laughed.

He saw now where he rated in her estimation. He rolled away and flopped onto his back. Once she was gone he could deal with the unrequited lust she left behind. But she surprised him by leaning over and cupping his manhood through his trousers.

"We'd best polish this sword first." She unbuttoned his flap and set to licking and sucking as though he were her favorite treat. He didn't know why he had caught Sabrina Bittlesworth's eye, but he could no longer regret it. As he had known intuitively the first moment he saw her, she was the only woman for him. Perhaps her lineage didn't matter. Perhaps nothing mattered but being with her.

Nineteen

They practiced with tipped foils. The first quarter hour was spent in essentially play. Showing off, observing each other's style. After that they focused more seriously on form and technique. Sabre was willing to admit that Quince knew far more than she did on the subject, her humility at least partially because it was so rare to find someone who did. He had not only studied in France, Italy, and Spain, but Hungary as well. She had a special interest in Hungarian sabre fighting. Its focus on the wrist and speed appealed to her, but she had not met a practitioner. The duke promised to teach her everything he knew.

As she smiled up at him she thought that her prediction to Jack was already coming true. She could fence with him any time she wanted. Watch him any time she wanted. Now all that was left was to become his duchess. He stopped what he was saying to grin back at her, looking baffled at her brilliant smile. She kissed him and encouraged him to continue what he was saying.

That night as they snuggled on the balcony Quince said, "I'm not sure what to do about Jessica."

"Jessica?"

"My sister. I know bringing her here would not protect her any better than being at the school."

Sabre sat up and looked down at him. "Robert could dispatch men to protect her. Have you told him of this note yet?"

Quince skimmed his fingers over her arm. "I'm not sure I trust Robert."

Sabre seemed suspiciously quiet and Quince looked into her eyes. Her brows were furrowed and she seemed to be struggling to say something. "That is probably wise," she allowed.

His senses went on alert. There was a truth here. He could sense it. "He wants to see the handwriting. I suspect he will know who it is based on that alone. I also suspect he won't tell me, and that concerns me."

Sabre looked out at the starry night. "That wouldn't surprise me. I've thought for awhile that he's playing a deeper game here."

Quince asked the question he had loathed considering. "Did he send you here to Belle Fleur?"

She turned her attention back to him, smiling sadly. "No. But he does know that I'm here." She looked at the sky again. "That day my horse had a stone in his shoe? Robert had his men seize me so that he could speak with me."

"He did what?" Quince could feel his heart stutter with worry about how she had been treated. He didn't take her as a woman who would use a word like "seize" lightly. No wonder she had hugged him as she had upon return to Belle Fleur.

"It's all right. I'm quite used to Robert and his ways. He's worried about me. But there is something more afoot."

"As much as I love having your here, how could he stand to let you return?"

She raised a brow at him. "That's the term he used. Let. That indicates a level of authority I don't allow others to have over me."

He chuckled. "Really? Saying that was a strategic mistake."

She became very still. "What do you mean?"

"That's hardly a statement to attract a husband."

She laughed and gave him her most flirtatious smile, leaning down until her breasts pressed up against his chest. "Perhaps not for a typical man, but you are not a typical man."

Prior to meeting her he might have agreed with her statement. But now he knew himself to be far more typical than he had ever hoped. He struggled daily to keep himself from using her for his own pleasure, and hearing her so clearly state her independence both irked and frightened him. How could he keep her safe if she would not submit to protection? Which only served as a reminder that Jessica needed protection as well.

His distraction must have reminded Sabre of their original conversation. "If you won't trust her to Robert, then who would you trust?"

He put his arms around her. "I only trust two people and the most logical candidate, Gideon, is far too wrapped up in Parliament to send off to Chippenham."

"Well, then who is the other one?"

He looked at her to confirm that she truly, innocently did not know. "Yes, that's an excellent question, isn't it?" he asked.

Rather than take his bait she sulked and said, "I've been meaning to ask you about Gideon."

"Ask what about him?"

"I don't like the way he treats Jack. He's so high-handed and authoritarian. And that's when he even bothers to be around, which isn't often. I don't understand why Jack puts up with it at all."

Rather than defend his friend, which was very tempting, Quince mildly asked, "Was there a question in there somewhere?"

"Yes! Why does he act like that? Why does she put up with it?" She seemed genuinely upset so he refrained from chuckling at her.

"Attraction does funny things to people."

She gave him a sour look. "Attraction makes him an overbearing ass? I argue he was already that way."

Now he did chuckle. "Yes, Gideon has always been an overbearing ass. He's actually less so with Jack's influence."

"Small miracles," she muttered. She plucked at the front of his shirt, obviously discontent.

"I saw it the first time he introduced me to her," he said.

"Saw what?" she asked, looking up with curiosity.

"How right they were together. It's like studying a painting, watching how people are together. It's all about balance."

The look she gave him was skeptical at best. "That makes no sense to me."

"What I'm saying is of course Gideon annoys you. The two of you wouldn't balance out at all."

"But Jack has *changed!* She used to be independent. She valued her freedom. Now she won't do *anything* without checking with Gideon."

"Are you upset for her or for yourself?"

"Beyond my annoyance, yes, I am upset for her. Why would I want her to become a shadow of what she once was?"

"Have you asked her if that's how she feels?"

"I don't need to *ask* her, I can see it!"

Quince was quiet for a moment. "You are disturbed that she surrenders some of her freedom and independence to please Gideon? Has it ever occurred to you that she exercised her freedom and independence to please you?"

Sabre's mouth dropped open. "That's not…That's silly! Of course she didn't…"

But he saw that her mind was considering it, turning the thought around and about to see what flaws it held. Rather than argue further she laid her head on his shoulder. After a few minutes of silence she petulantly said, "That's poppycock."

"Me for suggesting it or Jack for doing it?"

She raised her head again and gave him the most autocratic look he had seen from her to date. "I don't want to talk about that anymore. How shall we protect Jessica? Who is this sainted second person who has managed to earn your trust?"

He stroked the corner of her mouth. "I can certainly see how we balance. The things I see most clearly are where you have blind spots."

That only served to make her frown more fiercely. "I'm not particularly known for my blind spots."

He smiled at her. "It's you, Sabre. The second person is you."

Only moments earlier Sabre had thought to herself *Quincy Telford can be annoying*. And he was, certainly. Quite annoying. The smile he had given her after announcing she had blind spots had been downright patronizing. She hated patronizing men. Then he had said, "It's you, Sabre." Simple. Direct. That he trusted her more than almost anyone in the world. As though it were blindingly obvious. As though it were a given. She heard the blood rush in her ears, felt her heart squeeze in her chest. She was a bit dizzy and glad they were already lying

SUE LONDON

down. She had discovered that her heart was quite willing to do foolish things to make him smile at her. But for his trust? She would do irrational things. Unwise things. She felt both invincible and fragile.

Not sure how to respond she laid her head on his shoulder and waited for the dizziness to pass.

Later that evening Quince watched Sabre brush her hair. This would be their fourth night sleeping in the same bed. Before they left the balcony he had asked her if she would like to stay with him. She had enthusiastically agreed and gone to retrieve her nightgown. Now she was seated in a chair and brushing the curls out of her hair. He lounged on the bed watching her. He had a moment of clarity that this was what the rest of his life held. That in forty years he would be here on this bed watching her brush her hair. It filled his heart with a warmth he had never known before.

When she set her brush down she saw that he was watching her. "What?" she asked.

He held a hand out and she came to him, crawling up on the bed to join him.

"What?" she asked again, more softly.

He cradled her face in his hands and drank his fill of her beauty. He realized he had yet to see her, all of her, as he had dreamt about.

"May I take off your nightgown?"

He saw her brow furrow in worry. "Quince, I'm not sure-"

"We won't. I just want to see you."

She nodded hesitantly. He pulled the hem of her gown up, kissing her briefly, sweetly. She raised her hips as he continued to pool the fabric up at her waist, then sat up so that he could

140

pull the voluminous fabric over her head. He sat back on his heels, stunned. She was even more beautiful than he had dreamt. Her proportions were perfect. He couldn't decide whether he wanted her portrait just like this, nude and lounging back against her arm, or if the idea of anyone else seeing her like this would kill him.

"Quince, what are you thinking?"

"You're perfect," he said in a strangled whisper.

She gave him the sweetest smile he had ever seen. "Now let me see you."

"Sabre, I'm endeavoring to keep my promise not to touch you."

She tilted her head as though considering his words. "I want you to touch me. I want to see you."

He nearly tore his shirt in his haste to remove it.

Seeing him, all golden muscle, long and sleek, lying with him skin to skin, Sabre had wanted him so desperately. She begged him to join with her. He seemed torn between his desire and his need to protect her. At last he had given in to her begging but on his first thrust she knew she had made a terrible mistake. It hurt almost as much as the first time, although it didn't surprise a scream out of her. She bit her lip and held onto his shoulders as he thrust into her over and over. The pain subsided a bit but she never experienced the pleasure she had been led to believe would occur. That her own body seemed to promise her every time he touched her, kissed her.

When he grunted her name on his final thrust she hugged him and kissed his shoulder.

He cradled her face. "Are you all right?"

"I'm fine."

"Was it any better?"

"Some." She kissed his shoulder again. "It will get better. Did you enjoy it?"

"Beyond all things."

She felt a warm glow. "Then that makes me happy."

But he still looked worried.

Twenty

When Quince awoke, Sabre was no longer in their bed. His first instinct was to jump up and prowl around until he found her. After lying in bed for a quarter hour trying to control the impulse he finally gave in and pulled on trousers and a simple shirt. Hopefully she hadn't gone far. She wasn't in their sitting room or the duchess's quarters. She wasn't in the rose-colored guest room. He went downstairs and didn't find her in the dining room or study. He finally stopped to address a footman.

"Where is my...guest?"

"Miss Bittlesworth is in the kitchen, your grace."

Quince cocked his head to the side. "Indeed? And...where would I find the kitchen?"

"This way, your grace," the footman said, leading him past the dining room and down a narrow hallway. They descended a short flight of stone steps and as they approached the kitchen Quince could hear chatter and laughter. He could hear *Sabre's* laughter.

When he entered the room one of the maids spotted him and exclaimed, "Your grace!" and dropped into a deep curtsy. The chatter and laughter stopped, with all of the servants addressing him as "your grace" and bowing or curtsying as though he were on parade. Sabre had been rolling out piecrust on the center table and didn't curtsy, but did give him a blindingly happy smile. She wiped her hands on her apron and walked over to him.

"Good morning, love," she said, pulling his face down for a kiss.

"Good morning." He felt foolish for charging around the house looking for her. Doubly foolish for interfering in the work of the kitchens. Work that he hadn't realized she involved herself in. And to be kissing in full view of the servants? He was behaving like a man who had no care for her reputation at all.

"We thought you might fancy a kidney pie for lunch. Havers assures us it's a particular favorite of yours."

It was a particular favorite of his but he didn't remember ever expressing a preference. Apparently the old butler paid attention to which dishes went back barely touched and which earned a clean plate. He looked at all the expectant faces peering at him, awaiting his slightest sign of pleasure or discontent and realized what a horrifying employer he had been. They wanted to please him and all he had wanted to do was avoid them. He looked back at Sabre. "I've never had a bad meal at Belle Fleur," he assured her. "But yes, kidney pie is a favorite."

She looked as pleased as a mother whose child had won a prize, and he found himself unreasonably delighted. "I've told them that the kitchen is exceptional," she said, "but I'm sure they are happiest to hear it from you."

In that moment he realized he had found his chiaroscuro, the light that balanced his darkness. "I'll leave you to it, then," he said. "And perhaps track down my valet so that I may be presentable for the breakfast table."

As he left he heard the excited chatter start again, first in a hushed tone and growing louder as he made his way up the steps and into the hallway.

Sabre sat across from the duke and admired him. He was more than presentable for breakfast. Other than the fact that he was wearing a morning jacket, he was polished enough to attend any ball in the *ton*. She had a hard time concentrating on her breakfast while thinking about how he must smell like lemongrass.

He paused in picking up his glass. "Are you all right?"

"Yes." She moved her eyes to her plate in hopes that she could get some breakfast down and deal with the pressing matters at hand well. "My thought is that I should fetch Jessica and take her to Gideon and Jack. It's hard to imagine anyone breaching the Wolfe household when they are on alert."

Quince was silent for too long and Sabre looked at him again. He looked troubled. "Gideon doesn't know about my siblings. He would hardly take it well to have one of them thrust upon him without warning."

"What do you mean Gideon doesn't know? I thought you were friends."

"We *are* friends. I didn't find out about these siblings until after my father died."

"That was four years ago. What did you do, shove them into a bedside drawer?"

"I suppose you would look at it that way," the duke said testily.

"I'm beginning to have some sympathy for poor Gideon."

145

"He's not the easiest person to talk to."

Sabre gave a frustrated sigh but realized this line of discussion wouldn't be fruitful. "All of this aside, what will we do for Jessica? And your mother?"

"Robert did send men to check on my mother."

"And you trust that, yet do not trust him to have his men fetch Jessica?"

"It's just a feeling. That I shouldn't show him this most recent note from the blackmailer. That I shouldn't involve him any more deeply. Not yet."

Sabre blew out a frustrated breath and sat back in her chair. "At least half of your problems are of your own making."

"You were the one who said you wanted to help."

"And I have helped! If it weren't for me you would have missed your meeting at White's and most likely wouldn't have had any papers to string him along with at all."

"For all the good it's done us! In case you have forgotten, he is threatening my sister."

She folded her arms. "Something he was already planning to do if he could respond like that in under an hour. If I asked Robert to have Jessica protected, even without revealing her true identity, he would do it, no questions asked."

"He might not ask you any questions but I'm sure it would raise his curiosity."

Sabre had to admit that he was right about that. "Well, then we are at an impasse."

They sat in an angry silence, picking at their food. Sabre finally made another suggestion. "I could send John and either Laura or Lizzy. Perhaps both. Having servants pick up Jessica may actually be much less notable."

"Who are John, Laura, and Lizzy?"

"John is my coachman. Laura and Lizzy are two of your maids. They seem levelheaded enough to be up to the task. The only question after that is where on earth we can put Jessica that she would be safe."

Quince closed his eyes, putting his fingers to his temples.

"Are you all right?"

"Shh, I'm thinking."

Sabre sat back in her chair again. Yes, Quincy Telford was quite annoying.

When he finally opened his eyes again he gave her such a brilliant smile that she almost forgot how to breathe.

"I've got it," he said. "I don't send her to Gideon. You send her to Jack."

Sabre frowned. "Doesn't that accomplish the same thing?"

"No, because Giddy would never question anything Jack would want to do. And Jack would never question anything you would ask of her."

Sabre smiled. "I stand corrected. You can be devious."

"I have my moments. Now, I just need to write a letter to Jessica asking her to conceal her identity while with the countess. And you need to write a letter of introduction for Jessica to Jack."

"If she can't go by Jessica then what name should we use?"

Quince thought for a moment. "Celia Frederick."

Sabre smiled. "When in doubt quote the Bard?"

"Always."

"And while Jack is quite likely to pick up on the implications of the name, Gideon is not."

"Most likely not."

She felt better knowing they had a plan, even though the stress of the situation seemed to be wearing on both of them. At least she knew she could trust John implicitly. He had been the boy who had taught her to kiss all those years ago. What was it? Thirteen years now. He had never been untoward but it had been clear that he had a soft spot for her ever since. And if she invoked the Haberdashers code to ask Jack to look after Jessica, then there would be no question of it being done. Yes, this plan would work. She would write the necessary letters this very morning and send John and the girls on their way. Quince would need to write the letter to Jessica. She looked over at him, resplendent in a soft gray morning coat and snowy white cravat, rather precisely cutting his meat. Certainly she could count on him to be hasty in writing a letter that ensured his sister's safety. Certainly.

Quince sat at his desk, pen in hand, thinking about what to write to Jessica. Sabre ostensibly browsed his book collection, but nearly vibrated with energy in her interest to get their plan underway. She had already brought him all of the items she had drafted so that he could review them. A letter to her friend the countess, rather carefully worded, and letters of reference for each of the servants that would be traveling for him to sign. She was, in short, even more managing than Gideon. He was sure that if he sat here long enough she would seize the pen from him and draft this letter as well. It was tempting to find out how long that might take. But tempting as it was to torment her, Jessica would be most receptive to something written in his own hand. He bent to finish his task.

Dearest Jessica,

It is not something I can explain at present, but I need you to go with the three servants who bear this letter and stay with my good friend, the Countess of Harrington. Please remain there and be attentive to her instruction until I fetch you. Keep the maids with you at all times you are not directly with the countess and do not speak to any strangers. You are not to tell anyone who you are and travel under the name Celia Frederick. Please burn this letter before you leave the school, so that no trace remains.

With deepest love,
Your brother Quincy, Duke of Beloin

It was hard to imagine that the letter itself wouldn't panic her, but what else was there to do? He could only hope she would be a sensible girl and do as instructed. It was difficult not to just take the ducal carriage and sweep through the countryside to gather all of his family. If he thought he could keep them safe, he would. But he strongly doubted that the safest place was near him. The way the blackmail letters had been delivered indicated at least one person in his employ was not to be trusted. And where there was one there could be many. Was he wrong to trust these maids, Laura and Lizzy? He looked over to where Sabre was reading a small book of sonnets, stolidly demonstrating a patience she obviously didn't feel. He trusted Sabre. Not that he could exactly explain why, but that was often the case with things that were important. He just knew them. He trusted Sabre and she spent far more time with the servants than he did, and she had recommended these girls to protect his sister. He would try to be at peace with that.

He saw her slide her gaze over to his desk and quickly folded the letter and set to sealing it before she could offer any suggestions for revisions. Managing girl.

Twenty-One

*B*y mid-morning Sabre had seen John, Laura, and Lizzy off for their mission. The carriage included a good number of items to be of comfort for a young lady. She gave stern instructions to the staff that they should do their best to conceal the girl's identity when she left the school, covering her with a shawl and keeping the curtains on the carriage drawn. It wasn't certain, but most likely the blackmailer was having the school watched and any edge they could gain against him would be helpful.

Undoubtedly Jack would spoil the girl to no end, even without knowing that she was Quince's sister. Now, after a flurry of activity, there was nothing to do but wait. Worry. To Sabre the whole blackmail affair felt like trying to play a game of chess with at least half the board obscured. Who were the remaining lords of The Four? What were they really capable of? What sort of resources did they have?

Unfortunately, due to Quince's own stubbornness, the pieces he did have available to him were not yet in play. Gideon Wolfe could undoubtedly be useful but Quince had yet to confide in him. Although originally involving Robert, Quince was now withholding information from him as well. This morning, when Quince had folded up the letter to his sister without inviting her to read it, Sabre had realized that Quince was perfectly fine concealing information from her. Not that she expected him to allow her to review everything, but she had shown him all of her letters. He had said he trusted her. He had said he trusted both she and Gideon. Yet if she were to judge by his actions, that wasn't the conclusion she would draw. So here they were, with sparse defense and no movement, waiting for a move from an obscure but potentially powerful enemy. Potentially deadly enemy.

The duke's lack of action might drive her insane.

One of Sabre's favorite games as a child had been War. She had made up most of the rules herself and would play it with anyone who would indulge her. War was far more complicated to set up and play than chess, and included the element of chance. It entailed setting toy soldiers on a terrain, declaring troop movements, and rolling Crown and Anchor dice to determine outcomes. They had reenacted many famous battles from history over the years, those being a particular favorite for Jack. They had also created wars whole cloth, with made up nations and generals.

If she were to compare this to a battle in War, it was as though she and the duke were in a valley, knowing that the enemy was over the next rise but unaware of whom it was, how many they numbered, or how they were equipped. The logical move was to fall back and send a scout or two ahead. But how were they to gauge the enemy's strength without even knowing precisely where to search? Mulling over their potential resources she kept coming back to the people they knew. She kept coming back to Robert and Gideon.

The only one who could ever beat her at War was Robert. Clever, ruthless Robert. It would be helpful to have him on their side. Especially if this enemy turned out to be even half as clever and ruthless as Robert could be. But she couldn't discount Quince's unease about her brother because she shared it. No, as powerful a resource as Robert might be in this instance, it would be a mistake to involve him in their movements. It was too much of a risk until they knew more.

That left Gideon Wolfe, Earl of Harrington. The duke's best friend. He was recognized as a powerful presence in the House of Lords and rumored to be wealthier than Croesus. Using him to protect Jessica was wise, but most likely an underutilization. Certainly there was any number of things that he could do to help Quince if he desired. If he knew what there was to be done.

All that brought her back to Quince. If she weren't here he would be in this valley by himself. Refusing to take action, refusing to enlist the help of his friends. If she were to help him, it would be to get him out of this valley before his enemy descended upon him. No matter how she turned it about in her mind she didn't see any path that he would want to take. Which left her to figure out which path he would find least offensive and convince him to take it.

She needed to think.

As she didn't trust that a horseback ride wouldn't be circumvented with another abduction, she settled for walking the gardens of Belle Fleur.

Twenty-Two

Quince had been in his study for some time, lying on the couch and thinking, when he realized that the house seemed strangely quiet. Still. Perhaps even lifeless. He sat up and concentrated on listening. No sound but the longcase clock in the front hall. He swiftly rose to investigate. Before long he discovered staff quietly employed at their chores. But no Sabre. He checked her room. His room. The duchess's quarters. Not sure where else to look he ventured out onto the suite's balcony. And that was when he saw her. Wandering among the flowers, her fingers reaching to touch a bloom here and there.

The house was quiet because she was quiet. A rare contemplative mood. In her pale blue dress and straw bonnet she was the ideal of a young English girl admiring the gardens. Resting his elbows on the balustrade he settled in to watch her. After some time she seemed to sense his gaze and looked up at him. She smiled and moved more directly below the balcony.

She called up, "But, soft! What light through yonder window breaks?"

Quince laughed. "Aren't those my lines?"

"You're the one on the balcony." She shaded her eyes against the bright sunlight as she continued to look up. "Is it time for luncheon yet?"

"I suppose that it is. Would you like to dine in the gardens?"

"Dine al fresco? How positively continental of you."

"I beg to differ. Nothing could be more English than taking more time to admire the gardens."

"For either reason, I accept."

He smiled down at her. "Then I shall be down presently."

He barely had the patience to order their luncheon served before joining her outside. As they ate Quince knew this would be a memory he would treasure all of his life. They dined in a spot of shade on the side of the manor. A breeze blew periodically, wafting the scent of the flowers over them and ruffling the lace edging on Sabre's dress. Cook had outdone himself with the kidney pie. The conversation was filled with nonsense and laughter. If there were an hour that he could preserve forever, it would be this one. With Sabre's eyes full of mirth and his heart full of love for her. His fairy queen.

He kissed her hand and twined his fingers in hers. "Hear my soul speak. Of the very instant that I saw you, did my heart fly at your service."

She smiled. "The Tempest."

He could tell by her easy acceptance that she thought he had only found a quote to recite to her. Not that he was telling her of his heart, of his love. If they were lucky he would have time to convince her of that love later. But for now he was content to have this short, idyllic break in the otherwise consuming task of out-thinking his opponents.

Sabre thought that luncheon was an excellent example of how she could be charming without being mentally present at all. She still worried over what the best next action would be to remove Quincy from danger. Meanwhile, he chatted and flirted with her as though they were in the bosom of the *ton* without a care in the world. She was beginning to think that he could fiddle while Rome burned.

Not that she wouldn't enjoy his company immensely if there weren't some horrid blackmail plot hanging over their heads. A plot her father was likely involved in. A plot that she had yet to divine her brother Robert's role in. Not that she thought Robert would do anything at their father's behest. To say that the viscount had a strained relationship with his eldest son would be a vast and laughable understatement. Sabre didn't know the exact source of the discord, but it seemed very obvious. The two could be in the same house, the same room, and it was as though the other didn't exist. She hadn't seen the two of them exchange a word in at least ten years. Robert doted on his two siblings. Even, to a lesser degree, their bastard brother Justin. He was unfailingly polite with her mother, their father's second wife and Robert's step-mother of these past twenty years. But it was as though he could neither see nor hear Father. And Father treated him exactly the same way. It was left to Charlie to ferry messages if anything of import needed to be communicated.

The greatest question in Sabre's mind was what sort of resources this blackmailer had. His letter had intimated that he was in contact with Quince's mother. That was either hubris on the part of the blackmailer, or an indication that he didn't have the funds to hire someone to watch her rather than do it himself. The letter about Jessica, however, hadn't directly indicated he had seen her or visited her school. Of course, he could have acquired at least the school name from her mother if they were on friendly social terms. It came back, however, to a suspicion that he wasn't so well off that he could hire men to do his bidding. Perhaps. Again, it could be ego. And if it was ego, that was a weakness to exploit.

While that debate chased its tail in her head she also considered what they knew, or thought they knew, about The Four. It would be easier for her to put the pieces together if Quince would give her more information, but based on what he had told her she didn't know that she wanted to hear any more about the group. Further, as they had already discussed, hearing about the depravity they were capable of while out of the light of Society didn't particularly help to know what they acted like while they were *in* Society.

Honestly, it would be easier if there *were* some papers that his father had left behind describing these men. Giving some clue to their identities. She had hoped the business papers she had pored through would reveal some business partnerships his father had made that could give them a list of suspects. Far from it.

Everything his father did had been handled at an arm's length and the list of businesses and solicitors she had made would only help if she could run down the connections. That would only be possible in London. Since she was wary of giving Robert more information, she had to hope that Justin, in his new role as Harrington's clerk, would be able to find the information. She did find, however, that although Quince didn't seem to keep the bulk of his papers here, it was readily apparent that he had a business partnership with Harrington. One that yielded a hefty return based on the one statement she had run across. If this was ducal poverty she had no idea what he thought his holdings should be worth. But if the duke was cash poor then that was also a consideration for any strategy they might employ.

Thus her mind spun round and round over the central concern; how do you conquer an unknown enemy? How do you judge his strength? How do you anticipate his next move?

She smiled indulgently at Quince while thinking she might throttle him if he didn't become more serious about the trouble that he was in.

Sabre wasn't quite sure where Quincy had disappeared off to after lunch but as she had wanted to spend more time reviewing his father's papers she decided not to worry about it overly. She had sufficiently cowed his steward to be granted free access to the study and took the opportunity to dig deep into the drawers and cabinets. Surely there was something here that would help. She was so bent on her task that she barely noticed a supper tray had been brought for her. Eating from it absently, she continued to read and organize the papers. Quincy hadn't been facetious in saying that his father kept detailed journals about everything including the growth rate of crops. There was a journal regarding the gardens of Belle Fleur that spanned more than fifty years. Journals that related to the profitable business of the lands had been maintained, if sporadically, after the older duke's death. This journal for the gardens ended abruptly with the autumn entry for 1810. Early in the book the duke's crabbed and angular handwriting had been interspersed with a more flowing and rounded hand that Sabre suspected was the first duchess. It made her unaccountably sad to see the journal not kept up. As she had spent all morning walking through the gardens and was quite familiar with them now, she took up the steward's ink and set to creating the entry for spring 1815. She was just completing notes for the early roses when she heard the door open again. Expecting it was a servant returning to remove the tray, she hadn't even looked up yet when she heard the duke's voice.

"I wondered where you'd wandered off to. Don't we have a steward to see to that? Whatever it is?"

He sauntered closer, raising a brow as he looked down at the journal she was still holding open. Sabre felt herself flush to the tips of her toes. Partially because it felt a bit naughty to not only be looking through, but updating, the duchy's papers. But mostly because he didn't ask if *he* had a steward. He had said *we*. Flirting and quoting the bard struck her as meaninglessly romantic. But saying *we* when referring to the household? When the only possible *we* would be the two of them? That was very meaningfully romantic. She finally realized what else he had said.

"I thought you knew where I was since you sent in a supper tray."

He sat in the chair opposite from her. "Indeed I did not. The staff informed me that you were taking a tray and I assumed you had requested it." He tilted his head as he considered her. "I couldn't ascertain why you would want to avoid dining together."

Sabre busied herself with cleaning the quill before setting it aside. "I didn't mean to, I just got caught up in reviewing the papers here and then wanted to update this journal. It's about the gardens at Belle Fleur."

"Yes, I know what that journal is about."

She glanced up at him through her lashes. He wasn't precisely angry, but whatever he was feeling was in the neighborhood of it. A blackmailer was threatening his family and he chose to be testy about whether or not she came to the dining room?

"My apologies that I lost track of time, your grace."

He sighed and looked off to the windows where the pink streaks of the sunset glimmered against the darkening sky. "I wasn't looking for an apology, Sabrina."

She felt his emotional withdrawal as an almost physical pain. Not naturally being a creature of emotion she hadn't noticed the attachment growing between them. Hadn't noticed how she immediately turned her attention to him when he entered the room. Hadn't noticed that she hung on the slightest sign of attention and affection from him. He had arrived irritated but curious. Now his tone and posture communicated that he had shut her out. Sabre felt a completely unexpected surge of panic. But fear always had the peculiar effect of stiffening her spine.

"I find that I'm looking for one, your grace," she said in a prim voice.

That bold statement proved sufficient to return his regard to her. "Beg pardon?"

"That hardly sounds like a sincere apology," she admonished.

The irritation had returned. "What am I apologizing for, exactly?"

She gave him her most grave and imperious stare. "If I have to explain it to you that somewhat reduces the effect of the apology, doesn't it?"

His features settled into a neutral, haughty expression. Raised to be a duke, he would be her match at this game. "Then you shall have to suffer through a reduced apology. Explain."

Although she tried to keep her face impassive she felt her lips quirk at the corners. It wasn't her fault that the man was so damned adorable. Especially when he was being The Duke. Now it was Sabre's turn to tilt her head with some curiosity. He did treat his title more as a role to be played than an essential part of who he was.

He raised a brow. "As enchanting as your Mona Lisa expression is, I am waiting to be educated on what you think it is I need to apologize for."

"You have left me on my own for hours without so much as a kiss."

Now his brows both flew up. "Would you rather have an apology or a remedy?"

She smiled and pretended to consider his question, staring at the ceiling. "Perhaps the latter."

He stood and leaned over the desk to cup the back of her head, lowering his lips to hers. The kiss was sweet, surprisingly sweet after such cross words. She sighed and leaned into him, grasping the lapels of his jacket. He took hold of her arms and hauled her onto the desk.

"Quincy! The ink!"

He pushed it aside and set to kissing her again. Her lips, her throat, nibbling on her earlobe. His hand caressed up and down her ribcage, brushing the side of her breast. She wanted desperately for him to cup his hand over her breast. Or better yet, for him to kiss her there.

"Quince," she panted, "please touch me."

Finally his hand was fully on her breast, stroking her nipple. She felt her body catch fire. Surely if they joined it would be better this time? It had to be better. Her body insisted that it would not only be better, it would be glorious.

"Take me to bed?"

He cupped her face in his hands and pulled back to look at her. His eyes were shadowed with worry. "It's not just about that. You know this, yes?"

"It's not about that all the time, but right now..."

He laughed and kissed her forehead, then drew her into a hug. She nestled into his shoulder. It should probably worry her, she thought, that his touch could rule her emotions so easily. That he could make her want, could soothe her. She gave a sigh of contentment. His arms were strong and warm around her. His scent of lemongrass and male were like a tonic that made her forget her worries. She wanted all the rest of it to be over. For there to be just this, just him.

"Are you ready for bed?" His voice was a soft rumble.

"Yes."

Twenty-Three

Quince watched Sabre in the pale lamplight and thought that perhaps it was fear of loss that made everything more poignant, more perfect. Even though his soul told him that there would be many more nights like this in their bedroom, nights to touch and love her, logic dictated that it couldn't be true. Usually he trusted his instincts but he found that any possibility of losing Sabre seemed like too much of a risk. The fear preyed upon his mind. But it also made every moment that much more precious.

He met her in the middle of the room. She looked up at him, confused and curious, but didn't speak. He untied the sash of her white silk robe and pushed it off her shoulders to pool on the floor. That earned him one of her smiles. He ran a finger over her cheek, along her jaw. His fairy queen. His beautiful, beautiful fairy queen.

Untying the ribbons on her lace nightgown, he sent that to the floor as well. She stood before him nude and lovely in the candlelight. Her nipples had hardened, begging to be suckled. In that moment he thought he finally understood all the poets. She was everything. The only thing greater than his want of her was his love. She could have him on his knees. She could make him beg. He would do anything to protect her. To please her. Rather than frighten him, these thoughts, these feelings, only made him feel stronger. Made him more certain. He had spent his life searching for meaning and somehow, unexpectedly, he had found it in her.

She lost patience and reached out to untie the sash to his robe. He wore nothing beneath and she stepped closer to wrap her hand around him. Her small, warm hand stroking him felt like heaven. She moved closer still to kiss his chest, his throat. He tilted her face back and kissed her with all of his passion, all of his love. She returned the kiss eagerly. He backed toward the bed and she followed, bumping into him in their haste.

By the time they fell onto the mattress they were both laughing from the awkwardness. Their laughter slowed as they stared at one another. Stretched out next to her he ran his hand over her side and down her hip. As he caressed the top of her thigh she raised her leg to hook over his. They began kissing again. Slowly. Leisurely. He pulled her closer, his hand curving over her bottom and squeezing. It was tempting to believe that they would have forever, that nights like this would stretch out in their future endlessly. But that wasn't possible. For all he knew they might only have tonight. And if it were only tonight then he would do his best to please her.

He kissed his way down her throat, cherishing every mewl and shiver he wrought from her. As his kisses descended to her breast she rolled onto her back, arching toward him. She clutched at his hair as his suckled first one turgid tip and then the other. He wished that joining gave her the same impossible pleasure that it gave him, but as it didn't he would concentrate on what did give her pleasure, and his suckling and nibbling on her breasts made her moan breathlessly. Certainly that was a good sign. Her hand moved to clasp at his waist, pulling on him.

"Quince, please."

"Please what?"

"Make love to me."

"I am making love to you."

She huffed in frustration. "You know what I mean."

He raised his head to look at her. "Not tonight. I don't want to hurt you."

"I know it could hurt, but I want to."

He shook his head. "No, my love."

"I don't like that word."

"Which one?"

"No. It's a beastly word. It only means someone is going to try to stop me from doing something I want to do." The testiness of her words was undermined by the delighted gasp she gave at the end when he brushed his palm over her nipple.

"I would stop anyone from hurting you, Sabrina. Even you. And especially me."

"I thought you believed in a woman's right to make her own choices."

He chuckled. "You're in my bed, aren't you? Right where you chose to be."

"Almost," she whispered. "Almost right where I choose to be." She wrapped her fist around his cock again. He was so hard and ready that his hips instinctively rocked against her touch. She slid her hand up and down in a gentle rhythm that made his whole body tighten with need. She was such an amazing blend of innocent and knowledgeable.

He pressed his cheek into her shoulder. "Sabre, please stop."

"Wouldn't you rather be inside me?" she whispered.

God's teeth, yes! But he wouldn't hurt her again. Instead he focused on the intense pleasure of her hand caressing him and spilled his seed onto her thigh while grunting her name. When he raised his head to look at her she gave him a wry smile and pulled him down for another kiss. He sank into the delight of her lips. She was all he wanted. All he would ever want.

Still intent on giving her at least a portion of the pleasure she gave him so effortlessly, he trailed kisses down her neck again on his way to her lush bosom. It was certainly no sacrifice bringing her pleasure by suckling on those beautiful breasts. He could feel his cock already twitching to life just thinking about getting his mouth on her nipple again.

"Quince?"

"Yes, love?" This time, instead of going directly to the nipple, he kissed around the side and underneath. She shivered and dug her nails into his shoulders.

"Shouldn't we talk about what we're going to do about the blackmailer?"

He stopped kissing her and drew back to rest on his elbow, looking down on her. "Beg pardon?"

"We haven't discussed it all day. At lunch you were silly and tonight you've been thoroughly distracting."

He considered distracting her further. Squeezing and kissing her breasts until she writhed in pleasure. Finally sliding into her as she had already begged him to do this evening. He didn't want to talk about the blackmailer, think about the blackmailer. He wanted to be submerged in the pleasure of his...whatever she was. Mistress wasn't a fine enough word for her. Consort? The word wife crossed his mind. He looked down to see her brow furrowed while awaiting his answer, her skin flushed and rosy from their bed sport. He felt himself frowning.

Most likely frustrated by his silence, she said, "I've been thinking about it all day and we don't have enough information to plan an effective strategy."

"I agree. That's why I've decided to send a letter to your father."

"What? Why?" She sounded alarmed.

"He's the only one I know who is in The Four. Receiving something directly from me will make him contact the others. It will cause some sort of movement outside the original plan."

"No," she said, shaking her head. "That is too dangerous."

"How is it more dangerous than what we're already facing?"

"This could be suicide. I forbid it."

"I'm sorry, did you say that you *forbid* it?"

She pulled the sheets over to cover herself. "Yes, I forbid it." Her skin had paled and her eyes looked huge and dark in her face. She looked far too upset for him to argue with her, even if her choice of words had left him irritated.

"Don't worry so much, love," he said.

Sabre moved from worry to outright panic with Quince's announcement that he was going to contact her father. She understood the strategic possibilities. It could flush out The Four. She could ask her most trusted friends among the servants to tell her who her father spoke to after such a threat, what was said. But no. All day she had been trying to figure out how to get him out of the figurative valley he was in. Now, instead of retreating, he wanted to charge over the hill toward the enemy. Her entire body felt chilled. Her heart felt brittle in her chest. All she wanted to do was wrap herself around him and beg him to never, ever let himself get hurt. The realization was humbling. Frightening.

When playing War while growing up, Jacqueline had always been frustrated that Sabre won all the wars. Sometimes it would seem that Jack was winning all the key battles, but inevitably the tide would turn and Sabre would win. Although they would discuss strategy at length, Sabre had never told her friend why she was really winning. It had to do with Jack's heart. Jack would always form an attachment to some of the "characters" in the war. It might be a historical general she particularly admired, or a soldier that had survived long odds in the present game. But Jack formed an emotional bond and would alter her play to protect the figures she had become attached to. It made her predictable. It made her weak. It made her easy to defeat.

Now Sabre had an attachment. But this was no game. If she thought Quince would listen to her counsel she wouldn't feel quite so helpless, but she could tell by the look in his eye, the tone of his voice, he had made up his mind and wouldn't be dissuaded. If he had only confided in her while he had been thinking of this plan then she might have convinced him otherwise. But now he was committed and she was sure that it was the most dangerous thing he could choose to do. If it were just a game she might consider it. At times risky decision paid off. But this wasn't a game, this was Quince. The man she loved. The man she couldn't live without.

She couldn't let him continue without at least trying to help. "Certainly..." Her voice sounded dry and raspy. She swallowed and tried again. "Certainly there are some other alternatives. We should discuss them before you commit to this course."

He curled his arm over her waist and settled against her side. As though this were just a friendly conversation. As though he weren't trying to break her heart. "I've thought about it quite a bit. Almost exclusively since I received the first note. With some," he smiled at her, "notable distraction."

"I believe it unwise to contact my father."

He narrowed his eyes at her, drawing back from the cozy posture. "So you've said already. Is there some reason you don't want me contacting him? Are you and Robert planning something? Would contacting the viscount give me information you don't want me to have?"

Sabre's lips felt stiff and cold but she forced them to continue speaking. "No. If Robert is planning anything I'm not privy to it. As for my father," she paused and sighed. "There are stories. People who have disappeared. People who inconvenienced him."

"It's hard to make a duke disappear, love."

She wanted to throttle him. He seemed to have no regard for the danger the situation presented. She scooted away from him and stumbled out of the bed. Searching the floor she found her nightgown and robe. He stayed on the bed watching her. Ever patient. Ever willing to let her do as she liked. She almost sobbed as she pulled the nightgown over her head. She tied the sash with a double knot.

Looking at him one last time she raised her chin and said, "You're making a terrible mistake." With that she left the room. If he wanted to kill himself she didn't think she had the heart to watch.

Quince watched her go, fighting every impulse to follow her, argue with her, make love to her, kiss and tease her until she admitted her feelings for him. He fisted his hand in the bedclothes, frustrated with how the evening had ended. But she

had been upset with his plan to contact her father, much more
so than he would have predicted. It was best to let her go back
to the Rose Room and cool down. He would see how she fared
at breakfast.

Twenty-Four

Even though he hadn't slept well, Quince awoke earlier than usual. Something was wrong. There was a terrible silence again. He checked the pillow beside him to make sure he wasn't imagining it. He was alone in bed. Rising from the sheets, he stood in the middle of the room and warred with himself. Should he ring his valet and prepare for the day? That would be the logical course, as surely he was only imagining that Sabre was gone. He was only upset that she hadn't been there, at arm's reach, upon awakening.

Or should he follow his instincts and search for her now? After another moment of indecision he found himself once again putting on the simplest of clothing to go searching for his love. At this rate he thought he would soon earn a reputation as the mad, barefoot duke. He didn't find her anywhere upstairs. Jogging down the steps he found Havers to greet him at the bottom. The butler seemed anxious.

"Where is she?" Quince asked without preamble.

"The Miss left this morning. In the wee hours." Havers was literally wringing his hands. "We didn't know if we should wake you."

Quince felt himself go cold. "If it has to do with Miss Bittlesworth you should always wake me."

The butler nodded, looking close to tears. "She went to the barn and had a horse saddled. She didn't want anyone to go with her but Bill, the groomsman, followed her to make sure she was safe-"

"And?" Quince prompted, impatient to hear the conclusion of the story.

"He returned not thirty minutes ago, your grace. She's... she's gone to London."

Quince nodded and looked down at the floor, hands clenched. He understood now how dangerous a job it was to be a messenger. He wanted to rage. He wanted to hurt someone, anyone who stood in his way. He wanted to curl into a ball on the floor and weep. She had left. She had left him. Was she so frightened about him writing to her father? Was it something else? How had he misread her so completely that he hadn't expected her to leave? He realized he was still staring blankly at the floor and lifted his chin.

"Have my horse saddled."

"Yes, your grace. Do you want any outriders?"

Quince had already turned to take the stairs two at a time. "I don't bloody care!"

In short order he was dressed, mounted, and on his way to London with four riders trailing him. Bill the grooms-man had received the shock of his life when the duke asked for him, then gave him a hug in thanks for ensuring Miss Bittlesworth's safe arrival at her destination. Bill's description of the house meant she had headed directly where he thought she would.

It had been near dawn when Sabre arrived at Robert's townhouse. She had felt slightly guilty rousing his groomsmen to take her horse. She made sure to tell them it was the property of the Duke of Beloin and that she would eversomuch appreciate it if someone could take it to the duke's London stable soon. Sneaking into the house, she made her way quietly up to her room.

This was one of the times when she particularly appreciated her brother. Shortly after he had purchased the townhome one of the first things he had done was bring her and Charlie here to show them where their rooms were. To tell them that they would never, ever be guests. They were family and would always have a place with him. Only being fourteen at the time she had, of course, asked where Justin's room was. Robert had explained that however much he cared about their half-brother, it wouldn't be appropriate for him to have such an open door policy with a bastard brother, especially as their father had not made provisions for him to be acknowledged in Society. When she had fussed and stomped her foot Robert had promised that Justin could always come to him for anything he needed. Although Charlie had maintained his bachelor's quarters and hadn't, to her knowledge, made much use of his room here, she, on the other hand, had come to see the room as a sanctuary, her personal haven over the past year.

Quietly opening the door and slipping inside, she smelled the lingering scent of her perfume. It reminded her of innocence, youth, and her own strong-willed nature. But it didn't smell like lemongrass and the duke. For a frantic moment she wished she had taken his shirt or cravat. But wouldn't that make it worse? It felt like there was a band tightening around her chest and her throat was choked with unshed tears. She didn't take off so much as the jacket of her riding habit, just walked straight to the bed and burrowed face down in the pillows. Pillows that didn't smell like Quincy. She finally shed the bitter tears she had been holding back. How had she fallen in love with a man who had no sense? A man who would most likely be dead before the month was out.

Within an hour Sabre heard a knock on her door. "Go away!" she protested.

The door opened and she knew it must be Robert. It sounded as though he lingered in the doorway.

"The staff said you had arrived." His voice was soft. Perhaps out of deference to the early hour, perhaps because he sensed from her posture that something was amiss. When she didn't respond he prompted her. "Sabre?"

"I heard you," she said, her voice still thick from her crying jag. "I have arrived."

She heard his footsteps come closer, then felt the bed tilt slightly as he sat on the edge. He placed his hand on her back. "Sabre, what is wrong?"

His voice was clear, calm. Kindly, even. She recognized it as his first stage of extracting the information he wanted. "Nothing is wrong, Robert."

That received a wry laugh. "We both know that's not true. What did he do?"

"Nothing. And we both know that I have no patience for a person who won't do anything."

"So he didn't do…anything?"

Sabre knew what Robert was asking. And knew that she couldn't answer honestly. But thinking about what they had done only caused her a new batch of tears. She missed him already. They had been together only hours before but she missed him as though it had been days. Months. She wanted to answer her brother, but couldn't through her sobs.

"Sabre?" Robert moved to kneel beside the bed near where she had buried her face in her pillows. His voice had an edge of panic. "Sabre, please look at me."

She didn't want to, but knew that a contest of wills between them would quickly make an unpleasant situation worse. She wiped her eyes and nose on her sleeve and looked over to him in the pale light of the early morning. His expression of concern hardened into something more dangerous.

She grabbed his hand where it rested on the edge of the bed. "Please don't hurt him," she said. "Please? Swear to me."

He looked at her for a long, silent moment. She knew that tears continued to leak at the corners of her eyes. His hand was warm but tense in her own.

"Please, Robert. Don't hurt him. And if it must be said, don't have anyone else hurt him." She furrowed her brow and held back another sob. With a small voice she added. "If possible, don't let anyone hurt him at all."

He rose and tried to extract his hand from hers. "I'll let you rest."

"No!" she said, clinging to his hand tenaciously. She could hear hysteria in her own tone. "Promise!"

He sighed, using his free hand to smooth her hair. "I promise," he said softly.

"Don't let him be harmed," she insisted.

"I'll do my best," he agreed.

She finally let his hand go. He leaned down to kiss the top of her head. "Get some rest, Sabre."

She nodded and burrowed into the pillows again. Pillows she wished smelled of lemongrass.

Quince arrived at Robert Bittlesworth's townhouse shortly after dawn. While his men milled in the street he sprinted up the steps and pounded on the door. It was promptly opened by none other than Robert himself. The younger man did a credible job of looming in the doorway considering that they were of a size.

Quince tried to push through anyway. "Is she-"

"She won't see you. You aren't welcome here." Bittlesworth's stance was solid. His stare flat and implacable. The stare of a predator.

The duke blinked. "I don't understand."

"That's hardly my problem." Bittlesworth began to close the door.

"Wait, stop! What happened? I don't even know why she left!"

Robert planted a hand on the duke's chest and pushed him back. "That's hardly my problem," he said again, closing the door with a solid snap.

Quince pounded on the door for a good five minutes but there was no other response from the occupants. Backing up he stared at the second floor, wondering if any of the windows were to Sabre's room. Realizing he was being a good deal more foolish than he should be, especially for a public street, he rejoined his men to lead them to the ducal London home. His gaze stayed on the Bittlesworth townhouse until it was out of sight.

Twenty-Five

*A*fter spending the morning pacing restlessly, Quince sat down to write a note to his friend Gideon Wolfe, Earl of Harrington. He knew he needed to calm his mind to ensure that what he wrote would make any sort of sense. Lord knew if he wrote anything while in an agitated state it would lead Giddy to descend upon him like a mother hen. He'd made that mistake when his father died and it had taken a fortnight before Giddy had left him alone. So now he cleared his thoughts and set to writing.

G,

Returned to London and fancy a drink. Will you be At Home this evening?

Q

Simple. Certainly nothing that would alarm the earl. Quince dispatched a footman with the note to track down Gideon, whether at Parliament or home, and return with a reply. Exhausted, he took to bed. And spent a long time staring at the empty pillow next to him.

Sabre had fallen into a half-sleep but roused when she heard footsteps in the hall. After a lifetime of hearing it, the knock at the door was familiar.

"Go away, Jack," she said waspishly. "I don't want to talk to you."

"Sabre, what happened?" her friend called through the door. At her silence Jack continued. "Robert called me over here because he's worried about you. Is it," her voice became hushed. "Is it Quince?"

Sabre pushed herself from the bed and stomped over to the door, flinging it open. "I don't want to talk to you because you didn't tell me it would be like this. All your talk of *love*. Love doesn't make you happy. It makes you weak. It makes you powerless."

Jack had drawn back with a hand over her mouth, eyes wide. Sabre slammed the door again. And locked it.

Jack stood in the hallway, shocked. She had never seen her friend in such a state. Hair falling from its pins, eyes red and swollen, clothing mussed. Sabre wasn't like that. Sabre was steady, determined. Remembering what she herself had gone through with Gideon, she wondered what on earth Quince could have done.

Quince wasn't like her husband. The duke was, well, mild-mannered. Clever. Perhaps he had rejected Sabre's suit. Her friend usually didn't allow anyone to thwart her plans. Then again, she had never tried to ensnare a duke before. Or fallen in love. Jack touched the door, wishing she knew what to do for her friend.

"She won't let you in?"

Jack's heart tripped to hear Robert's voice so close behind her when she hadn't heard him approach.

"Indeed not."

"I don't know what happened." He looked frustrated and Jack knew that he hoped she would be able to draw the story out of his sister.

Jack sighed. "Love."

Robert raised a brow at her. "What do you mean?"

"It does funny things."

He looked at the door again, still irritated. "Last week she said she wanted to marry him. She didn't say anything about falling in love with him."

"She told you? You approved?"

"I thought I did."

Sabre's voice came from the other side of the door. "Stop talking out there as though I can't hear you."

Robert tried the handle and found it locked. "Sabre, open this door."

"No!"

"Sabre, open this door before I open it for you."

Jack heard the soft click of the door unlocking again. The door remained closed and after a few moments Robert opened it. They found Sabre looking out her window over the back garden. She had taken some time to smooth her hair and skirt, and had removed the jacket of her riding habit to lay it on the bed.

"Sabre," Robert said. "We don't know what to do for you unless you talk to us."

"There's nothing you can do," she answered, her voice sounding hollow.

He stepped toward her. "Sabre, you don't know-"

She spun to look at him, hand clasped into fists at her sides, eyes dark with anger. "You needn't tell me what I don't know! I don't even know if you're part of why he's in danger. Why would I tell you anything?"

"Quince is in danger?" Jack had asked the question without thinking and now had both Bittlesworth siblings staring at her coldly. She heard boots in the hallway and turned to look over her shoulder. She didn't think she had ever been happier to see Charlie Bittlesworth in her life. She hadn't seen him in at least a year, but he was still as lanky as she remembered. He'd let his blonde hair grow a bit longer and it fell into his eyes like it had when he was a child. And as she caught his eye he smiled at her. Thank God for Charlie. The only sweet-natured Bittlesworth in the lot.

He paused in the doorway to take in the tableau. His two dark haired siblings looked ready to fight one another. Jack appeared, she knew, somewhat lost and out of place.

"Hullo, Jack," he said. "Robert."

The two brothers nodded to one another.

Stepping into the room he said more softly, "Hullo, little bird."

The fight seemed to drain out of Sabre. She sobbed and dashed across the room into his embrace.

Jack linked her arm in Robert's and pulled him from the room. When they descended the steps she realized it now felt rather odd to walk again with someone closer to her own height. If he was taller it was only by the merest inch or two. She looked over at him and he seemed deep in thought.

"How is Quince in trouble?"

Her question pulled him from his rumination. "I'm sure that's something the duke would prefer I didn't tell you."

SUE LONDON

"What makes you think that?"

"Because otherwise you would already know."

"Does Giddy know?"

He shrugged.

"Robert, you're not being very helpful."

He gave her a frosty smile.

She told him sternly, "Well, I shall have to tell Gideon about this, so don't be surprised if he comes here demanding answers."

"He can do as he wishes."

Jack scowled. Robert was being vague and willful. "Why does Sabre believe you could be involved in Quince's troubles?"

He leaned closer, his lips almost to her ear and she felt his warm breath as he whispered. "Because she is very, very smart." At that he drew away from her. "I have work. I'm sure you know how to let yourself out."

Jack shuddered. She had grown up with Robert. Idolized him. Adored him. He had been her first crush. But just now she realized that perhaps she didn't know him at all. She let herself out of the townhouse and fled for home.

Twenty-Six

"What are you doing abed at two in the afternoon?" The earl sounded testy. Well, Quince thought, the note hadn't been as casual as he'd thought, then. Somehow he needed to severely curb the number of people who felt comfortable storming his room while he was trying to rest.

"It seemed wise as I didn't sleep last night and had an engagement scheduled with the Earl of Harrington this evening."

Gideon loomed over the bed and frowned. "You look like death. Are you ill?"

The duke sat up and scrubbed his face with his hands. "Get out of my room, Gideon. Wait in the parlor. Or in the kitchen for all I care. I can't stand your hovering when I'm not yet awake."

The earl looked displeased but nodded. "Downstairs, then. I'll be in the study."

Quince sighed as his friend left the room. He might yet regret seeking Gideon's counsel, but what else was he to do? Sabre had deserted him. He didn't trust Robert. His own household staff was suspect after the way the notes had been delivered.

Once downstairs he did, indeed, find Gideon in his study poring over his journals. Perhaps the earl and Sabre would enjoy a party wherein they did nothing but read from the ducal accounts. Just the thought of trying to do that gave him a headache. The earl's eyes tracked him as he crossed the room to flop down in one of the side chairs along the wall.

"You don't look like yourself," Gideon said.

"Oh really? Then who, pray tell, do I look like?"

"A scoundrel who has stolen the duke's cast off clothes. Even your hair is disorderly."

Quince ran his hand through the mop. "I thought you knew that artfully mussed hair was all the rage."

"Yes, and usually you are a model of the fashion. But right now you just look untidy."

The duke scowled and steepled his hands across his abdomen while he slouched in the chair. "Egads," he said drily. "We all know that the worst sin is to be untidy."

Gideon came around the desk and sat in the chair opposite. "All right, out with it."

Quince sat forward, elbows on knees. "You're going to wish you had waited until a more reasonable hour for drinking."

Gideon gave the duke an appraising look, then crossed his legs and settled in to wait for the story.

Quince rubbed his face again and looked at the desk, the carpet. Most anywhere but at Gideon. "I have things to tell you and some of them have been a long time in the telling." As the earl remained quiet, Quince continued. "The most pressing concern is fairly recent."

There was a long pause as Quince forced himself to look at his friend. Gideon's expression was still impassive. Patient.

"I'm being blackmailed."

"By whom?"

"I'm not sure."

"When did this start?"

"Almost three weeks ago."

"What steps have you taken?"

"I asked Robert for his help."

Quince saw a muscle in Gideon's jaw flex but all he said was, "That seems wise."

"Actually I'm not sure it was. I've begun to suspect that he's somehow involved."

Now Gideon leaned forward. "I know that you don't like Robert, but-"

"It's not about that, believe me. And I don't dislike him precisely. In fact," now he smiled down at his clasped hands, "I'm under the impression that he has a far greater dislike for me than I ever entertained for him."

"What makes you say that?"

"Among other things, the nickname. Although I presume you know it."

"If Robert has a nickname for you, I'm not aware of it."

"Interesting. He called me Gideon's Angel. He seemed quite offended by all the times I dragged you out of the gutter. I think he stopped just short of calling me a fishwife."

Gideon snorted. "It's nothing that Robert or Charlie wouldn't have done for each other if they hadn't both been face down in that same gutter together. But Robert aside, you still haven't told me what the nature of this blackmail is."

"There's something else I have to tell you first."

"Something worse than blackmail and having the Hero of the Home Office irritated with you?"

"You recall, of course, that I hadn't been aware that my mother was still alive until after my father's death?"

"Yes," Gideon chuckled. "She detested me, if I'm not mistaken."

"She doesn't care for overbearing men, and after my father I can't entirely blame her. When he realized how headstrong she was he banished her to a townhouse in Bath and forbade her to have any contact with me. He would still visit her from time to time, though. Hoping that along with his heir, he could have a spare."

"It's good to know that your father was as charming in his personal life as he was on the floor of the Parliament."

"She managed to conceal three children from him. She was afraid he would take them all away as he had me."

Gideon sat up, alert. "Wait, you have siblings? How long have you known?"

"Two years. It took awhile for her to even confide in me."

Gideon strode to the side table and poured drinks. Handing one to Quince he said, "So I suppose the correct term is congratulations? It isn't often that one finds an entire family."

"Thank you. It has been interesting, to say the least."

Gideon resumed his seat. "Although I knew we had our differences I will admit to being surprised you haven't told me about them before this."

"Don't take it too hard, Gideon. There were a lot of things I needed to work out for myself." He saw the muscle tense in Gideon's jaw again, but the earl didn't say anything so Quince continued. "Then I quietly set about ensuring that my brother, Jeremy, is in line for the succession. As my father hadn't been aware of him, it posed something of a legal challenge but I think it's resolved now."

Gideon squinted, thinking. "And that means your cousin Lionel is no longer a marquess. Is he aware of that?"

"Not yet. But soon." Quince turned the glass in his hands as he saw Gideon start drinking from his own. "And that is part of why I'm coming to you now. What I'm involved in could be dangerous. If anything should happen to me I would look to you to ensure that Jeremy is granted his title. That he has someone who can help him in taking on his new duties."

"Why do you think this is dangerous?"

"We'll get to that momentarily. Do I have your pledge to look after Jeremy?"

"Of course. You needn't even ask."

"That is a weight from my mind."

"How old is he?"

"Sixteen."

Gideon considered it. "Is he more like you at sixteen or me at sixteen?"

Quince laughed. "Somewhere between, I think." He watched Gideon mull the implications of that statement.

The earl finally said, "I still should hope he wouldn't have to ascend at such a young age."

"Nor would I, particularly."

"And why are we concerned that he might need to?"

"The blackmailer is unknown to me but the only person that I'm fairly sure is involved to some degree is Viscount Bittlesworth. I plan to bait the bear in his den to see if I can gain more information."

Gideon frowned. "Blaise Bittlesworth?"

"Indeed."

"He is…unsavory, to say the least. But tell me more about this blackmailer."

Quince recited the text of the notes, including how they were delivered. Upon recitation of the third one Gideon rose from his chair.

"Dammit man, how can you be here if your sister is being threatened?"

"I thought being near me, or even mother, wouldn't be the safest place for her. As such, I'm having her sent to the safest place I can think of."

"Where would that be?"

Quince sipped his wine and grinned. "Your house, of course. Although she will be delivered to your wife, with instructions from Miss Bittlesworth. As I wasn't sure we would have this conversation in advance of her arrival we thought it best it be between the two of them."

Gideon had begun to pace but stopped to stare at the duke. "You were going to tell my wife about your sister before you told me?"

"Not really. There was no indication of the relationship. Simply one Haberdasher asking another to look after a young girl."

"And how, exactly, did Miss Bittlesworth get involved in this affair?"

"By inserting herself. She has been at Belle Fleur for almost a fortnight."

Gideon's frown became fiercer. "You've had the girl at your estate? Was she chaperoned?"

"No. Although apparently Robert knew where she was."

Gideon poured himself more brandy. "Then I suppose more congratulations are in order."

"I'm not going to marry her."

"The hell you aren't."

"I'd rather hang than see Blaise Bittlesworth have the satisfaction of his daughter becoming a duchess."

"You should have thought of that before you let her reside at your estate!"

"I love Sabrina, and I will do right by her as far as I am able. But it won't include a title."

"What do you mean you love her? You barely even know her."

"Really? How long did you know your wife before you fell in love with her?"

Gideon resumed his seat and looked at the ceiling, calculating. "Well…" he said. "It *seemed* like a long time."

Quince smirked into his wine. "I'm sure it did."

"It took more than a fortnight."

"No surprise. You never were the sharpest knife in the drawer."

"And it certainly didn't happen before we had achieved a certain level of intimacy." Gideon was silent for a long moment as Quince took another sip of wine. The earl narrowed his eyes. "If you've touched that girl I'll drag you into the church myself."

"Sabrina was most persuasive on the subject of intimacy."

"You're marrying her. This isn't negotiable."

"As much as you like to act like my older brother you, in fact, are not. I'll do as I please in this matter."

Gideon sat forward. "Quince, the blackmailers are the least of your concern. When Robert figures out what you've done, what you're doing, Jeremy will ascend in short order. Unless you marry the girl."

"I saw Robert this morning and I believe he knows. Yet here I sit, still among the living."

"The man trains spies and assassins. You're most likely one convenient accident from death."

Quince felt a chill and instinctively knew Gideon had the right of it. "Surely not."

The earl sat back again. "An accident would be the only way to rid oneself of an intractable duke. Meanwhile, I'm sure he'll see Miss Bittlesworth married off to whoever will have her."

"She wouldn't stand for it."

"She won't have a choice."

"You speak as thought Robert is head of the family."

"In many ways he is. His father is a selfish, arrogant snake and rarely pays attention to the true work of running a household."

Quince grimaced and took a sip of his wine. Snakes were similar to dragons in many ways. "I'm not sure she would have me at this point, in any case."

"Why do you think that?"

"She left. Last night. Thus why she's presently at Robert's."

"What did you do?"

Quince sighed. "Told her I planned to write to her father about the blackmail. Although at this point I think it would be better to visit him. And thank you for the vote of confidence, old boy, assuming that *I* had done something."

"That will be my first piece of marriage advice to you. Always assume you've done something, even if you think you haven't."

"Yes, I can see why you're inclined for me to marry. You want someone to commiserate with."

"Don't get me wrong, marriage also has much to recommend it."

"Such as?"

Gideon gave him a wolfish grin. "I told you, I don't want you thinking of my wife that way."

Quince snorted.

"But there are other things, too." Gideon stared down into his glass. "Everything I see, I ask myself 'Would Jack like that?' Or if I hear a bit of news I wonder what she will think of it. And there is a...peace of mind that comes from knowing she's there."

Quince nodded. "Then perhaps you understand how I feel about Sabre leaving last night."

Gideon looked at him keenly for a moment. "What are you doing here rather than knocking Robert's door down to get her back?"

"I wanted to this morning. But as I've thought about it, much as I'm sending Jessica to you for safekeeping, I should let Sabre stay with Robert. I would not want her put in harm's way if there is any danger."

Gideon smiled ruefully. "If she's anything like Jack, it's danger that will bring her running." He paused, considering. "If she loves you. She does love you?"

Quince shrugged. "She hasn't said so. It's possible that she loves the title. I was very clear there was no money to speak of."

"We're working on that."

"But the duchy will never, in my lifetime, have the funds one would expect of it."

"Especially as Robert will have you killed before the week is out."

Quince laughed, raising his glass. "Especially because of that."

"I'm not entirely joking."

Quince took a hard swallow of the wine. "Yes, I know."

Twenty-Seven

S abre was back to staring moodily out the window of her bedroom. It had taken to raining this afternoon, which suited her mood perfectly. She had cried all over Charlie but refused to talk. Safe, familiar Charlie. As usual he had cuts and bruises from the rough work he did in the stables and entertained her with stories of this year's batch of colts and fillies. Rather than press her for what made her sad, he contented himself with making her smile and laugh. Thank God for Charlie.

Later she had heard Robert downstairs grilling her poor middle brother about what he had learned. To Charlie's credit, she heard him defend her right to puzzle through her own feelings. Which left her considering that, for the most part, she had lived a life relatively free of strong feelings. She had thought she had feelings before, but now she recognized that they were really ideas and principles. She had never before made a decision based purely on emotion. Knowing the duke could get hurt had terrified her. Knowing that she was powerless to change his course from what she saw as disastrous had made her feel weak. And that he could die? She knew it could destroy her. She truly was angry at Jack for not telling her that love could wound so deeply.

On his second glass of wine Quince decided he had imbibed enough to broach one last item with his friend. "Gideon, I would like for your advice on something else."

The earl grunted. "If it is whether or not to redo this room, then I wholeheartedly support it."

Quince looked around at the antiquated gilt-covered chairs. "It is bloody awful. But as I don't spend much time in here it isn't high on my list of priorities."

"Then perhaps you won't notice if I replace everything wholesale."

"Perhaps not."

"If you don't want my advice on decorating then what, pray tell, is there beyond what we have already been discussing?"

Quince poured a third glass and thought that he may have started the conversation too soon. "Something you are very qualified to advise on and hopefully something I will live long enough to use."

"I already manage your money, we rarely agree on politics, and that only leaves one thing." At Quince's uncomfortable silence Gideon said. "No. Certainly you don't mean that."

"You'll have to admit you've made rather a study of, you know," Quince waved his hand, " how to please a woman."

"We're practically the same age, you could have been doing the same studying. Will this be like school all over again with me doing all your readings?"

Quince laughed. "As long as you don't take the test."

"We've been to the same whorehouses. Did they teach you nothing?"

Quince looked up sheepishly. "About that."

Gideon leaned forward. "What do you mean 'about that'?"

"It has never been my interest to be with a woman who has lain with many men."

"What did you do? Play whist?"

That forced a small smile that Quince covered with a swallow of wine. "At times. I'm sure they thought that I had...other interests."

"You didn't sleep with any of them?"

Quince gave an involuntary shudder. "No."

"You propositioned Miss Bittlesworth when you thought she was Robert's mistress. Why would you do that if...Why *would* you do that?"

"Curious, isn't it? I surprised even myself that day. As is typical, my soul knew things that my mind had not yet comprehended."

Gideon sat back with a frustrated look and downed the brandy in his glass. "You don't even like to talk about sex. You say it disturbs your digestion."

"As we're drinking our luncheon I'm sure I'll be fine. If it makes you feel any better, imagine I'm Charlie."

Gideon snorted. "Charlie would have the good sense to visit the whores and find out for himself."

Quince smiled down into his empty glass, not quite sure when he'd drunk it. "Very well. Don't worry about it."

But Gideon was intrigued now. "How many women have you slept with, then? Have you been preying on the virgins of the *ton* and I've somehow missed it?"

"Sabrina Bittlesworth is the only woman I've ever been intimate with."

Gideon stared at him. After a long moment of silence the earl rose to fetch the brandy bottle and brought it back to his chair. He refilled his glass a generous amount and downed more than half of it in one go. "All right, then. What do you want to know?"

"She experienced a great deal of pain the first time, which I'm given to understand is common?"

"It can be, although there are ways to reduce the pain."

"I wish I had known them. There was a good deal of blood."

"Ah. There may not have been much you could have done then."

"That, at least, is reassuring in a way." Quince thought for a moment. "Although could the position have caused greater pain?"

"I'm baffled to consider what position two virgins could start with that might do so."

"Standing up, with her back to the wall."

Gideon's eyebrows rose. "I'm impressed."

Quince chuckled. "It was her idea. She said 'don't worry, I know what to do.' I didn't have the heart to tell her that I was glad one of us did."

"Are you sure she was a virgin? The blood could have been her menses."

"There was resistance. I definitely felt something break or tear."

Gideon nodded. "All right, then. Jack didn't bleed as much but I have no other experience with virgins. Women are different in other ways, so it would make sense they are different in this."

"The second time she still had pain. She was sweet about it, but I could tell I had hurt her. Is that normal?"

Gideon sighed. "Again, I have limited experience with virgins. How much time had passed?"

"Two days."

"As she bled more than Jack it would make sense that she had more of a wound and would need longer to heal."

"How long did you wait with Jack?"

Gideon smiled at the memory. "I had planned to wait two days. I think she only waited about two minutes."

Quince chuckled. "What interesting women we find ourselves in company with."

"Indeed." Gideon poured more brandy into his glass. "Were those all your questions?"

"No."

Gideon waited a moment, then prompted. "And?"

"I want to be able to please her, and I think I do somewhat, but," Quince trailed off, unsure how to continue.

"What have you done that seemed to please her?"

Quince could feel himself blushing. Better to finish this now than have to start the conversation again some day. "She enjoys kissing very much. And she enjoys when I kiss or fondle her bosom."

"And have you kissed her below?"

"You mean on her...? Ah, no."

"It's rare for a woman not to enjoy that. Although it is an acquired taste, I will grant you. Bring marmalade to bed if you need to."

"I suppose it would only be fair."

"She...? Bloody hell, how did she know how to do that?"

"She claims you can learn all manner of things from the servant girls."

Gideon shook his head. "I suppose that's true. Especially at her father's house."

That thought sobered him significantly. "I can't marry her, Giddy. I can't be that man's son-in-law."

"You have to, Quince." After a few moments of moody silence between them Gideon said, "All right, pay attention. It may take me the rest of this bottle of brandy, but I'm going to tell you everything I know about pleasing a woman. And, God willing, I won't remember this come morning. Should I become senseless, promise me you will deliver me unto my wife before she becomes frantic as to my whereabouts."

"Why would she do that? Sabre said you're hardly ever home."

Gideon looked offended. "I dine and sleep with my wife every night. We ride together almost every morning. Although in her condition I hope to curtail that soon. The only time I am not at home is if we have a social engagement together."

"You never go to White's anymore?"

"If there is a conversation I need to have for Parliament I will go there between supper and bed, but I don't stay out carousing."

Quince looked at the brandy bottle that Gideon had been steadily consuming. "I suddenly feel like a horrible influence."

"Come to think of it, the last time I drank better than a half bottle of brandy it was your doing. Perhaps a fallen angel, then."

"Before your wedding? If I hadn't been there you would have had a full bottle."

Gideon thought for a moment. "That's probably true."

"I suppose the hangover wasn't helpful for your wedding night."

The earl smirked. "Not only did I not anticipate my vows, something which probably shocks you to no end, I also did not enforce my conjugal rights that night. It was near a fortnight after the wedding before we became intimate."

"You're right, I am shocked." Quince grinned. "And it makes me think you're not as skilled at seduction as I had thought."

"See here, man, I will not be so insulted. As I said, listen closely and I will illuminate you."

"I'm hearing nothing yet."

"The first thing is to know what she likes. What she wants."

Quince poured some more wine for himself. "Yes, you're being so helpful."

Gideon raised a brow but continued, slouching down more comfortably in his seat with the brandy bottle propped on one knee and his glass on the other. "Your first encounter tells me she's adventurous. The type who would probably enjoy a change in location. In a field on a summer day, some closeted room at a ball. And her personality tells me that she might enjoy dominance games."

"Beg pardon?"

"Oh, you know, hold her down. Tie her up."

Quince shuddered. "No, I don't believe I'll be doing that."

"You didn't ask me advice on how to seduce you, now did you? But let her tie you up, then. See how she likes it."

The duke raised his own brow in return but didn't say anything, content to sip his wine and let Gideon continue.

"As you are a complete novice I will assume you need some instruction on a woman's body. You are already familiar with the appeal of lips and breasts. After all, who could miss them? But there are any number of places that both you and she may find erotic. The nape of the neck. The back of the knee. The important thing is to explore and see what she responds to. And know that it's not just where you touch her, but how you touch her. She may enjoy a feather light caress, or she may want a masterful grip. She might like both at different times or in different places."

"You approach women as you do billiards. All strategy and finesse."

Gideon looked contemplative. "Interesting analogy." He sipped his brandy. "Most likely accurate. At least until now."

"It's different now?"

"I lose my head with Jack. I don't focus on it as...as an event." He smiled a bit blearily, the brandy taking effect. "But I have a sufficient amount of practice that I can do that without losing sight of her satisfaction. I assume that you, my friend, do not have that luxury."

"How do you know when she's satisfied?"

"You know, I have a book to share with you, but you must promise to return it or Jack will be heartbroken."

"Of course."

"It usually takes longer for a woman to reach her peak, but when she does it is a beautiful sight to behold. Especially when it's the woman you love. God, I hope I don't remember this conversation in the morning."

Quince chuckled. "Have sympathy for me, then. It's in my best interest if I do."

"Tell me, how did you make it to this age without taking a woman to bed at least once?"

"That's a story for another time. I don't want to interrupt you now that it's getting interesting."

"What was I saying?"

"What a woman looks like when she reaches her peak."

Gideon smiled, his words beginning to slur lightly. "Oh, yes. Well. Different things bring them to completion and they express it differently. Some moan or scream. Others are quiet. Some scratch." He frowned. "That can get bothersome at times. But the best part is when they look at you as though you've discovered something about their body that they never suspected."

"Bloody hell, you are full of yourself, aren't you? How does Jack stand you?"

"She likes me quite well, thank you."

"If you're just going to sit there looking self-satisfied then I'm taking you home."

"I thought you wanted the advantage of my gathered wisdom."

Rather than reply, Quince stood and put out a hand to haul the earl to his feet.

Gideon finished the brandy straight from the bottle before standing. "I may be sufficiently drunk enough now to tell you what I would do were I to find myself in your position."

After steadying Gideon on his feet Quince said, "Then I suggest you use small words. The larger ones seem something of a challenge." He set the empty brandy decanter aside before the heavy crystal could get broken.

As Quince helped Gideon up the steps of the earl's town-home he had to admit that some of the insights shared on the carriage ride could prove useful. Provided that he had the opportunity to try them.

"But we are brothers, aren't we?" the earl asked again.

"Of course, Giddy. You can be sure that if Charlie had the ability to disavow Robert as his older brother, at times he would."

Dibbs opened the door before they gained the last step. "Good evening, your grace."

"Just like old times, eh Dibbs?"

"Indeed, your grace."

"Give my apologies to the countess for returning the earl in such a state."

"As you wish, your grace." The butler bowed deferentially to the duke as two footmen materialized to help Gideon into the house.

Quince decided that, as he was already out and about, there was no time like the present to pay a visit to Blaise Bittlesworth.

Twenty-Eight

"*D*ammit, Sabrina, you need to eat." Robert was prowling around her room as though he expected to find some source of worry hidden in the corners.

"I'm not hungry."

"The staff said you sent everything back today untouched. When was the last time you ate?"

She thought about the tray she had nibbled from the night before. "I had supper last night." She sighed. "It's late. I just want to go to sleep."

He narrowed his eyes at her. "It's only eight o'clock and you've slept a good portion of the day."

"Robert, you're being tiresome."

"And you're not acting like the sister I know. It's well within my purview to be concerned about you."

There was a polite knock at the open door and Sabre turned to see one of Robert's footmen hovering impatiently. Robert went to talk to the man in hushed tones. When he turned back to her his face was an impassive mask but his eyes burned with a dark fire. "Get some rest. I have to go out."

She nodded and rubbed her forehead. All the men in her life were tiresome.

Quince had never set foot in Blaise Bittlesworth's house before but somehow the staff seemed to be very much aware of who he was. Even though he had walked up the street alone, looking easily the most disreputable he ever had in his life, the butler had bowed him in with murmurs of "your grace" and he had been installed in what was a really quite lovely parlor on the second floor.

When he heard the door open he considered rudely remaining in his seat but what he saw made him shoot to his feet with alacrity. For a brief moment he thought it was Sabrina and his heart started pounding painfully in his chest. The petite, dark-haired woman glided toward him and curtsied.

"Your grace," she said with a slight accent he couldn't place. She was even smaller than Sabrina, like a lovely little doll.

He bowed over her hand. "Lady Bittlesworth."

She settled onto a silk loveseat and he sat in the chair opposite her. He couldn't stop staring. She looked so much like Sabrina that it hurt. So much that he thought he might already love her, too.

She smiled at him as though the hour and his appearance didn't make the situation awkward. "We are pleased to receive you, your grace. I have asked for tea to be brought in and hope that is acceptable to you?"

Surely tea would help to clear the fogginess of his brain after the four glasses of wine he had drunk with Gideon. "Thank you for your hospitality, Lady Bittlesworth."

Just then the staff brought in the tea tray and arranged it on the low table in front of the viscountess.

"How do you take your tea, your grace?"

"Two lumps, please."

She prepared his tea with a delicacy and grace he couldn't imagine Sabrina using. He wondered at the relationship between mother and daughter. Sabre had never mentioned anything about her. Once he had tea and two lemon biscuits he realized the evening wasn't at all going in the direction that he had imagined it would.

"I was hoping to speak to the viscount."

She almost arched a brow, but didn't quite. As though she were controlling her reaction. "I'm afraid he is at his club for supper. As usual."

"Ah."

With another smile she said, "Are you here to ask him for Sabrina's hand?"

The shock of the question made him swallow his tea the wrong way and he started a coughing fit. The viscountess fluttered over him. "Your grace, are you all right?"

He held a hand up to ward her off and nodded as he worked to control his breathing.

"My apologies, your grace. I just thought...I mean a young man such as yourself..."

"You have nothing to apologize for, Lady Bittlesworth."

She resumed her seat again, taking her teacup in hand. Her hair was as dark as Sabrina's but her eyes were a lighter blue, like aquamarines. He realized he was staring again and struggled to find something to say. "Your husband was a friend of my father's and I found some documents that he should find interesting." Might as well plant the seed however he could.

The door opened again and the butler announced. "Mr. Bittlesworth."

Robert strolled into the room as though it were an appointed visit. Lady Bittlesworth rose to greet him and Quince rose as well to accommodate the lady.

"Robert!" she said happily, holding out her hands to him.

"Maman," he said, kissing her hand and escorting her back to her seat. Nodding briefly at Quince he said, "Telford."

There it was again, that familiarity that might be insult. "Robert," he responded coolly. Two could certainly play this game.

Robert took the chair next to Quince, which had him sitting so close the two were almost touching. Lady Bittlesworth set to making her stepson a cup of tea, obviously acquainted with his tastes. Settled with his refreshments Robert asked, "So what brings you to visit our maman?"

There was an edge to his voice. Subtle, but clear. Quince was trespassing in an area that Robert called his own.

The lady replied for him. "I'm delighted to receive a visit from his grace."

"Had I known of your beauty and charm," Quince said to her, "I would have visited far earlier."

She smiled prettily at him but Quince was fairly sure that Robert would have growled if he had thought it socially acceptable. They passed a half hour in somewhat convivial company. It was to Lady Bittlesworth's credit that she kept the conversation lively. At last Quince surrendered on the point of waiting for the viscount to appear and made his farewells to the lady.

"I'll walk you out," Robert offered. Quince knew it was more threat than hospitality. His assumption was borne out in the first shadowed length of hallway when Robert pushed him against the wall. "What are you thinking, coming here?" the younger man hissed.

"Let go of me or we shall come to blows."

Robert obviously didn't believe him because he continued to push the duke against the wall. And didn't protect himself against the first undercut punch. The two fell to brawling as though they were in a tavern instead of a Mayfair townhome.

"Robert!" Lady Bittlesworth's outraged voice split them apart faster than a douse of cold water. She walked up to her stepson. "That is outside of enough." She surveyed him in the dim light. "You may go home now. Tell Sabrina that I shall see her tomorrow."

"She may not receive you."

Now Lady Bittlesworth did arch a graceful brow. "Tell her I shall see her tomorrow." Although covered over with a great deal more grace and charm in Lady Bittlesworth, it was clear that a good portion of Sabre's steel in fact came from her mother.

"Yes, maman." He slid his gaze to Quince. "I must give the duke a ride home as he arrived without a carriage."

"Then wait outside."

"Yes, maman."

Once Robert proceeded down the steps Lady Bittlesworth said, "I must apologize for my son, your grace."

"Think nothing of it. That fight has been brewing for six years at least. My only regret is that you had to see it."

"Why did you come here today, your grace?"

"I hoped your husband could help me."

She smiled sadly. "Then I can assure you it was a wasted trip."

"You will tell him that I was here, though?"

"If you wish."

"Indeed I do."

She nodded and he bowed over her hand again before taking his leave.

When Quince boarded the carriage Robert was already seated in the far corner.

"This seems a bit cramped for a second round," the duke said, "but I'm game if you are.".

"That would be counterproductive."

Quince frowned. "What do you mean?"

"I'm only here because I promised Sabre I wouldn't let anyone hurt you."

The duke took a moment to digest that information. "How is she?" he asked softly.

Robert huffed out a breath and turned to watch the oil streetlamps they passed. "I don't know," he finally answered. "She's not herself."

"I see. However, I'm glad," Quince paused, finding it painful to say. "I'm glad she has a place with you where she will be safe. I fear that resolving this blackmail will be difficult." He wished that her place were by his side. He wished that he could keep her safe.

Robert turned his attention back to the duke and watched him for a long, silent moment. "I will keep her safe. Whether she cares for it or not."

Quince nodded. "Thank you. That is what is important."

"You mustn't approach my father again. It is counterproductive. And not at all safe."

"Counterproductive?"

"I have found some interesting information. Things I might have told you earlier today if I hadn't wanted to beat you senseless for upsetting my sister."

Quince was quiet. Robert had *found* some interesting information? Or was finally ready to release some interesting information?

Robert spoke again. "My only consolation is that you seem no better off than she."

Now Quince turned his attention to the window. He didn't want Sabrina to be hurting, but if she was then it meant she at least cared for him a bit. Didn't it?

They spent the rest of the carriage ride in silence. Quince didn't ask after Robert's supposedly interesting information. He didn't feel he could trust anything the Bittlesworth scion had to say.

Jack poked her husband. "Gideon, wake up."

He grunted and wrapped the pillow around his head.

"No, you've had long enough to sleep it off. Wake up. I think Quince is in trouble."

Gideon sat up suddenly and then gripped his head as though it might fall off. "Oh bloody hell. Quince."

"Yes, Quince. Are you awake?"

Rather than respond he reached over and pulled her into his lap, wrapping his arms around her in a ferocious hug.

"Gideon, you're crushing me."

"Quiet, woman, you're louder than church bells."

She surrendered, simply enjoying his warmth. He had loosened his grip a bit, but still held her quite tightly. She could feel his breath on her neck and it tickled. Oh, how she loved him. If she had tried to dream up her perfect husband she would have guessed completely wrong.

"Giddy?" she said softly while idly tracing patterns on his warm bare arm. "Robert frightened me yesterday."

He pulled back to look at her. "What do you mean he frightened you? When did you see him?"

"I received a note from him that Sabre was upset and could I please come see her."

Gideon stared at her intently as though willing the rest of the story out of her.

"She was quite upset and accused Robert of putting Quince in danger. Later when I asked him why she would say that, he said it was because she was smart." Jack gave an involuntary shiver. "The way he said it, Gideon, it sounded like a warning."

The earl narrowed his eyes. "It sounds like it is time for me to pay Robert Bittlesworth a visit."

"I've known Robert my whole life, Giddy, and he's never unsettled me before. What is going on? Did Quince tell you?"

Gideon put his forehead to hers and sighed. "Quince told me a good number of things last night. For one we will be hosting his sister for a time."

"Quince has a sister?"

"He apparently has a number of siblings I was unaware of. It is not common knowledge and we are not to share it. But she needs our protection."

Jack felt herself frown. "She shall, of course, have it."

Gideon smiled at her staunch support, then scowled before he said, "And for another, Quince is being blackmailed."

Jack gasped.

"That is also not common knowledge and not to be shared."

"But Sabre knows?"

Gideon shrugged. "One assumes?"

"I never should have let her go to him."

"You knew?"

"Of course I knew. Who else would she depend on to cover for her absence here in London?"

"Why didn't you try to stop her?"

"I didn't say I didn't try. But Sabre is notoriously headstrong."

Gideon chuckled. "As are you, my sweet."

"Oh, Sabre makes me look docile by comparison. We should all be happy she didn't set her sights on a prince or she would be running a country in short order."

"She set her cap for him?"

Jack sighed. "Yes. She's probably the only woman in England who would fall in love over someone getting past her guard."

"She fell in love with him at the duel?"

"Not love, perhaps, but she was intrigued. Obsessed. One of the first things she said after we got in the carriage was that she would marry him."

"Quince doesn't want to marry her."

"Good luck to him on that. But why?"

"Her father. I've never know the exact conflict between Quince and the viscount, but it has been enduring."

"Ah. Well, you know what they say. *Omnia vincit amor.* Love conquers all."

"It has yet to conquer this hangover."

"Oh, my poor husband." She laughed but rubbed his temples. "Why did you drink so much?"

"There were reasons, believe me. But it didn't seem to have the desired effect." He sighed and leaned into her hands. "That feels good. Please don't stop."

Twenty-Nine

Quince tried thrice more to intercept the viscount: once at Parliament and twice at White's. He finally heard that Bittlesworth had withdrawn to the country. It was hard to determine whether the seed he had planted had already taken root and caused Bittlesworth to withdraw from his regular routine, or if the viscount was simply continuing on with whatever plans he already had. Left without any further options for influencing his supposed blackmailers, Quince completed his parliamentary work and left for the country himself. Belle Fleur, of course, as it was convenient to London. His seat in Northampton was two full days away and he didn't feel that being so far from London would be wise.

Shortly after arriving at the estate he received a letter from Gideon that seemed primarily about their shared investments but cleverly mentioned a fruitless conversation with a mutual friend and the happy arrival of Jack's guest. Robert wasn't being helpful and Quince's sister was safe.

Meanwhile, he missed Sabre every day. He mooned about in the Rose Room for much of the first day he was home, and then requested that all of her items be moved to the duchess's suite. Except for the shawl she had been wearing when she arrived, which he kept in his own room. It still smelled lightly of her scent. When he awoke each morning he looked for her before remembering she was gone. At night he would lie on the balcony staring at the stars and wish she was with him. If this was love, it was damned inconvenient.

He was beginning not to care much at all about the blackmailer. His sister was safe with Gideon. As for his mother, it was most likely the secret of her additional children the blackmailer was hoping to use, and that was something that would become public in accordance to his own plans. Whatever role Robert had in the affair was unfortunate, but he found he simply couldn't care about it anymore. His lassitude was such that he had to force himself to prepare for the trip back to London for the Harrington ball. The ball where he had invited the blackmailer to make further contact. As the news of his brother's existence was already being fed to the papers this week, the threat of the letters didn't seem as great. Without a great deal of enthusiasm, he was packed and prepared for the trip to London two days before the ball was to occur.

"Miss Bittlesworth, may I present Miss Frederick. Miss Frederick, my good friend Miss Bittlesworth."

Sabre looked at the young girl curtsying to her and felt longing pierce through her. The child looked so much like Quince it was hard not to leave off from curtsying and simply hug her. She must be frightened. Confused. But she had enough of her brother's backbone to look reserved instead.

"It is good to meet you, Miss Bittlesworth."

Really, any moment now she would hug the girl and be done with it. Oh, sweet Lord, was she not going to be able to say anything without being choked up? This would never do. She took a deep breath before saying, "And you, Miss Frederick."

Jack was looking back and forth between them and said, "Miss Frederick, Sabre, rather, Miss Bittlesworth and I will be doing some shopping this morning so Emmy will be your companion for today. You will, of course, both stay inside?" Jack looked at the girls until they both nodded agreement. "Perhaps you two would like for us to bring you some ribbons?"

Emmy's eyes lit up. "Oh, yes, my lady. Green, if you please."

"What color do you prefer?" Jack asked the girl.

The young 'Miss Frederick' seemed to consider it as a very serious question.

"Celestial blue," Sabre announced. She stepped forward to tip the girl's chin. "To bring out those lovely eyes."

That succeeded in making the girl smile. "If you're sure."

Jack laughed. "Sabre is always sure."

Sabre felt her lip quiver. No, she was not always sure. Right now she was hardly sure of anything. She had thought that washing her hands of Quince's plans would lead to an eventual lessening of her concern for him. Nothing could be further than the truth. She missed him constantly, as though a splinter had buried deep into her heart and was festering. Leaving him was supposed to lessen her concerns, not increase them! Would she never be free of him? Would she never stop missing him? Worrying about him? It had been the better part of a fortnight and she still felt hollow, bereft. Perhaps she could convince Jack to visit Floris, the perfumery. Surely they would have some lemongrass scent on hand that she could purchase. But would that only prolong the agony? No, she wasn't sure of anything anymore.

The morning was clear and warm, as good a day for travel as one could hope. Quince's staff had fussed over him a bit. He had not only had a good breakfast before he left, but a basket of treats tucked under the carriage seat. His driver and footman were up top, while three outriders were arrayed around the carriage. Hopefully in two hours he would be at his London townhouse. Within twenty minutes he had started to doze when he heard rapid hoof beats riding off to the west. A moment after that the carriage rattled onto the short bridge that spanned a creek. He was drowsy and slightly irritated by being awakened.

A loud explosion rocked the carriage violently. He heard splintering wood and a horse screaming. His conveyance surged forward, and then tipped over as more explosions erupted. He tried to brace himself but was flung forcibly against the opposite seat as the carriage crashed on its side and he was unable to keep himself from falling backwards through the air. He heard glass breaking, men shouting, and suddenly all was darkness.

"Your grace? Your grace?" He felt someone shaking his arm and wondered who had decided to invade his bedroom this time. Then he noticed the noise. Men shouting, horses stomping. A shot rang out close by and he sat up abruptly. His footman, Averton he thought, backed away quickly. Light streamed in above him where the door to the carriage was open. There was a stabbing pain in his head and he felt so horrible he thought he might cast up his accounts.

"Who is shooting at us?" the duke demanded.

Averton glanced toward the front of the carriage. "They had to put down the second carriage horse. Can you stand, your grace?"

Although moving quickly seemed unwise, Quince put a hand out and pushed himself to his feet. He stood, dizzy and trembling.

Averton looked him over. "How do you feel, your grace?"

"Furious."

He jumped up to grab the sides of the door and pulled himself out. Sitting on the carriage he surveyed the scene. It was grim. Both carriage horses appeared dead, the first most likely not surviving the explosion. The driver was on the ground, bloody, with one of the men seeing to him. Quince looked back over his shoulder at the bridge. A good portion of it had been shredded apart by the explosion and spikes of jagged wood were everywhere. It looked as though the first explosion had been under the front left wheel and left horse. It was quite likely that the second horse bolting in terror had saved his life.

"Can I help you, your grace?" Averton called up from below.

"No," Quince said, then added in a murmur, "it seems no one can."

He jumped to the ground, which jarred his aching head. But he drew himself up and approached the man crouched over the driver. "How is he?"

"He'll be fine, your grace," the outrider said, but his eyes gave a different story and encouraged no more questions. "Stanford went to fetch the doctor. Hopefully they'll be back soon."

"Averton," Quince called.

"Yes, your grace?" the young man said, having extracted himself from the carriage.

"In my trunk, there should be some laudanum. Bring it for the driver."

"Yes, your grace."

Quince looked down at the outrider. "I'm sorry, but I've forgotten your name."

"Cosgrove, your grace."

"Cosgrove, as you seem to know what you're about I will leave you here to care for him as you are able. Averton will be here to assist you. Where is the other outrider?"

"Platts is trying to track down the rider we heard running off before the explosion."

"When he returns tell him to follow me to London."

Cosgrove stood. "Your grace, you shouldn't go alone."

Quince gave him a quelling stare and would grant that the man didn't back down easily. His familiarity with treating wounds made Quince assume he was a soldier, now it seemed likely he had been an officer.

"You're bleeding, your grace. At least let me see to that first."

A delay tactic, but a good one. "It doesn't signify," Quince said and turned to gather the reins of Cosgrove's mount. At least the time to London would be shorter as a single rider. He jumped into the saddle, gritted his teeth against the pain still throbbing in his head, and set the horse to a canter.

Thirty

Quince made good time and sailed through the front doors of the Home Office in under an hour. He presented his card and asked to be escorted to Robert Bittlesworth. The staff, a bit overwhelmed by both his title and rough appearance, scrambled to do his bidding. Within moments they had taken him upstairs and bowed him into a well-appointed room where Robert was speaking with another man. They both rose to greet the duke as he was announced.

Sparing not a glance at the other man, Quince focused on Robert. "I need to talk to you. Alone."

"The ambassador-"

"I don't care if he's the bloody King of Prussia." Finally looking at the second man, who seemed a bit shocked, Quince said to him, "Get out."

The ambassador and staff exited hastily. Robert frowned and came around the desk toward him. "Telford, I'm not sure what you're about-"

Quince shoved the younger man against the wall and held him there, forearm braced across Robert's throat. "The correct address is 'your grace.' I wouldn't think that would be hard to remember. You know more of my case than you have divulged.

You will tell me all or I will see to it that you are hanged." He didn't see fear in Robert's eyes, but he did see calculation.

"Yes, your grace."

There was a knock at the door of an unusual cadence and Robert said, "That is one of my agents. The knock signals that it will pertain to you. Shall I let him in?"

Quince released him and backed away. "Yes. I'll be curious to hear what he has to say."

Robert straightened his jacket and called, "Enter."

A small, nondescript man slipped in the door. He seemed shocked to see Quince and bowed low. "Your grace."

"Report," Robert said sharply.

The man's glance flicked back and forth between them. "There was an attempt on the duke's life this morning, sir. I didn't know he'd survived until now."

"What sort of an attempt?"

"At the bridge crossing on the Mimmshall, m'lord. I was following at a distance when there was an explosion at the bridge. Saw a rider galloping away. The duke's man chased him and I followed at a distance, sir, but was unable to catch up to them. Came here to report, sir."

Robert looked appraisingly at Quince then turned back to his agent. "Anything else?"

"No, sir."

"You are dismissed."

The man nodded and slipped through the door as quietly as he had come, leaving Quince and Robert to stare at each other. Robert finally turned to his sideboard and prepared drinks.

"Hell of a morning for you then, your grace." He handed the duke a tumbler of scotch. "How can I assist you?"

Quince swallowed a hearty amount of the liquor and took a seat. "You know how you can assist me. So out with it."

Robert sat across from the duke and rolled his own tumbler between his hands, having not yet taken a drink. Staring down into his scotch he said, "Sometimes I wonder, in God's accounting for your soul, what matters most. Intention, action, or result?"

"What do you mean?" Quince asked.

"Any of those things can be good or evil. A good intention can lead to an evil action. How many have murdered in the name of the church? An evil action may lead to a good result. What if a murder saved hundreds of other lives? So which matters most? That you meant to cause harm? Or that you caused harm? That you meant to ease suffering? Or that you eased suffering?"

"Admittedly this isn't something that I've thought about a great deal."

"Of course you haven't," Robert said with a ghost of a smile. "Angels have no need for redemption."

"Explain to me how this is salient."

"Although this affects you, it was never about you. And I certainly never intended for someone to make an attempt on your life. Especially now." He frowned down into the glass. "Especially now that Sabre's feelings are engaged."

"If it isn't about me, then who is it about, Robert?" Quince was feeling the warm pressure in his gut that told him an important truth was in the offing. "What is going on?"

Robert finally looked up at him and his expression was one that Quince couldn't place. "It's about my father."

Quince sat forward. He was beginning to wonder if he would have to physically pull the story out. "In what way?"

Robert looked down into his drink again. "He's not a good man, my father." That made him smirk. "Of course, there are people who would say that about me."

"If you want the viscountancy there should be easier ways to go about getting it than this."

The younger man's expression became hardened, vicious. "If I wanted him dead he would be dead, have no doubt about that. I want him to suffer. I want all of his friends to turn away from him. I want the remainder of his life to be as mean and desperate as he deserves." Robert finally took a drink, schooling his expression back to the calm neutrality he usually displayed. "I want him exiled. And that is where you, my dear duke, come in."

Quince leaned back in the chair. "In what way?"

"You were uniquely qualified to carry this out." Robert frowned, seeming to draw into himself as though contemplating. "You have the power and authority of your title, and I knew that whatever you lacked in political clout, Gideon would be willing to lend you. It is rumored that you are one of the Prince Regeant's favorites although you eschew his company as much as you do anyone else's. It is also fairly well known that you abhor my father. Although I'm not sure why, I assume it is for many of the same reasons I do. Among them, because of The Four."

Now Quince felt a tingling along his extremities. There was both truth and danger here. "Who are the others?"

Robert shook his head. "I have only divined our fathers from the group. They were wearing masks when I saw them."

"You saw them?" It came out in a near whisper as Quince felt a dread come over himself. To hear the stories was torture enough. But to be there?

"Only the once. My father had hoped to induct me, as Draco had been inducted by his father."

"Your father isn't Draco?"

Robert shook his head. "My father is Cygnus. But he is the only one I knew by name. I suspect your father was either Ursa or Leo?"

"Leo."

Robert nodded, considering.

"So you went to one of their..." Quince repressed his need to shudder, "parties."

The younger man looked at him keenly. "You did not?"

"No. Undoubtedly my father realized that it would not be the best fit for me to participate. When did you go?"

Robert's brow furrowed. "Ten years ago now."

"And you saw such acts of degradation that you planned for ten years to rid yourself of him?"

"Not exactly, I had decided that long before." He finished his scotch. "But seeing what The Four were doing made it clear exactly what kind of man my father was. And gave me ideas on how to punish him."

Quince contemplated Robert's choice of words. Punish. "And it took this long to start your plot?"

Robert smiled. "It took this long to put together the pieces of my plot. To find the key that would unlock this solution."

"The key?"

"You. I finally uncovered a second member of The Four, your father, and that led me to you. Who better to mete out judgment than an angel?"

"And rather than ask for my help you conspired a plot against me."

"I'm usually quite good at this. It's possible that in my fervor to see this done I made mistakes. But the motivations of all the players was evident. The outcome inevitable."

"Unless they had managed to kill me this morning."

"Unless that," Robert conceded. "I was concerned how Father would react to the more direct threat of you visiting his home. Whispers, innuendos, anonymous letters. Those are easily handled at a distance. Not that I know this morning's incident was my father's doing. But it could have been."

"But we know the letters are not from your father. You wanted to see them because you think you can identify the handwriting."

This caused Robert to pause for a moment. "Yes, I know the handwriting of every lord in the realm. If one of the other Four wrote it himself I would be able to identify him."

"And so you started all this? With whispers and innuendos?"

"What could a group such as they fear more than evidence of their deeds? They were ripe for influence. I knew that fearing exposure by you would make them react. I knew that pressure from them would make you retaliate. Again, the outcome seems inevitable. My next gambit was to tip the identity of my father as one of The Four. But you already knew."

It was Quince's turn to frown and consider. "If you had told me what you wanted to do then we could have found a solution together."

Robert sneered. "Yes, I'm sure that you would have stepped up to do so."

"Most likely. Especially if you had convinced Gideon first."

"I judged that too much a risk. Sometimes you will refuse to do things just to annoy Gideon."

"Not if it's important. Whatever Charlie would do for you, I would do for Gideon. Why do you think I fished him out of the gutter so many times?"

Robert shrugged. "I couldn't be sure of that path. And certainty is something I value."

"Well," Quince continued, "as you did not involve me or speak to Gideon, we will negotiate. You want your father exiled? I want some things in return."

"Such as?"

"Your sister."

"That's acceptable."

Quince tossed back the remainder of his scotch. "I don't plan to marry her."

The younger man narrowed his eyes but only said, "I'm sure she'll learn to adjust. What else?"

"I lost two carriage horses this morning. Perhaps two of Charlie's finest?"

"Done. What else?"

"What else would you give me?"

"Anything within reason."

Quince gained his feet and leaned over Robert's chair. "Keep your horses and know this. Giving away your sister to be kept as some man's mistress is not within reason. Even should I not survive today I can guarantee you that any attempt to give her to a man in such a way will be met with fitting punishment. It is best for you to remember that when God wants to punish the wicked he doesn't hire an assassin." He slammed his empty tumbler down on the table next to Robert, making the younger man jump. "He sends an angel."

Thirty-One

"Are you sure it's all right? It's not too revealing?"

Jack watched her friend turn in the mirror, trying to catch the dress from all angles. Sabre had lost weight and looked wan. If Jack didn't know better, she would assume recovery from a long illness. Thank goodness they had come in for a final fitting because the dress needed to be taken in again.

"It's lovely and perfect for you. No one can wear coquelicot quite like you can." The poppy red color did indeed help to put some brightness in Sabre's cheeks. Jack wished that Sabre would talk about Quince but she had been obstinately silent to date. Considering the anxiety with which she studied her gown, Jack knew that her friend both hoped and dreaded that the duke would make an appearance at the ball.

Jack couldn't stand the tension. "We can't even be sure that he'll be there."

Sabre became completely still, pausing in smoothing down her bodice. "He'll be there," she said softly.

Jack wasn't sure whether she would rather shake Sabre for not being herself, or throttle Quince for whatever it was he had done. Instead she took a deep, calming breath and turned to the modiste. "Do you think it needs to be pinched in at the waist a bit more?"

"*Oui, madame.*"The modiste stepped in to pin the adjustment.

"Do we have time?" Sabre asked. "The ball is the night after tomorrow."

Jack looked at the modiste beseechingly. Certainly adjustments for her new gown were a much better thing for Sabre to focus on than when and if she would see Quince.

"*Oui, madamoiselle*, there is still time. We can deliver it to you in two days? *Oui?*"

"*Oui,*" Sabre agreed.

The modiste continued her pinning and Jack sighed. Now what else could she distract Sabre with before the ball? It also helped to divert herself from the fact that she was hosting her first London ball and wanted terribly much to make a good impression. Perhaps she could convince Sabre to eat by tempting her with her favorite treats.

Quince entered Gideon's office at the Parliament and received yet another reminder of how his life had already intertwined with Sabrina's when the earl's clerk looked up and then stood to receive him. The clerk who just happened to be Sabre's younger, bastard brother.

"Your grace," Justin said, bowing low.

"Mr. Miller," Quince said. The boy already stood taller than himself and looked well on his way to outgrowing even Gideon. "Is Giddy about?"

The boy took out his pocket watch. "He's currently on the floor, your grace, but should return shortly. Can I get you some refreshment?"

Quince considered that he had already had a tot of scotch this morning. "Tea, if you please."

"As you wish. Would you like to wait in the my lord's office?"

"Don't mind if I do."

Once inside the office Quince found that he couldn't settle into a chair. He paced, fussed with the gewgaws Giddy had set around the place, and generally felt like a nuisance. He wanted to be practicing his sword, or at least out riding, or...He stopped short. Was this the source of Gideon's ceaseless energy? Was he furious a good portion of the time? What a curious thought.

The efficient Mr. Miller delivered not only tea and a light repast, but provided a mirror, towel, and basin. Quince finally took stock of his injuries. A small gash on his jaw that had bled onto his cravat. A scrape above his right eye. Based on his aches there were undoubtedly bruises yet discovered. But all in all he was in surprisingly good shape for a man who had just survived a personal Gunpowder Plot.

"Hullo Quince, Justin said you weren't feeling quite..." Gideon trailed off. "What happened to you?"

"When you get to the bottom of it, it turns out the answer is Robert Bittlesworth."

"What do you mean?"

Quince sighed. He had never told Gideon of The Four. Of what his father, the elder duke, was truly like. What he knew of Viscount Bittlesworth. Although it would give a greater context for what had occurred, he still couldn't find the words to admit what he had come from. What he had grown up seeing, hearing. "Robert wants his father exiled. He thought the easiest path to that was causing a friction that made me want to use my power, and if necessary, yours, against the viscount. His miscalculation was that I approached the viscount directly to address it. And that the viscount reacted with violence."

The earl's expression turned progressively grimmer as the duke spoke.

"I'm sorry, Quince. I always thought of Robert as a friend and never would have expected this of him."

"It's all right, Gideon. I can respect it, in a way."

"Don't be ridiculous!"

Quince felt torn between rage and despair. He looked down, unable to meet the earl's eyes. "Our fathers were friends, Gideon. Robert's and mine. They ran with a group that made anything you've done look tame in comparison. Depravity you've never conceived of." Quince finally looked up again, seeing that the earl was solemn but not judgmental. "Robert wants them, especially his father, to be punished. They are terrible men who did terrible things." Quince scowled down into his empty teacup. "My fear, when you ran with the Bittlesworth boys, was that your path would lead you to something like that, and that they were a bad influence that would take you there. However, I suppose if Robert were that way then he would have been inducted in their group and not had time to go drinking with you."

"Are you sure he's telling you the truth that he didn't join them? We have no reason to believe much of what he says at this point."

Quince shrugged. "It's difficult to say for certain, of course, but I do believe him."

Gideon nodded. "Very well. What do we do now?"

How very like Gideon to want to focus on what could be done. In an odd way it made Quince miss Sabre all the more keenly because she would want to examine all the options and discuss the potential effect of any actions.

"I think there's nothing we can do but wait for the ball. Whomever the original blackmailer was, they will be expecting to contact me there."

"May I say, I'm delighted you invited them to my home," the earl said in a dry tone.

"They are lords. You most likely invited them yourself."

"Speaking of invitees, I'm sure Robert is on the list. Would you like for me to ask him not to come?"

Quince sighed. "Angry as I am at him, he will most likely be useful. You know what they say. The enemy of my enemy is my friend."

"Friend isn't something I can imagine calling Robert ever again."

Quince spent the majority of his time waiting for the ball in practice with his London sword master. The exercise kept him from doing something unwise, like going to Robert's house to start in on fisticuffs again. Or trying to see Sabre. It also gave him time to think. It sounded like Robert had made up the idea of papers as a whole-cloth lie to fit the fears of The Four. But it was an effective lie precisely because it was so believable.

When he took over the duchy he, Gideon, and an army of stewards had gone through piles of papers in setting the estate to rights and nothing in those papers had even hinted at what Robert was suggesting, at least nothing that had come to his attention. But as he thought about it more deeply, he realized his father was a man who had concealed the location of a cellar where he held debauched parties for decades. Had delighted in doing so. As far as Quince knew the secret of that cellar's location had died with him. If his father had kept papers regarding the activities of The Four, they were most likely hidden. Although it was possible they were secreted somewhere at the ducal seat, it still seemed far more likely that they were at Belle Fleur. It was where his father had spent a large portion of his time. Alone. Well, alone save for the staff.

Quince had never been particularly close with any of his staff, but Sabre had developed something of a relationship with the ones at Belle Fleur. Could he capitalize on that to find out if any of them knew anything? Suspected anything? It would be easier if Sabre could just come back with him to speak to the staff, but no. He couldn't put her in harm's way. Thanks to Robert's machinations, The Four were squarely focused on him and, obviously, at least one of them was willing to use deadly force.

Thirty-Two

S abre had never felt so awkward at a social event in her life. She forced herself not to pick at wrinkles in her dress or pat at her hair. It wasn't like her. Usually she would wander and flirt, never self-conscious, always at ease. Tonight she felt like, well, she felt like she imagined her friend Jack usually did. Yet there was Jack, veritably glowing while standing next to her husband receiving guests. They made a handsome couple, both towering above the average attendee. It was like arriving at a ball to be received by two gods. Sabre had arrived with Robert but her brother had disappeared. She had yet to see Charlie. Or…him.

It would be best not to think about the duke. He would undoubtedly be in attendance, if for no other reason it was Jack's first London ball and he would lend his title to the guest list. For Gideon's success. She would never understand his relationship to Gideon, which seemed both loyal and rife with animosity. Her best friends were just that. Best friends. They didn't keep secrets or harbor resentments. She couldn't dream of discovering siblings and not immediately telling Jack and George about it. Then again it seemed there were many things the duke would do that she would never dream of doing. It was undoubtedly best to continue her plan of removing him from her thoughts.

"Are there any dances left for me?"

His voice made her heart race in her chest. She looked over her shoulder to see that he had come in from the receiving line while her mind had wandered. He looked perfect. The very image of an English aristocrat. From his artfully tousled hair, to his fitted black jacket with snowy white cravat, and down to his dancing shoes. But seeing him she only wanted the unshaven, drowsy man in an open shirt who would want to lie in bed with her all day. If she wasn't careful she would make herself cry or, worse yet, beg.

With a half-smile she lifted her wrist so that he could inspect her dance card. Save for the first dance claimed by her brother, it was empty.

"It is obviously my lucky day." He set to scribbling his name on two dances.

Standing so close she could smell his cologne. It was difficult not to lean in with her eyes closed to enjoy the scent. Then she noticed his jaw.

"What happened?" she asked, lifting her hand to hover over the healing wound.

"Robert didn't tell you?"

"No, did he...?"

The duke smiled vaguely. "Indirectly, perhaps." He bowed over her hand. "Until our dances, Miss Bittlesworth."

As he walked away she checked her dance card. Both waltzes. It would be torture. A most delightful and terrible torture. It was somewhat inappropriate to dance both waltzes with the same man, but she didn't care. Perhaps she would pretend that all was well, just for this evening. That he had asked her to be his duchess. That she didn't worry constantly that his enemies were closing in on him. Those enemies would be here tonight, she was sure of it. She realized that if nothing else she could observe the attendees in the hopes of finding some clues. Watching people always provided an entertaining diversion anyway.

Quince knew Gideon's townhouse as well as he knew his own. The staff didn't interrupt him as he ducked through a side door and up a set of back steps to the hallway with the bedrooms. Once there he set his hands on the wall to brace himself and just breathed. After a few moments the band of pain that had trapped his chest eased a bit and the rapid beat of his heart slowed. Sabre had looked fragile, like a pale and saddened shadow of herself. And she had been so quiet. If another man had done this to her he would have killed the bastard without remorse. But it hadn't been another man. Somehow he had done this. And he knew that he would do anything to set it to rights. There was no room for pride. He would do anything for her, give anything to her. By God, give *up* anything for her. He felt tears gathering at the corners of his eyes. No, no. There was too much at stake tonight to spend it weeping in a darkened hallway. He straightened his impeccably tidy jacket and returned to the party.

Sabre had a completely full dance card by the time the music began. In her first dance with Robert she attempted to ask about the duke's wound but her brother had been even more mulish than usual. Her dance with Charlie had been full of laughter and teasing, which she enjoyed even though she regretted how it interrupted her focus on cataloging the attendees of the ball. And cataloging she was, now that she had put her mind to it. Names, faces, clothes, mannerisms. It was a challenge but, as she already knew many of the attendees, it wasn't unachievable. She also tried to track who spoke to whom, who danced with whom.

Then it was time for the waltz to start and she knew that she wouldn't be paying any attention to the other guests. If the duke ever appeared to dance with her. She hadn't seen him since he signed her dance card. But there he was now, making his way across the room to her as the first notes were being played. Arriving at her side he bowed and she curtsied.

"Shall we?" he asked.

She nodded and he swept her up into the steps of the dance. They hadn't danced before and it only served to remind her of fencing with him. Or, if she were to let her mind wander into dangerous territory, being intimate with him. She trained her gaze on his left shoulder and tried to focus on having pure thoughts. It was difficult to do while feeling the warmth of him, smelling his cologne. All she wanted was to step forward and burrow into his embrace. But he was getting ever closer to danger, she was sure of it. He didn't even want to marry her. Why torture herself with what could never be?

They didn't speak. She didn't even look into his eyes. When the music ended he bowed over her hand and then he was gone. She felt her throat close tight in despair, tears pricking the edges of her eyes. Her heart shuddered in an irregular beat, yearning for what could never be. Damn him. Damn her treacherous heart.

After a few moments, collected, she went back to observing all the attendees.

Quince was usually quite good at waiting. Too good at it, perhaps. He had oceans of patience that could sometimes lapse into downright laziness. But not tonight. Tonight two important things were to happen. The blackmailer would contact him. And he would get to dance with Sabre again. He finished his third glass of wine and continued to argue with himself about whether to approach Jack and demand to know why Sabre was so withdrawn. But he would probably hear something about himself that he didn't want to hear. Although he would like to point out that she left him. There was no good reason for her to be moping about it.

"You broke her heart, you know."

The duke almost jumped. He hadn't heard Robert approach, but now the younger man stood beside him to look out on the dancers in the ballroom.

"She kept throwing it in front of me. I was bound to trip over it eventually."

"I don't think I care for your cavalier tone in regards to my sister."

"Two days ago you were willing to trade her for cooperation and now you don't like my tone? Pardon me if I consider your fraternal rights a bit curtailed as you don't have her best interests at heart."

"You can ask either of my siblings, I don't have a heart. I do, however, have eyes and it is perfectly clear that what she wants is you. Why shouldn't I try to gain your cooperation while also giving my sister what she so desperately wants to have?"

Quince's voice was rough as he said, "If she wanted me she could have me. She's the one who walked away."

Robert was quiet for a long moment and when he spoke again it was to change the subject. "Any contact from our friends yet?"

"No. I've expected at any moment to receive a note, since I doubt they would be so bold as to approach me on the ballroom floor. Unless," Quince added with suspicion, "you are my contact?"

"Although I instigated their actions, I can assure you that I am not involved with them."

"Perhaps I should warn you that Gideon is displeased with you."

Robert smiled. "That became clear earlier when he shook my hand and nearly crushed it."

"You should be delighted that he still considers you a good enough friend to shake your hand," Quince mused.

"Perhaps I should, your grace."

"Now if you'll excuse me, I believe the second waltz is about to start." Quince handed Robert his empty glass and set out across the floor to find Sabre.

He found her in conversation with her other brother, Charlie. She was laughing and swatting Charlie on the arm with her fan. The young man teasingly stumbled back as though she had dealt him a mighty blow. Then he caught sight of the duke and his demeanor changed. His eyes glinted with challenge and he straightened to his full height.

Quince slowed his step. Whereas Robert seemed frustrated and at a loss over his sister's behavior, Charlie was furious and protective. Sabre looked over her shoulder to see what had caught Charlie's attention, and then went up on her tiptoes to whisper in her brother's ear. Whatever she said made him look down on her with an affectionate smile.

Quince bowed to them. "Miss Bittlesworth, Mr. Bittlesworth."

With the slightest of bows Charlie said, "Your grace. What brings you to this side of the ballroom?" He had put a possessive arm over Sabre's shoulders.

"A dance with your lovely sister, Mr. Bittlesworth."

Charlie looked down at her in mock confusion. "Did you not promise the second waltz to me?"

"I didn't and you know I didn't."

He rubbed his chin with his free hand. "No, I am fairly certain you promised it to me. Unless, of course, you would prefer to dance it with his grace?"

"He is far less likely to step on my toes on purpose."

Charlie chuckled. "Come now, I only did that once."

"And the bruise lasted for a week."

"How was I to know you were such a delicate little flower?"

Sabre elbowed him in the stomach. "You already knew you were a big clumsy oaf. Now let go of me."

"So you chose him over me? As you wish, my martial little sister. But do tell me if he steps on your toes and I will have words with him. If you leave anything of him after your own retribution."

It was a relief to see Sabre with some of her spark back. And Charlie Bittlesworth was making it very clear he would do anything for his little sister. It was good to know that at least one of her brothers would.

Quince bowed over Sabre's hand and, with a nod to Charlie, led her out to the dance floor.

"Your grace, I'm sorry my brother is..."

"Protective?"

She laughed. "I was thinking rude."

"Manners take the hindmost when one is protecting one's family."

She sobered. "Have you seen your sister yet?"

"I thought it best not to emphasize the connection as it could be a danger to her. Hopefully Jacqueline is keeping her cloistered. Have you seen her?" He could hear his own voice roughen at the end.

Sabre smiled. "Indeed I have. She's a lovely girl, but a bit shy."

"Do you consider that a cardinal sin?"

"Cardinal, no, but a pity."

"I was shy as a child so she may yet grow out of it."

"That's no measure, you're still shy now."

Quince was surprised. "I am not."

Sabre arched her eyebrow at him. "No? Excellent. Then I have a great number of people I would like to introduce you to this evening."

He frowned and looked out across the ballroom floor at the other dancers. "Don't mistake misanthropy for shyness."

"Hmph!" she said, as though that were her final word on the subject.

He looked down at her and she still had an arch look on her face. He found himself speaking before he could stop it. "I miss you."

She blushed bright as her dress and lowered her gaze to his cravat. He hoped she wouldn't withdraw as she had during their first dance. Suddenly he realized he couldn't stand it if she were to withdraw again. He maneuvered them through the dancers and to the hallway. Grabbing her hand he led her deeper into the house.

"Where are we going?" she asked with a laugh.

Perhaps Gideon was right. Perhaps what she wanted was a little adventure. "I've heard a great deal about the seductive properties of libraries."

"Quince!"

Oh thank God, she had used his name again. They were already in the unlit portion of the house, kept dark to discourage the guests from wandering. Backing to the wall he pulled her against him, lowering his head to capture her lips. The sweetness of kissing her almost brought him to his knees. His beautiful, bold Sabrina. She wrapped her hands in the lapels of his jacket and he heard her whimper.

Breaking the kiss he said, "We're almost there."

He took her hand and led her to the library. The heavy oak door was already open, the room dark. Pulling her inside he shut the door and backed her against it. He wanted her desperately. Perhaps this memory could replace their first, somewhat disastrous, encounter. As he kissed her he thought perhaps the leather couch would be better. He kissed her throat, her lovely shoulder.

"Quince?"

He could tell from her tone that something was wrong. As much as he was loath to, he took a half step back. "Yes, love?"

"We...I need to stop. I..." there was a catch in her voice and she finished in a whisper. "I'm trying to recover from you."

It was as though icy water had been poured down his back. He released her and took another step backwards. "Beg pardon?" he asked dumbly.

"I'm sorry," she whispered, then opened the door just far enough to slip through and away. The opening at the door let in a sliver of dim light from the hallway. Even that, he thought, was brighter than what was in his heart.

Thirty-Three

Quince couldn't believe that Sabre had left him again. "Sorry, old boy, but maidens are notoriously fickle."

The voice came from behind him. It was a mild voice, plain, but there was an undercurrent of bitterness that carried across the room like a fetid wind. Quince had never heard this voice before, but somehow he knew, without doubt, that it was the blackmailer.

Regardless of how little he felt up to it, the duke knew this exchange would be vital. He could show no fear, no weakness. "Fortunately there are a good deal of them out there on the dance floor. Like fishing from a stocked pond, really."

"Yes, but remarkably few of them are Bittlesworth's head-strong daughter. I imagine bedding her would give you a great deal of pleasure. You've made no secret of how much you detest him."

Quince suppressed his need to defend Sabrina and focused on divining where the accursed man was in the room. "All pleasures are short lived, my lord. What I seek is satisfaction."

The blackmailer chuckled. "A quicker wit than your father, I see."

Quince was fairly sure that the man was standing across the room near the windows. Had he entered from outside? Or from the hallway? The door had been open when they came in. "My father was not slow witted, he simply didn't have as much levity as a typical hedgehog."

"Is that how you see yourself? As a hedgehog? Are you rooting about in my garden, Leo?"

The duke felt his blood run cold. "I have no right to that name. You may address me as Beloin, or your grace. Or hedgehog, if you like. I'm sure there are some pests in your garden for me to devour."

The blackmailer was quiet far too long for Quince's comfort. When he spoke again he had moved across the room. "You don't have any papers, do you?"

"No. But I do have a determination to see Bittlesworth suffer, you're correct about that. And I will keep digging, turning over rocks to find the crawling nastiness beneath, until I am able to punish him."

"Punish him?"

"With exile at the very least."

"Odd that he has been the one to raise your ire. But no matter. Is that your only demand? Bittlesworth?"

"Yes." Quince was intrigued that the blackmailer seemed to indicate that one of the other members had been more detrimental to him than Bittlesworth. But at this point the duke only wanted to play out Robert's goal and bring an end to this debacle.

"And you have no papers or evidence?"

"No."

The blackmailer gave a contemplative sigh. "With his attempt on your life I feel that he has shown a shocking lack of judgment. I will give you the evidence you need, provided that you guarantee me that you will stop…digging in my garden."

"You have my word."

"I'd best. Surely I don't have to explain to you that I would not bumble like him. That lovely child upstairs would suffer, for instance. Meanwhile, I shall have a packet delivered to your man of business before the week is out. Do with Bittlesworth as you wish."

Then there was silence.

Quince called out, "My lord?" He pushed the library door open to allow what dim light was available to pool in the room. He heard nothing. Saw nothing. Had the damn man vanished?

After leaving the library Sabre stumbled up the steps to Jack's sitting room. She just wanted to get away. How could it hurt this much? It felt like she had a knife in her heart. But surely if she stayed, if she allowed herself to love him, it would be worse. He was playing a dangerous game with ruthless men. He could be hurt or killed and didn't seem to care. Staying with him would drive her mad. And, if she were being honest with herself, she feared the power he had over her. She would refuse him nothing. It humbled her to know that he could ask anything of her and she would not have it in her heart to refuse him. She curled up on the settee, weeping.

"Miss Bittlesworth?" a small voice called.

Sabre sat up, dashing at her eyes with her knuckles. "Is that you, Emmy?"

"Yes, and Cici."

She gave a watery laugh. "Oh, it's Cici now, is it?"

Emmy and Cici sat on either side of her. Emmy took her hand. "Why are you crying?"

Cici, really Jessica Telford, leaned forward to tell her new friend, "You can't ask someone why they're crying, that's rude."

Emmy gasped. "I'm sorry, Sabre, I didn't mean to be rude."

Now Sabre laughed in truth, and pulled each girl to her to kiss on top of the head. "You can, in fact, ask friends why they are crying. Especially good friends."

"Are we good friends?" Emmy asked softly. Raised most of her life on a farm, she was still a bit hesitant in her role as companion to a countess.

Sabre joined hands with both of the girls, lacing her fingers with theirs. "We are the best of friends."

"Then why are you crying?"

"I'm very sad."

"Why?"

"Because my heart has betrayed me. It insists on loving a man that it shouldn't."

Cici finally spoke again. "That doesn't make sense."

"Nothing about the heart has ever made sense to me, I'm afraid."

"No, I'm saying that you should trust your heart."

Sabre sniffed and smoothed the girl's hair back. It was even lighter and silkier than Quince's. "What makes you say that?"

"My heart has never led me astray, but many times I have thought myself into trouble."

Sabre resisted the impulse to tell the girl that at her age she had hardly seen enough to make such a determination. She didn't want to ruin the coze that was making her feel better. Perhaps it wasn't her Haberdashers, but sitting here with the young ladies had a familiarity that comforted her. Instead she asked, "What sort of trouble have you thought yourself into, love?"

"When I was a little girl I became convinced that our father hated us, and that was why he never came to see us."

"What did your heart tell you?"

"It remained stubbornly silent on the subject. That's why my mind made up stories. Then one day an older brother I had never met came and my heart knew him. He was as familiar to me as my other siblings. When my brother told me that I was lucky to have never known my father, lucky that mother had hidden us away, I believed him."

Jessica spoke with a calm, clear confidence that Sabre had rarely heard. After a moment she realized where she had heard the tone before. Herself. But whereas Jessica derived her greatest confidence from her heart, Sabre had only ever trusted her mind. Trusting her heart would be a tremendous leap of faith that she wasn't sure she was capable of. However, one of Jessica's statements kept ringing in her head. *My heart knew him. My heart knew him.* Sabre's heart knew him. Right now, considering for the briefest moment that she go running back into his arms, she felt her heart burbling with happiness. Which was the greater risk? The possibility of losing him to danger? Or the surety of losing him by turning away as she had for the past fortnight? Even as she tried to free herself of him, she continued to worry about him. Just this evening she had taken on the task of observing all the guests in the hopes of identifying the blackmailer among them. In the hopes of helping Quince. She ran back through the assortment of facts she had put together this evening about the attendees of the ball and suddenly gasped. "Oh no! I saw him!"

"Saw who?" Emmy and Jessica said together.

She stood up. "I need to find Quince."

They heard a door close in the hallway. "Emmy? Cecilia?" It was Jack's voice. Followed closely after by Quince. "Jessica?"

The girl looked at Sabre with a knowing smile. "Ask and ye shall receive."

"We're in here," Sabre called. A light filled the doorway as the ever-practical Jack had actually brought a candle. But Quince preceded her into the room.

Thirty-Four

he blackmailer's threats had left Quince in a panic over his sister and Sabre. He had collected Gideon, Robert, and Charlie to scour the downstairs looking for the blackguard and asked Jacqueline to take him to his sister. But upon checking both her room and Emmy's they had been missing. Unable to find either Sabre or Jessica at that point he had been ready to tear London apart, if necessary. Now here they were. Both girls were taller than Sabre, yet somehow she managed to have them safely under her wings. Not trusting himself to speak, Quince walked forward and hugged Jessica. Sabre leaned into him and he put his arm around her as well.

"Quince," she said. "I think I saw him."

He drew back to look down at her. "Who?"

"Draco."

"How do you know?"

"His own arrogance. He was wearing a pin. Jack, what's that symbol called? Where the serpent is eating its own tail?"

"Ouroboros," Jack supplied.

"Right. Ouroboros was also called a dragon. And there was a gem in the middle of it. Red tigerseye. Also known as dragonseye."

Quince mulled that, fighting his need to pull her to him. "Perhaps. What did he look like?"

Sabre closed her eyes. "He wasn't very tall. Older, perhaps the same age as Jack's father. Light brown hair going to gray. He wasn't particularly notable other than his dark green jacket and that pin."

Quince looked over at Jack and she nodded. "I'll go tell them."

"Tell who what?" Sabre asked.

"Someone was in the library," Quince said. "He spoke to me after you left and then he seemed to disappear. Gideon and your brothers are looking for him. If the man you saw was the same one who spoke to me, then the description will be helpful to them."

Sabre looked worried but after a moment she merely leaned against him again, resting her head on his shoulder. He held both her and Jessica close.

Quince had left his sister upstairs with additional footmen posted outside her door but had to repress the instinct to go check on her again. The search of the house had turned up nothing. After the earl and countess bid their last guests a good evening they joined the group gathered in the library. Both Bittlesworth brothers were present, as well as Sabre. The duke looked at Robert, wondering what he would be willing to say in mixed company. The younger man seemed to take that as a signal and rose to speak.

"I am afraid that I have caused his grace, and all of you, a great deal of trouble. His grace has received threats over the past month because I spread rumors that he was in possession of some papers that he was not."

Gideon spoke up. "That was a damn sight more than threats, Robert."

"What do you mean?" Sabre looked at Quince. "What does he mean?"

The duke shook his head. "It doesn't signify."

Sabre jumped to her feet. "Don't you dare! This is exactly what I was afraid would happen."

She tried to reach out and touch his jaw near his wound again, but he captured her hands. Frowning, he said, "I'm fine."

The earl spoke again. "The greater question to me is whether you are still in danger."

Quince shrugged. "The man I spoke to tonight seemed to indicate no. He has offered to provide the evidence that Robert needs on his original target."

Robert, now leaning against a table with his arms crossed, considered that information. "In exchange for what?"

"Leaving him alone. He was very clear that the threats to my mother and sister remain should we do anything to discomfort him."

"I don't trust him," Gideon said.

"Nor do I," Quince agreed. "He blamed the incident the other day on our original target, but I'm not sure I believe him."

"Agreed," Robert said. "The style isn't fitting. Although one can never account for the creativity of employees."

Charlie finally spoke up. "It's quite obvious that some of you know a few things the rest of us don't. Is that how this conversation is going to go?"

Quince and Robert eyed each other and the duke finally nodded that it was Robert's call on what to say.

Robert stepped forward again. "My original target was our father. I seek to get him exiled."

Charlie's eyebrows shot up and then he nodded, considering. "I can understand that."

"Oh, Robert, I'm not that mad at him." Sabre said, referring to her fury over their father not allowing Justin to go on Tour. The reason she had retreated to Robert's house.

He gave his sister an indulgent smile. "I know, poppet. But I am."

She looked confused and shifted her gaze from Robert to Quince. The duke shrugged. As if he knew what went through Robert Bittlesworth's mind. It was interesting, however, that Charlie accepted the news so easily.

"So who is the other man?" Charlie asked.

Quince and Robert looked at each other again. "We don't know."

"He threatens your family, makes an attempt on your life, and you're just going to let this lie?" Charlie pressed.

"What else would you have me do?"

"Find him. Make him pay."

"And any misstep in finding him will alert him that we have not left him alone, therefore putting my family in even more jeopardy."

"I agree with Charlie," Gideon said. "We need to do something."

"It's my family and I say it is too dangerous to pursue."

Charlie stepped forward. "Considering your relationship with our sister, I would say it affects our family as well. What if there is another attempt on your life and we lose her?"

"Robert, I was hoping that Sabre could continue staying with you. Fortunately, when he saw us in the library he suspected that I was attempting to seduce her as a jab at your father."

Robert gave a dry laugh. "He ascribed his own motivations to you. Obviously he has not studied you at all."

Charlie glared at Sabre. "What were you doing in the library with the duke?"

She patted her brother's arm. "It doesn't signify."

Her light-haired brother glowered at Quince, obviously not satisfied with her answer.

Jack finally spoke. "Sabre? What do you think the right thing to do is?"

She pursed her lips and looked thoughtful. "We can't do anything until we've assessed his strength, and that means we have to find out who he is. Without him realizing that is what we're doing."

Quince felt a pain in his heart as he thought of how his sister could be affected. "It's too risky."

"Which is the greater risk? Trying to defeat him or living with an axe hovering over your head?"

Robert added, "With a man like that, he will start using his power over you to extract favors."

"You would know, wouldn't you?" Quince asked acidly. Turning to Sabre he said, "Any risk to my sister is unacceptable."

"Quince, she is at risk so long as this man is free to do what he likes. And he won't know what we're doing, not if we're careful. Let's start with what we know. I think that I saw him. Although I'm sure I would recognize him again, his looks are too pedestrian to be notable. It would be difficult for me to describe him to someone else in a useful way."

"I didn't recognize his voice," Quince said. "And that means he's not active in the House of Lords."

"Good," Sabre said, nodding. "Any other thoughts?"

Robert spoke up. "Based on the details from his second letter he may be on speaking terms with your mother, which may mean that she would have further information if supplied with his description. We might get a name that way. Even if a false one, it could prove useful."

"Good," Sabre said again. "And we can probably get that information from her without alerting her to why we need it. To ensure she doesn't accidentally tip him to what we are doing. What else?"

"We know..." Quince paused and looked at Robert. "We know he has two unsavory friends, one of whom he is willing to condemn in order to save himself. So there is an additional person to be on the lookout for."

"And we don't know what that person's motivations might be," Robert added. "The group seemed solid for years, but with one turning on another? Anything could happen."

"We also know," Gideon added with a frown, "that the man has bought his way in, or otherwise infiltrated, at least two houses. Between the way Quince's notes were delivered and how he managed to disappear here."

"And knowing that my sister was here."

"Could that have been a good guess on his part?" Sabre mused. "Rather than actual intelligence?"

"What do you mean?" Quince asked.

She shrugged. "It's a classic chess move. When the king is threatened he withdraws into his castle. Anyone with a sufficient knowledge of how your household is run could surmise that you would remand your sister to Gideon for protection."

"But it seemed rather specific knowledge," Robert countered. "Describing her as being upstairs when she could just as easily be at Kellington or somewhere else. Typically someone who is guessing will hedge their bets with a more general description in the hopes of being nearly right rather than completely wrong."

"On the other hand," Quince said, "if this is the dragon, my impression is that he is more of a gambler than most. He might make a bold statement at high risk."

"I'm sorry," Charlie said, "the dragon?"

As Quince and Robert exchanged another look, Sabre said, "Do you know what a Hellfire Club is?"

Charlie nodded. "Yes."

"That's essentially what this group of men was, a Hellfire Club."

Jack raised a brow. "Demon worship?"

"We haven't seen any evidence of that." Robert said, then sighed. "Yet."

Quince nodded. "And we say the dragon because the four of them took nicknames from constellations in the spring sky. Leo, Ursa, Draco, and Cygnus."

"And do we know who any of them are?" Charlie asked.

"Our fathers," Quince answered, indicating himself and the Bittlesworth siblings.

Gideon snorted. "Your fathers were in a Hellfire Club, yet somehow *I* got the nickname Lord Lucifer?"

"I don't like the sound of this," Jack said, moving closer to Gideon. "Robert, isn't there anything the government can do?"

"Not without evidence."

"Which, if I'm following correctly," Charlie said, "the dragon is willing to provide against our father?"

"Correct," Robert said.

"And which one is our father?"

"Cygnus. The swan."

Charlie turned to Quince. "And your father was?"

"Leo. The lion."

"Which," Jack said, "leaves Ursa the bear completely unaccounted for, so far."

Charlie shrugged. "Perhaps he passed on, like his grace's father did."

Quince and Robert had another pregnant pause that prompted Jack to say, "What?"

"Draco," Quince said, "is a second generation member."

Charlie frowned. "How does that work?"

"His father inducted him into the group," Robert said. "For some years they were referred to as Draco Senior and Draco Junior. Until the elder Draco passed on."

Charlie's eyes widened. "Did father....?"

Robert nodded. "He took me to a meeting some years ago. It did not hold the appeal to me that he had expected."

Sabre turned to look at him. "That's why you don't speak to him."

"I have not spoken to him directly since that night, no."

An uncomfortable silence descended on the room.

"Is there anything more we can do this night?" Jack asked.

Quince shook his head. "I think not."

"Jack, can I stay here?" Sabre asked. "I can help you keep an eye on Jessica."

"Of course."

"It might be best," Gideon said, "if we continue to refer to her by her alias."

"Agreed," Quince said. "If he isn't certain she is here then there is no reason to verify his assumptions by having her name commonly enough used for the information to be bought off the servants."

Gideon looked affronted at the insult to his staff but didn't say anything.

"Come on, Charlie," Robert said, clapping his brother on the shoulder. "I'll give you a ride home."

Quince bowed to Jack. "It was a lovely ball, Lady Harrington. My apologies that this drama has shadowed it."

"Don't worry," Sabre said. "Jack loves mysteries ever so much more than balls."

Quince bowed to Sabre as well. "Miss Bittlesworth."

She curtsied. "Your grace."

Quince turned to Gideon to bid him good evening but was cut short by the earl saying, "I'll walk you out."

Once they gained the hallway, Gideon stopped him with a hand to the shoulder. "Are you all right?"

"Of course I am."

His friend gave him a grim look. "No one knows you better than I do, Quince, and I know that you are not all right. That was simply an invitation to tell me why."

"It's perfectly obvious why."

Gideon blew out a breath. "Much as I'm loathe to admit it, talking about it might help. I now wish I'd forced you to talk to me last month after the duel. I knew then that something was wrong."

Quince was irritated by Gideon's assumption that he could *make* him talk about anything. Besides, if it were true that talking about it would make him feel better, he knew there was only one person he wanted to speak with. And she would be here helping to protect his sister. "Don't worry about it, old man. When I need your help I'll ask for it."

Although he didn't look pleased, the earl let him leave without much further comment. Quince rode back to his townhouse in dark silence.

Thirty-Five

*A*fter the men had taken their leave, Jack crossed her arms and looked at her friend. "Well, are you going to ask for the use of a carriage, or will you endeavor to sneak out without me seeing you?"

"I'm that transparent, am I?"

"As glass."

"I need to find out about the attempt on his life."

Jack nodded. "I understand that."

"Do you know anything about it?"

"No. I'm sure they think they are protecting us somehow, but it's more than a little irritating."

Sabre nodded. "More than a little."

"How do you feel about Robert's plan to have your father exiled?"

"Strange. I've never been close to father but I've also never had the issues with him that my brothers do. Apparently I didn't know him as well as they."

"Charlie has issues with him as well? I've never seen that."

"It's a look Charlie gets when talking to him. Hard to explain but... Yes, Charlie has issues with him."

Not sure what else to do for her friend, Jack simply hugged her. "Please be careful."

"I'll try. But as you know, sometimes fortune favors the bold."

Jack shook her head. "Sometimes, Sabre. Just use the wisdom that I know you possess."

Quince stared at his bed. This was where the blackmail notes had been delivered. Someone had come into his home, his room, to leave messages of promised violence. It was a violation. Sabre was right that the threat would remain, like an axe over his head, until they found some way to neutralize it. What could be better than having a duke on a string? A duke liked by both the Prince and one of the most powerful men in the House of Lords. He had to find evidence against this man, this monster known as Draco. It wasn't too much to consider killing him outright. That wasn't something he had ever considered himself capable of doing, but now it seemed far more likely.

Was this how it started, though? Evil that could be justified? Certainly it seemed the greater good to simply remove a terrible person from society. By brute force, if necessary. But if he could consider such a thing, then perhaps he was more in need of Robert's ruminations on redemption than he previously thought. He had sinned already, taking a woman to his bed before marriage. He was considering a second sin so soon? And murder, no less.

He heard a light tap at the door before it opened.

"Your grace," Larkins said softly.

Quince turned to see his butler looking a bit out of sorts. He felt a thrum of anticipation. "Yes, Larkins?"

"There is a young woman here insisting to see you, your grace. She would not accept being turned out."

"Is she about," Quince held his hand level to his chin, "this tall?"

"Yes, your grace."

"Where is she?"

"I put her in the front parlor, your grace, I wasn't sure what else-"

Larkins stopped speaking as Quince pushed past on his way to dash down the stairs. His heart beat painfully strong in his chest. It had to be her. Please let it be her. He paused outside the oak door to the parlor, trying to gird himself for the disappointment if it wasn't her. If it wasn't Sabre.

Pushing the door open he saw a figure standing in the middle of the room, turned away from him, and covered head to foot in a dark cloak. She appeared to be studying the large portrait over the fireplace.

Leaning against the door frame he tried to discern from her height, the way she shifted her body...But was it just wishful thinking? "The portrait is of my father's first wife," he said.

"Quince!" She turned and hurried to him.

Oh, thank God. It was her. She was here. She wrapped her arms around his waist and burrowed against his chest. He embraced her and felt the burn of unshed tears in his throat. But she shouldn't be here. It wasn't proper. It wasn't safe.

"Sabre, I thought you were going to stay at the Harrington's."

She tipped her head back to look at him, the cloak's hood sliding off her hair. "No one believed that."

He laughed. "I believed it."

"Then you're gullible."

"Don't be rude. I might have you thrown out."

She raised a brow at him. "I, on the other hand, am not gullible and I don't believe that in the least."

He couldn't stop himself. He had to kiss her. Had to taste that sweet, saucy mouth. He stroked her jaw and ran his fingers into the hair at her nape as he sank into the kiss. Lord, how he had missed her. Missed this. He knew that for her own safety he should send her back to Robert's or the Harrington's. If Draco were to discover what she was, how much she was worth to him...It didn't bear thinking. He would handle Draco. He must.

She broke the kiss and his heart plummeted as he thought that perhaps she was once again pulling away. Leaving. It had only been earlier this evening she had said she wanted to purge all memory of him and perhaps she really did mean it.

Sabre smiled up at him. "Isn't there some place more comfortable we could be doing this?"

Relief washed over him. "Perhaps I could find a place." He held his elbow out to her and as she wrapped her arm around his and he looked down into her smiling face he realized that even the poorest, most common man must feel like a king when the woman he loves looks at him adoringly.

He took up a candle as they walked through the hallway and led her up the grand steps to the ducal suites. He opened a door that he hadn't opened in a long time and indicated that she should precede him. She entered, looking about her with interest in the limited light.

"This isn't your room, I take it?"

He set the candle on a table. "No, this would be the duchesses' suite."

"Thank goodness it's in far better shape than the one at Belle Fleur was."

Quince smiled, remembering the amusing picture she had made with an oversized apron tied around her waist, her hair in a kerchief, and covered in dust. When had he started loving her, he wondered. Had he loved her since the first moment he saw her and everything else had only helped to reveal that to him? He wasn't sure. It didn't even matter. She was here. She was his.

Looking at him again, she tilted her head. "Why are you so quiet?"

He smiled and walked towards her to take her hands. "Aren't I always quiet?"

"Not always. Sometimes. When you're thinking. What are you thinking about?"

He kissed her hand. "You."

She smiled but said, "What else?"

"There is nothing else. There may never again be anything else."

She giggled but drew back from him as he bent to kiss her neck. "No, there is something else."

Quince looked around the room for a brief moment. "It's just been a long time since I've been in here. I'm sure we can find something more interesting to talk about." He laced his fingers through hers and led her towards the bed. "Or do."

"Why did you come in here at all before?"

He sighed and began unbuttoning the cloak. "I never knew my mother. As a child I assumed she was dead, so I would visit her rooms to try to get a sense of her. To feel closer to her."

"That sounds lonely."

He paused in his work, looking at her. "I suppose it was, but it didn't occur to me to think that at the time." He gave her a self-deprecating smile. "And I don't think I have the need

257

SUE LONDON

to be with others like some do. I don't interpret solitude as loneliness."

Sabre chuckled. "I suppose I don't know much of solitude."

"No, I suppose you wouldn't. My father often wasn't home as I was growing up and I was actively discouraged from playing with the staff. By the time I got to school I wasn't much for playing, really. I was like a very small sixty year old man." He laughed, and then furrowed his brow. "Although I didn't... approve of my father, I did love him in my way. He was all I knew of a parent. When he passed I was more distraught than I expected. I still remember being out in the country and sending Gideon a letter to announce my father's passing, desperately hoping that he would see the inherent invitation and come."

"Did he?"

"Of course. But before he arrived, within a day of father's passing, there was a tremendous disturbance in the front hall. I had been in the study at the time, wondering what on earth I was supposed to do. And I heard a woman's voice, clear and distinct as a bell. I will never forget what she said. 'No one will keep me from my son now that the old bastard is dead.' I couldn't believe it."

Sabre grabbed his hands. "Oh, Quince."

"When I came out to the hallway I found her and ten of her footmen. They seemed ready to do battle. As soon as I saw her it was clear that she was my mother. We look too much alike for there to be any doubt. I felt all my blood rush to my head and it's a wonder that I didn't pass out from the shock. She must have just as easily recognized me and pushed through the staff to get to me. I can't tell you what that felt like, Sabre, to think that I had lost everything and then there she was. To me, back from the dead. She wrapped her arms around me and kept saying 'my baby' over and over. I was too numb to do anything."

Sabre wrapped her arms around him and pulled him close without saying anything.

Quince sighed, embracing her. "I don't know why I'm telling you this."

"Because I asked."

"You asked me what I was thinking, and I wasn't thinking about that. I really was thinking of you."

She pulled him over to the bed and encouraged him to sit. "Was that all of the story?"

He shrugged. "Mostly. She spent some time with me there. After Gideon arrived it soon became clear that I needed to keep the two of them separated. Once Gideon and I had the ducal accounts mostly settled I went out to Bath to see her again. She has a lovely townhouse and holds a salon for freethinkers and intellectuals."

Smiling as she removed the cloak from her shoulders, Sabre said, "She doesn't like Gideon and holds salons? I think I'm starting to like your mother already."

Quince leaned back on his hands, admiring again how the poppy red ball gown complimented her figure and coloring. "Yes, I'm sure you would get along."

"Is the townhouse hers or do you own it?"

"It's hers. I'm somewhat shocked that my father made that concession."

She paused in folding her cloak. "You consider that a concession?"

"For him, yes. It would not only bother him on a moral front, it's actually legally complicated to give a married woman property of her own. The rights to the property were much clearer with his death."

"I was," she said softly, and then steeled her voice. "I was hoping you would gift me with Belle Fleur."

Thirty-Six

Quince felt a *frisson* of worry go through him. "Are we discussing terms?"

Sabre lifted a chin a notch, looking both ferocious and vulnerable. She clutched the cloak to her midsection in an unconscious gesture of defense. "Yes."

"That doesn't align with my plans for Belle Fleur," he said. He saw her expression go blank and knew that perhaps he should rush to explain. "I had been thinking to foist the title on my brother and ask him to give us Belle Fleur."

She frowned. "Can you even do that? Give up your title?"

"Just because something hasn't been done doesn't mean it can't be done. And then," he reached out to take her left hand and caressed his thumb over her ring finger, "there would be no impediment to us being married."

She became brisk, pulling her hand away and setting the folded cloak on a chair. "Don't be ridiculous, your grace."

"Quince," he said.

"When you are being ridiculous it will always be 'your grace'."

"So you do not wish for me to give up my title to marry you?"

She crossed her arms and shook her head. "No. You shouldn't give up your title for anything."

"And to be my mistress you would only ask for Belle Fleur?"

Her lower lip quivered and she caught it between her teeth. Looking down at the floor she finally said, "I would ask for nothing."

"You're a bit worse at negotiation than I would expect."

Her eyes flashed as she looked back up at him again. "This isn't a negotiation! Don't sully it like that."

Stubborn as she was he suspected this was as close as he would get to her revealing her feelings for him. There she stood, prickly and proud, and oddly that endeared her to him even more. He sighed.

"I love you, Sabre. I would gladly give you everything I have if I could. That was true from the first moment I saw you. But as Belle Fleur is the only unentailed property left, yes, you may have it. You have only to tell me what you want and I will get it for you. Even if I have to beg, borrow, or steal it."

She had wrapped her arms around her middle while listening and he heard her make a muffled sob. He rose to embrace her.

"Quince," she whispered, "all I want is you."

He kissed her temple. "I guess you did warn me of that in the beginning."

She gave a watery laugh and he hugged her close, pulling her to sit in his lap on the bed. The passion from earlier had settled into an intimate closeness that he wasn't sure he wanted to disturb.

After a few moments she shifted. "Quince?"

"Yes, my beloved?"

"I could use some help getting out of this dress."

His body reacted instantly to her suggestion. "Yes, that is help I will always be willing to give you."

She stood and he followed her, hands on her hips as he couldn't keep himself from touching her.

"And…" she added softly, "could we go to your room?"

"Yes," he said, surprised, "but why? I thought your goal had been to claim the duchesses' suites."

"I like it when my pillow smells of you."

He ran his hand over her hip in an intimate, possessive caress and pulled her closer. "You could solve that by sleeping on top of me."

She giggled and kissed his chin. "You aren't nearly as soft."

He sighed, took her hand, and picked up the candle, leading her to the connecting door. "It will be as my lady wishes."

"You make me feel demanding."

"No, you are demanding and I'm just not polite enough to avoid pointing it out."

She laughed and said, "You are the rudest man I know!"

"That may well be true. But a duke is privileged with being able to say what he likes and you have missed your chance to change that."

Once in the ducal bedroom he set the candle on his bedside and began removing her dress. Within moments she was in her shift and slippers, the red dress laid aside on a settee. "I do love you in red," he said, kissing her shoulder.

She shivered in response to his light kisses. "Then perhaps we shouldn't have removed it."

He pushed the shoulder of the shift down, stroking his hand over her skin and then nibbling where the side of her throat met her shoulder. "I love you even more in nothing at all."

She gave a soft moan and tried to push his jacket off his shoulders. The tight evening jacket barely budged.

Laughing he said, "This may be significantly more difficult to remove than your dress. Shall I summon my valet?"

"No," she said with determination. She walked behind him and, placing her hands just so, peeled the jacket back off his shoulders.

"You would make a more than reasonable batman. Should I be concerned that you know how to get men out of their clothes?"

"Brothers," she said simply, tossing the jacket aside to join her dress.

He knelt to remove her shoes, pausing to kiss the side of her knee. Once standing again he kicked off his own shoes and unfastened his cuffs as she removed his cravat. He leaned forward to kiss her briefly. "We have too damn many clothes."

"You had at least a full hour before I arrived," she sniffed, "you could have undressed then."

He pulled his shirt off without unbuttoning it, throwing it aside.

She gasped. "Oh, Quince!"

He had honestly forgotten how horrid the bruises looked. "Not now," he said. "Please? I need you."

She nodded but he could see tears at the corners of her eyes. He pulled her close and began kissing her again. She relaxed into his embrace and kissed him avidly, but seemed afraid to put her hands on him.

Breaking the kiss he cupped her face in his hands. "Sabre, please touch me. I need you to touch me."

She tentatively stroked over his arms and shoulders. He set his forehead to hers with a contented sigh. "Thank you."

As he expected, her touch became bolder. She tipped her head to resume their kiss and he sank into the sweet pleasure of her lips. He broke the kiss again for a moment to remove her shift and reveled in the feeling of her soft skin pressed against his. As he caressed her back and sides, her questing fingers went to work on unbuttoning his breeches.

"Impatient," he murmured in her ear before trailing kisses down the side of her neck.

"Yes," she admitted.

He scooped her up, making her laugh in surprise, and deposited her on the bed. He stood watching her, enjoying her flushed cheeks and bright smile. "Are the pillows to your liking?"

She pulled one to her nose and breathed deeply. "Perfect." She waved her hand at him. "You still have on too many clothes."

He shucked off his breeches and knelt over her on the bed. Running his hand down her body he echoed her word. "Perfect."

She twined her fingers in his hair and tugged him forward for a kiss. He braced himself above her on an elbow as his free hand continued its journey over her body. She would shudder and clutch at him when his touch turned hard and possessive.

Kissing her throat he asked, "Are you ready?"

She nodded, "Yes."

But he knew from the tension in her body, the tone of her voice, that she feared it would hurt again. He smiled into her hair, knowing that he would surprise her. His hand skimmed down over her, coming to rest over her core. He cupped her there, gently, and then gave her mound a hard and possessive rub. She gasped against his throat, her hips shifting in her surprise. His thumb found her pearl as his first two fingers stroked inside her.

"Quince?" she said uncertainly.

He kissed her again, harsh and demanding. Her grip tightened in his hair and she met his assault with the same vigor. As he rubbed and teased her, she became impossibly wet and slick, his fingers losing purchase as she began to buck and writhe. He tightened his other hand in her hair to hold her head as he broke the kiss and moved to suckle her nipple. She gave a few gasping breaths and then her body bowed up from the bed on a sharp cry.

His touch turned soothing and soft, kissing her shoulder, her lips. He looked down to see that she was crying. "Are you all right?"

She nodded and gave him a trembling smile. "Why didn't we do that the first time?"

He chuckled and kissed her shoulder again. "You said *you* knew what to do."

She sighed happily and ran her fingers through his hair.

Damned if Gideon wasn't right. Having Sabre look at him as though he had discovered a great secret about her body made him feel like a mythic hero.

At last her body had fulfilled the promise of all the whispered secrets she had heard from the serving girls. Beyond that, really. She felt luxurious, cherished. Quince was skimming his hand over her flesh, kissing her softly in delicate spots that made her shiver. The inside of her elbow. Along her ribs. She felt as though she were floating on a sensual cloud made entirely of his touch, his smell. She never wanted anything other than this. Complete intimacy with the man she loved.

He shifted his weight on top of her and she felt his cock against her thigh. She still feared that joining would cause pain, but she wanted him. Pain was nothing, fear was nothing, as long as they could be together. She opened her legs wider in silent invitation, and while he nibbled on her ear he slipped inside her.

Oh, it wasn't like the previous times at all! It felt right. It felt good. Like welcoming him home after a long absence.

"Are you all right?" he asked softly.

She rubbed her cheek against his. "I'm wonderful. You're wonderful. Please, more."

He began to rock against her and she felt the fire kindle low in her belly again. Oh God, would joining lead to that intense pleasure she had felt under his hand? Her hips began to buck and thrust against him of their own accord and the more she moved in counterpoint to his rhythm the more her body tightened in response. This time the petals of sensation that unfurled in her center were slower to bloom, but deeper, more primal. She clung to him and encouraged him to go faster, panting his name. Then the knot of sensation broke apart and she was flooded with wave after wave of pleasure. She didn't know time or place or thought, only feeling. She heard him call her name. Hoarse, desperate, tender. She wrapped her arms around him. How had she ever thought that she could leave him, could get over him?

She would gladly be his mistress. It didn't matter what anyone thought. It didn't matter that she could no longer go out in Society, that her own parents might disown her. That even her brothers and friends might shun her. She, who had never done anything without weighing the risks and rewards first, knew that no risk could outweigh the reward of Quince's love to her. The only risk was losing him. She couldn't let that happen. Wouldn't let that happen. As he dozed next to her she lay awake in the coming dawn, planning how to keep him safe.

Thirty-Seven

S abre had dozed off herself because a knock at the door awoke her.

The duke called out without even raising his head from the pillow. "Not now, Larkins!"

"Your grace, I - no, sir, you cannot do that!"

The door opened and it sounded like a scuffle. Quince sat up, shielding Sabre and she couldn't see who it was.

The duke sounded furious. "Good God, Robert, have you no decency?"

She peeked around Quince to see her brother standing in the open doorway, shaking off the butler, holding a bundle of clothing. He looked unusually pale and haggard.

"I need Sabre to come with me."

"No." Quince's voice rang with a final authority. His ducal voice.

"My men report that Viscount Bittlesworth left for the coast this morning." His gaze shifted to Sabre. "And he took the viscountess with him. Against her will."

Sabre felt her heart stutter in her chest. Mother was usually too clever to openly defy father. His temper was short and at times violent.

"Thank you for bringing us the news," Quince said, still using his austere, commanding tone. He managed a surprising amount of poise for a man dressed only in a sheet. "I assume you and your men will handle it."

"I need Sabre with me."

"Why on earth would you take your sister into that?"

"Because she's the best shot, and perhaps the best fighter, among us. Further, she's the only one that father isn't likely to fire upon."

Even with the dire news, Sabre's heart glowed to hear her brother's compliment. But she knew he was gilding the lily to sway Quince to his plan.

"Are you sure that the viscount wouldn't shoot her?" Quince sounded both cynical and suspicious.

"Of course. He's not a complete monster."

But Sabre, who knew Robert so well, saw the truth. He had no such confidence that their father wouldn't be vicious to them if cornered. Yet they needed to try. And Robert, who had shouldered so much responsibility for seeing to her and her mother all these years was asking for her help.

"Don't be silly," she said to Quince, patting him on the arm. "I'll be fine. It's speed that is of the essence. We must catch them and ensure my mother doesn't get packed off in a boat. Then it would be so much harder to find her."

She determinedly kept her voice even and calm, to communicate that she wasn't worried at all about this mission. Inside, however, she was worried intensely. The fact that Robert seemed concerned was sobering. He dealt with vital international affairs with a steadier demeanor. What could his men have reported to him?

Quince finally turned to look at her. "I can't stand the thought of you being in danger."

"Don't be silly. I'm the one person who can do this and *not* be in danger. Pray for Robert and Charlie, father is much more likely to strike them." She looked back to her brother. "Thank you for bringing my riding clothes. Just leave them on that chair and I'll be dressed in a trice."

Robert set down the clothes, nodded, and withdrew.

Quince wrapped his arms around her. "I'm going with you."

She laughed. "No you're not. Father would definitely be happy to shoot you. I don't want you anywhere near him."

"You can't expect me to sit here and wait for you."

"No, I expect you to do something productive. Certainly you can think of something."

He held onto her tighter. "I don't want you to go."

She bit her lip to keep from expressing her true feelings. Her fear and helpless rage. "It's my mother, Quince. I have to go."

He looked down at her and nodded, rubbing her arms. "All right, then."

She was reminded of one of the first reasons she had fallen in love with him. His capacity to give others their freedom. No strings, no promises extracted. He offered an intoxicating blend of freedom and security. She had something she had to tell him, just in case.

"Quince?"

"Yes, love?"

She looked up into his spring green eyes, shadowed with worry for her. His blonde hair was tousled from sleep, his jaw rough with stubble. She cupped his face in her hands, careful to avoid the healing gash she had yet to learn more about. "I love you," she whispered.

He smiled and leaned his forehead on hers. "I know."

She laughed. "Rude!"

He caught her against himself and kissed her. Kissed her as though this could be their last kiss. Then he broke away, breathing hard. "You need to get dressed."

She nodded and ran to the pile of clothing that Robert had left. "So what will you do to be productive while I'm gone?"

He helped her on with her riding habit. "I have some things that I need to do at Belle Fleur." The answer was evasive, but she didn't have time to question him further.

"Perfect! Then I will meet you there after I have mother settled."

"You sound very confident."

"Of course. I always get what I want, remember?"

He chuckled. "How could I forget?"

She was ready and he had pulled on his breeches and shirt from the night before. Honestly, if everyone looked as good in dishabille as the duke it would set a fashion. He held out his elbow to her. "Let's get you downstairs before Robert wears a hole pacing on my carpets."

By the time she came downstairs Charlie had arrived with his best horses and there was a sweep of activity that had her mounted and riding out much faster than she would have wanted. She looked back over her shoulder to see Quince standing on the steps, arms crossed and lips drawn in a worried line. Not wanting to see him so grim she smiled and blew him a kiss. He gave her a half-smile in return, pretending to catch the kiss and hold it against his heart. The scene made her own heart trip and she faced forward again before she turned into a complete ninny and started crying. At least he would be safe from this confrontation.

"How did you convince his grace not to come with us?" Robert asked over the sound of trotting hooves.

"He trusts me."

"Well. I guess he'll learn better than that."

She glowered at her brother. "No, he won't."

Robert laughed. "At least you sound more like yourself again."

Quince wasn't able to settle himself for worry about Sabre after she left. Rather than continue to pace and climb the walls in London he called for his horse to be readied for a trip to Belle Fleur. He didn't fancy a carriage ride just now. It might be some time until he could enjoy travel by carriage again. Before he left town, however, he realized he should call on the Harringtons. They were as involved in all this mess as anyone now, and would appreciate an update. He dressed to be at least respectable enough to call on an earl and countess.

Dibbs took him in at once, of course, then intoned that he would see if his lord and lady were in for receiving. Quince waited in the front parlor. There were three paintings here that Gideon had purchased on his recommendation, so he did his best to focus on them despite his unsettled stomach. As well as being lovely to behold they would hopefully prove to be a worthwhile investment.

"Hullo, Quince. My apologies you had to wait." Gideon entered the room and slapped the duke on the shoulder, turning to look at the same painting Quince had just been studying. "I will never entirely understand the appeal art has for you."

"Undoubtedly."

Jack entered the room and held out her hands to him. "Quince!"

"How is Miss Frederick?"

"She's fine, would you like to see her?"

The duke shook his head. "I only wanted to give you both an update before I ride on to Belle Fleur."

"Has something happened?" Jack asked, betraying some tension.

"The Bittlesworth siblings have ridden out this morning in pursuit of the viscount. He has decided to flee and is taking the viscountess with him under duress."

Jack covered her mouth in shock. "Oh no!"

Quince gave voice to what was bothering him. "Of course, I didn't want Sabrina to go, but Robert insisted she was needed."

Gideon frowned. "Why?"

The duke frowned. "He said she was the best shot and further, the viscount is least likely to turn his anger against her."

Gideon raised a brow at his wife, "Oh?"

Jack caught her breath but said, "Yes, I can understand that."

There was something in the countess's reaction that made Quince worry but the earl distracted his attention before he could focus on it.

"Why didn't you go with them?" Gideon demanded.

Quince felt himself withdraw into a cool hauteur. "I have things to attend to at Belle Fleur."

The earl looked offended. "Things more important than keeping your wife safe?"

"They aren't married," Jack pointed out.

"They will be," Gideon insisted.

"As charming as this visit has turned out to be," the duke drawled, "I find I must be going."

"The hell you are. Explain to me how you'll live with yourself if something happens to her while you're spending your leisure at Belle Fleur?"

"Is that what you think I'll be doing?" Quince felt all the tension and worry bleed into fury instead. "Wiling away my time? Regardless of what you may think, Giddy, it was no easier for me to let her go this morning than it would be for you. The only difference is that I respect her enough for her to make her own decisions. And I *am* trying to keep her safe. Draco is more of a threat than Cygnus. I must find a way to neutralize the dragon and I think the key is at Belle Fleur."

"What makes you think that?"

"Because it has to be. If it isn't... The other alternative is less pleasant."

"What other alternative?"

"I will remove the threat in whatever way necessary."

Gideon paused. "Do you need help at Belle Fleur?"

"No, I need you to protect my sister."

The earl nodded in understanding.

"And if you could..." Quince swallowed and set his jaw. "If you could send word when the Bittlesworths return. Whether... whether Sabrina is all right."

"Of course."

After the duke left, Jack sat down heavily in one of the plush side chairs along the parlor wall. Gideon immediately came to kneel before her. "What's wrong? Are you feeling ill?"

She shook her head. "They lied to him. I don't know why they lied to him."

"What do you mean?"

"Sabre is a crack shot, but she's rarely bested Robert. She and I are about even with pistols."

"Why didn't you tell Quince that?"

"Because I'm sure Robert said it for a reason, I just don't know what that reason might be. Unless…"

"Unless what?"

She worried her fingernail for a moment. "One of the games we played as children was 'Rob the Coach'. It's possible Robert is thinking to use those tactics here. Since Quince didn't play he wouldn't know what to do, so they would discourage him from going with them."

"So you're telling me that the Bittlesworth siblings are considering using a children's game to save their mother?"

"Sabre's mother. Robert and Charlie's mother was the first viscountess. And we were all fairly serious about our games, thank you very much. Unfortunately for them, I was always in charge of 'Rob the Coach' because I wanted to be Robin Hood."

Gideon gave a wry laugh and took her hands, resting his forehead against them. "Of course you did. And you are not going after them to reprise the role."

"No. I wouldn't even know where to start looking for them."

He looked up at her, eyes narrowed in suspicion. "Promise me you're not going after them."

"Of course not. Why would I?"

He continued to stare at her until she fidgeted.

"All right, I promise."

He kissed her hand. "Thank you. One daring rescue is all that the future earl should engage in before his actual birth."

"It could be a girl, you know." She patted her stomach.

He stood and offered to help her up. "I shudder to think."

Thirty-Eight

"Well?" Sabre demanded as soon as Charlie was in earshot. A drizzle had been falling since they left London and she didn't want to simply stand around in it any longer than she had to. Her brother shifted his gaze around the stable yard of the inn before responding.

"It sounds like they came through here less than an hour ago."

Robert kept his head down as he adjusted the saddle on his horse. "They are headed for King's Lynn, then."

Sabre nodded. "Most likely. Do you think your men will be in place in time?"

Robert squinted up at the sky. "It doesn't really matter, does it? We're going to try anyway."

The siblings were solemn as they mounted their horses and rode out in pursuit of the viscount.

Quince allowed Havers to take his dripping greatcoat. The butler murmured, "We're happy to have you returned to us, your grace."

"Thank you. Please ensure that my riders have a hot meal, it's been miserable outside. How does my coachman fare?"

Havers paused for moment. "Not well, your grace," he finally said gravely. "The doctor has made him as comfortable as possible."

"Is he... Will he live?"

Havers' normally pleasant expression was etched into a deep frown. "That is not certain, your grace. The doctor believes his leg may need to be amputated and, well..."

The duke nodded. "I would like to see him now, please. And afterwards I will need to talk to you."

"Yes, your grace."

As Quince followed Havers to the servant's quarters he thought it was only by the narrowest chance of timing that it wasn't him lying in bed, broken and dying. How many people were going to suffer for this vendetta? The dragon needed to be stopped. And Robert had much answer for.

Sabre recognized the carriage immediately, even through the rain. Father had ten outriders, large brutes of men, which meant he had been expecting trouble. The bridge where Robert's men waited in ambush could be no more than a mile away. She looked over at Robert and he nodded at her. She spurred her horse ahead as her brothers pulled to the sides of the road. Once she had drawn close enough that she could be heard, she started shouting.

"Mama! Mama!" She tried to infuse her voice with the proper amount of feminine distress. As she truly was terrified both for herself and her mother, it didn't require much acting.

The outriders reacted as they had expected, with a few drawing together to face her as the others stayed with the carriage. The carriage itself sped up as she drew near. The first of her tasks done, alerting her mother to their presence, Sabre didn't try too hard to get around the outriders. The last thing she needed was for one of them to grab her reins or start a true confrontation at this point. Now she would move on to her second task and try to keep these four riders occupied as the carriage rolled ever closer to their trap.

She recognized one of the riders and addressed herself to him. "Gavin, you can't keep me from my mother!"

"I'm sorry, Miss Bittlesworth, but your father's orders were clear. Nothing is to stop them."

She swiped at her cheek as though wiping away tears, although the rain made it unnecessary to shed any. "How can he do this to me?" She gave a choking sob. "They say he is planning to stay on the continent. I don't know if I will ever see her again!"

The rider looked uneasily at one of his compatriots. "I'm sure you'll see her again, Miss Bittlesworth."

She sniffed. "How can you say that, Gavin? You know what he's like."

One of the riders narrowed his eyes at her. He had a hardened look that concerned her. "We don't have time for this little bitch's whining."

With his words she could see the attitude of the group shift. He had reminded them that they were not here to listen to the weeping concern of a daughter, but to protect the lord who paid them. This man had no sympathy in his eyes, no softness. Within a few moments he would shift the entire tenor of the group, most likely leaving one rider to control her while the other three rejoined the carriage. As her job was to help draw riders off the carriage, his influence was counterproductive. She drew and fired on him point blank before any of them knew what she was about.

Fortunately her powder was still dry, even with the rain, and her aim true. The rider reeled back, falling off his horse. The poor beast panicked and danced in the mud, stomping on the fallen rider while he writhed and groaned. Sabre held her gun hand up in a neutral position while the remaining outriders drew their pistols on her.

Her demeanor had changed as she said in a deathly still monotone, "We will be retrieving my mother, Gavin. If you try to stop us you will end up like him."

At her use of "we" the riders started looking around frantically, turning their horses in the squelching mud. The carriage was almost out of sight, but one of the outriders that had stayed with it was riding toward them, most likely in response to the sound of gunfire. She had drawn five of them now and hoped that helped. This was far more complicated and nerve-wracking than any game they had ever played. The dying man continued to moan and twitch on the ground as the riders surrounded her, still watching the trees with their guns on her.

The approaching rider called out, "What happened? Did you shoot the girl?"

Gavin called back. "She shot Pinsmail."

Sabre recognized the approaching rider as one of the more senior of her father's guards. "Hullo, Waghorn," she called.

Waghorn swung from his saddle and pushed the loose horse out of the way to check on the fallen rider. Standing he said, "Did you do this, Miss Bittlesworth?"

She found that she couldn't quite make her gaze lower to look at the man she had shot. "I'm here for my mother, Waghorn."

He gave a surprised laugh. "I don't think so, my lady."

She raised a brow at him. "How do you plan to stop me? Would you shoot a nobleman's daughter?"

"Aren't you a cold thing? And here I always thought you took more after m'lady than m'lord."

"An even better question," she said, leaning forward and lowering her voice, "is how do you plan to stop my brother?"

He looked at her, considering. "Well, which brother would that be, miss?"

She smirked. "Either of them. They're both here."

Waghorn took up his reins and made to mount. "Leave her," he ordered, "we need to get back to the carriage."

But the sound of gunfire made it clear that they were too late. The four of them set off at a gallop, leaving her with the dead man. Charlie came trotting out from the cover of the trees. "Are you all right, little bird?"

She nodded and blew out an unsteady breath. "We should go help Robert."

Charlie dismounted to catch the loose horse. "No, I'm charged with ensuring you stay alive. Something, I would like to point out, that you were making fairly difficult. They were too close on you for me to even attempt a shot from any distance." He smiled up at her. "And I didn't have the advantage of your fair sex if I were to close with them."

"They wouldn't want to shoot any of their lord's children."

Charlie laughed. "Second sons are merely inconvenient. Inconvenient to have and inconvenient to lose. You don't fire a servant over an inconvenience."

"Charlie!"

He patted her knee and looked up at her with a smile. "Are you sure you're all right?"

She looked at the horse he was leading. "I will be. Eventually." She looked back in the direction the coach had gone. "Are you sure Robert doesn't need us?"

"It's Robert, dearest. Stop worrying." He mounted his horse and tied the stray to his saddle. "He will send for us when he needs us. But we can walk in that direction if it makes you feel better."

She nodded and started off at a faster pace than Charlie. Then a thought struck her and she looked back. "Do you know what happened to Quince?"

"Quince?" he asked. "Do you mean his grace, Beloin?"

"Yes, the duke. How did he get those cuts and bruises?"

Charlie narrowed his eyes. "What bruises?"

Sabre huffed. "Charlie, just answer the question!"

"I am given to understand that his grace stumbled into a gunpowder plot. A bridge was blown out underneath his carriage."

She gasped. "Was anyone hurt?"

"Two fine greys died, which was quite careless of him. Other than that, not that I've heard of."

As she sat still, silent and frowning, he caught up to her.

"What is it between you and Beloin, then?" he asked.

"I love him, Charlie."

"Any idiot could figure that out. What are his plans?"

"I couldn't say."

"He'll not make you his doxy," he warned.

She smiled at him a bit sadly. "I love him, Charlie," she repeated.

His normally affable expression changed to something colder. "That's how it is, then? If these horses weren't so tired I would ride back to London now to beat him."

"Don't be like that Charlie."

"How do you want me to be, Sabre? You're my sister."

"I know, Charlie, and I hope that as my brother you will stand by my decision, whatever that might be."

He stared ahead, his jaw rigid. "Don't try to manipulate me into your way of thinking. It's wrong and you know it."

"Last month I would have agreed with you. Now…" She lapsed into silence, not sure how to explain her change of heart to her brother. She gave him a rueful smile. "I hope that when you fall in love it isn't so complicated."

"How can you love a man who would treat you like this?" he insisted.

Sabre realized she heard her own judgments of Jack reflected in Charlie's question. "I knew that I was in love with him when I couldn't stand the thought of him being hurt. I left him, thinking that if I broke it off then I would stop caring so much."

"Perhaps you didn't stay away from him long enough."

"It felt like a thousand years." She sighed. "I don't know how to explain it, Charlie. I have to be with him. No matter what."

They heard the sound of hooves in mud and tensed, worried that it might be their father's outriders again. Instead, Robert and his group of men rode into view. The viscountess was seated safely in front of her brother, and her mother's maid was astride a horse with one of his men. Sabre's heart sped in her chest. One small victory out of all the challenges they faced, but such a relief. "Mama!" she said, and heard her own voice break on the word.

"Sabrina! When I heard that shot I was so worried! Your father wouldn't stop the carriage but he sent his man back to check on you."

"I'm fine, mama." She hesitated. "Where is papa?"

Robert answered. "He has gone on to his ship."

"Sabrina and I have procured a horse for you, maman," Charlie said.

Robert raised an eyebrow at his brother and Charlie tipped his head in the direction of the original rider. Robert signaled two of his men to check on the fallen man.

"You know I'm not much for riding, Charlie," the viscountess said.

"Perhaps Sabre will let you double up with her, maman," Robert said. "Even the two of you together are hardly a load for any horse."

"Of course," Sabre said.

Robert dismounted to transfer the viscountess onto the back of Sabre's horse. "Take her to my house," he said. "Charlie, stay with them."

"Of course," his brother replied. He turned the reins of the stray horse over to one of Robert's men. Although some of the men nursed injuries it didn't look like Robert had lost any of them.

Sabre was happy to have her mother secured, but very much wanted to leave for Belle Fleur. Hopefully tomorrow she would be able to get away.

Thirty-Nine

Quince took a moment after visiting with his coachman, staring out the window of his study. The man had been delirious from pain and laudanum. It was impossible to know, even with the best care, if he would survive. It was sobering. Infuriating. Frightening.

"You wanted to speak with me, your grace?" Havers asked quietly.

"Yes," Quince said, turning his attention to the butler. "There is something I need to find and I believe it to be here. It is very important. If I don't find it then... Then I may not be able to keep Miss Bittlesworth and some other people safe."

Havers grew quite attentive when Sabre was mentioned, as Quince had expected. "How may I be of assistance, your grace?"

"I need you to answer some questions about my father."

Quince proceeded to query the butler and the rest of the staff about his father's behavior while in residence at Belle Fleur. It seemed that his father's habits weren't much different than his own. The elder duke would cloister himself in his rooms for hours, sometimes days on end. The only difference was that sometimes when the staff was fairly certain that he was in his room...he wasn't. Not that they had checked under the bed or in the closets. It was frankly odd at times to deliver a tray or some such and find his grace missing.

Although Quince had redecorated the room there had been no reconstruction. If there happened to be a concealed door in the room, it should still exist. He began to search.

After two days of searching Quince doubted his theory. He wasn't sure the last time he had eaten or slept. His only interruption had been to read letters he received from Gideon, letters reassuring him that both Jessica and Sabre were safe in London. He wished that Sabre were here because she would make this mystery solving bearable. But he couldn't have her here if she would be in danger. And that meant he needed to find the evidence that the dragon feared.

His frustration was such that he almost didn't hear the soft click when he pushed on yet another carved wall panel. He stopped and inspected it. Nothing seemed different. Putting both hands on it and attempting to push or slide didn't seem to affect it. He moved his hand down to where it had been the first time he had heard the click and pushed harder. When he released it the panel swung open on silent, hidden hinges. For a moment he just stared at the dark, dusty opening in shock. Then he lit a candle and stepped in.

Sabre loved her family, she really did, but their attempts to keep her from leaving for Belle Fleur almost drove her mad. On the third morning she simply arose early and left as though for a ride in the park. It was a risk traveling alone. However, she made good time and was at the duke's estate before luncheon. She hadn't seen anyone following her from her brother's house, but honestly she didn't really care. Havers opened the door for her and gave her a deep bow.

"Miss Bittlesworth, it is good to have you with us again."

Once over the threshold she couldn't help herself and hugged the old servant. "Thank you, Havers, it's good to be back. Is his grace in residence?"

The old man blushed pink to the tips of his ears but seemed well pleased. "Yes, my lady, he is. In his rooms."

"Very good," she said, and happily trotted up the stairs. She thought to stop in her room first to refresh herself, but after looking through the Rose Room she didn't find any trace of her previous residence. Had Quince sent her things back?

She walked to his suites. It seemed polite to knock, but it would be more fun to reenact that first morning when she had burst into his room and awakened him. This time if he were lying naked to the waist in bed she could do more than just flirt with him. Her mouth watered thinking about what they could do with that scene to play over again.

She opened the door, a smile on her face, but it was immediately evident that the duke was not in bed. The bed didn't even look slept in. She felt warmth in her chest when she saw that her shawl was folded at the foot of it. Then she heard a sob and the sound tore at her heart.

"Quince?" she called, feeling slightly panicked. She entered the room looking for him. She heard another sob and found him opposite the bed, sitting against the wall, knees drawn up to his chest, head down. She knelt down in front of him, rubbing his arms. "Quince, what happened?"

When he looked up at her his green eyes were shockingly bright in their red rims. He shook his head, then straightened his legs to pull her into his lap and buried his face against her shoulder. He held her tightly and she stroked his hair, trying to soothe him. After a few minutes of holding her close his sobs seemed to subside and he loosened his hold a bit. He lifted his head again to press his forehead against hers.

She framed his face in her hands. "What has happened, Quince?"

He shook his head. She wrapped her arms around him and tried to be patient while waiting for him to talk.

Finally, after long minutes, he cleared his throat and said in a husky voice, "I found the papers."

For a moment she was elated that another of their goals had been met. But why, then, was he so upset? She knew that he wasn't one to be rushed and tried to think of the best way to prompt him to give her more information. Before she could settle on a strategy he sat back against the wall, looking at her. He skimmed his fingers lightly over her cheek and jaw.

"You came back to me."

"I told you I would meet you here."

He kissed her hand. "How did your mission fare? Gideon wrote to confirm you made it back to London, but he didn't have details."

"Mama is safe at Robert's house. Papa should be somewhere on the continent now."

"No one was injured?"

She frowned. "No one in our party."

He was quiet for some time, just staring at her and running his fingers along her skin. His expression was bleak.

"Quince, what happened?"

He looked over at the wall as though something was there, but it just looked like a wall to her. "I really don't want you to read them, but I'm not sure I can read any more."

She scooted out of his lap and stood up. "Show them to me."

His eyes looked haunted. "You don't want to see them."

"I do. Where are they?"

He seemed to mull her request another moment, pulling his knees up to his chest again. "I'll let you read one or two. So that you can see what we're dealing with. And we can discuss what we want to do next."

With his title and connections Quince had the right to feel like one of the most powerful men in England but he seemed ill at ease. What on earth had he found in those papers? "Quince, you're worrying me."

He sighed and finally stood up. She followed him to the door she had left open, thinking that he was leading her out, but he simply closed it. She bumped into him in surprise. He reached out to steady her and they stood there for a moment, his hand lingering on her arm as he looked down on her solemnly. She stepped forward to wrap her arms around his waist, to feel his arms around her shoulders. He rested his cheek on top of her head and she finally felt him relax a bit.

"It's probably better if we get this over with and you just show me," she said, her voice muffled against his chest. He gave a short, bitter laugh and released her, walking back over to the wall she had seem him staring at earlier. He pushed on the panel and it sprung open. It surprised a short laugh from her. "A secret door!"

The smile he gave her was anything but mirthful. A grimace, really. She regretted her playful outburst and schooled her expression to be more somber. He lit a candle and gestured for her to precede him into the dark space. She stepped in, not even having to stoop, and in the dim light could see that it was a small but tidy office space. There was a desk and bookcases, all covered with a fine film of dust. A portion of the desk had been disturbed and had a disorganized stack of papers on it. She walked over to read them, but couldn't see the handwriting for lack of light.

"Bring the candle over," she murmured. Quince pulled the panel shut behind them, making it even dimmer yet, then came to set the candle on the desk next to the papers. Sabre's first impression was how much the document reminded her of the gardening journal she had updated. She recognized his father's handwriting and the template of date followed by short observations. But the subject matter was far different from gardening. She dug through the papers, stopping every third or fourth sheet to see that it was more of the same. Dark, disturbing information jotted down like observations about how the roses had wintered. She could feel the air backing up in her lungs. "My heavens, do you think this is all true?"

Quince had withdrawn to lean against the wall, arms folded. "If it is, if we can verify enough of it. They will all hang."

Sabre felt her heart beat heavily in her chest. Her father had escaped the country just in time. "How much of this did you read?"

"Not much. Enough. Murder, treason, stealing from the Crown..."

She looked around the room. "We need to go through it all. We need to know-"

"No!" Quince pushed away from the wall. "We don't need to know! Our fathers were monsters. Their friends were monsters. The only use we have for this is ridding ourselves of the dragon."

"But Quince-"

"No." His voice rang with finality. He picked up the candle, opened the panel, and signaled her to exit. She stepped back out into the bright mid-day light of his bedroom. The mood between them was tense, but she preferred his anger to the misery she had seen when she arrived.

"Have you had luncheon?" he asked, obviously grasping for the comfort of the mundane in polite exchange.

She shook her head. "I haven't even breakfasted."

He checked his pocket watch. "It should be served shortly if you would like for me to escort you downstairs."

"I was hoping to change but my clothing was no longer in my room."

He gave her an odd smile. "Of course your clothing is in your room."

She frowned at him. "I went there first and couldn't find anything."

"I suppose we should check again." He took her hand and rather than leading her to the hallway he led her through the sitting room and to the duchess's suite.

She poked his ribs. "You could have said something."

He raised a brow at her. "This wasn't the room you checked?"

"You know it wasn't."

He settled his arms loosely around her. "I was fairly certain you had claimed it the first day you were here."

Rather than answer she leaned into him and kissed his neck.

He sighed, relaxing a bit in her embrace. "Strange, but at the time I thought this room would mean you were too close. Now I think it is too far away. A shared sitting room is charming, but I would want you closer. At least our rooms in London are side by side."

Sabre looked up at him. His wit had returned, but his eyes were still shadowed and reddened. Although she was content breathing in his scent, warming under his touch, she truly was hungry. "I need to change," she said. He took a step back and began unbuttoning her riding jacket. Once he had removed it his fingers were slower in unbuttoning her shirtwaist. Although she could tell from his eyes, his breathing, that he wanted her, he simply removed all of her dusty riding apparel and set it aside, leaving her standing in her undergarments. Taking her hand he led her to the dressing room and the limited number of dresses she had to choose from.

"Which would you prefer?" she asked softly.

"Today? Perhaps the blue. Today needs as much innocence as we can give it."

He helped her don the dress with the same gentle patience he had used to undress her. She found that his sweet and loving care was undoing her more than any seduction could. Once she was dressed they walked hand in hand down to the dining room.

Forty

Although there were still many dangers, Sabre felt overall better about their strategic position. When she had quit Belle Fleur, it had been in fear that Quince was going to get himself killed, that he wasn't even using the resources they had available. Now they had a good number of allies in play with the Harringtons and her brothers. They had in hand the evidence that The Four seemed so anxious to keep from emerging into the light of day. Cygnus, her father, had left the country so his influence was at the very least severely diminished. The only thing left to discover, and it did give her pause to not know it yet, was who Draco was and what resources he had.

She hoped that going through the papers would yield some clue. Everything she had seen continued the tradition of only listing them by their names in The Four, but certainly there would be something. A reference to a location, a personality quirk, a physical trait. Something. Anything that would help them to identify Draco and Ursa.

Quince watched Sabre as she picked through the offerings on her plate. She seemed relatively undisturbed by the documents he had uncovered. He, however, was still disturbed. Deeply disturbed. He was, in fact, already on his second glass of wine with luncheon and strongly considering finishing off the bottle before trying to do anything else.

Sabre had opted for lemonade and seemed absorbed in her own thoughts. Should it bother him, he wondered, that she seemed unaffected by the morbid nature of the documents they had reviewed? The details were listed with the same detachment as a grain report, but in some ways that made it all the more horrifying.

29 April, 1794 ~ Draco brought a girl child he found in the London streets. He wanted to keep her at the Cellar but I said no.

What on earth had happened to that child? There had been no further mention of her that he had seen. He didn't want to think about the other entries where the disposition of women and children were much clearer. The Four's disregard for human life, for basic humanity, was staggering.

His father had always criticized him for being too sensitive, too gentle. And perhaps that was true. Because as he steadily made his way though this wine to dull his senses, a girl barely out of the schoolroom sat across from him without a seeming worry in the world.

"How old are you?" Quince asked.

Sabre looked at him and raised a brow. "Why do you ask?"

"Because I'm curious." He could hear the edge to his own voice and almost winced at it himself.

She stared at him a moment more. "Nineteen," she finally answered.

Nineteen? God's teeth, she was so young. He remembered himself at that age. Naive. Idealistic. Were the tables turned and his attraction had been to an older woman when he himself had been nineteen, he would have been a slave. He had to respect her firmness of mind in comparison.

"What's wrong, Quince?" she prompted.

"I didn't realize you were so young."

She gave him a flirtatious smile. "I thought men liked younger women."

"I can't speak for all men. For myself, I find a variety of women beautiful. But I have only ever wanted you."

That made her smile, but she was also looking progressively worried. "Quince, why are you being so serious?"

"Is there not enough to be serious about?"

"I've thought so for some time, but it didn't seem to matter to you before."

He stared at her and she returned his regard. He finally answered, "This is a very serious game and I don't want to lose any of you."

She cocked her head to one side. "It's a game?"

"It is to Draco. A game where the prize is more power and wealth. He thinks that his most recent winnings include the obedience of a duke." Quince could feel a cold fury even contemplating that. "But having played so deep he has set himself up with much to lose."

"If we can identify him."

"We will identify him. Then the question becomes what we do with him."

"After what we know he has done? Turn him over to the Crown for punishment. He'll be hanged in a fortnight."

"Giving him a fortnight to exact revenge. Even the most closely held prisoner can't be kept from everyone. He would find a way to plan what he would consider a fitting retribution. I shudder to think what that might be."

Sabre was quiet for a moment. "We could kill him outright."

Quince studied her. She had withdrawn to a blank, unreadable expression again. His little chameleon could be so good at only showing others what she wanted them to see. Did even he really know her? It would do well to remember that fairy queens were not known for their sympathy with the troubles of mortal men. Yet their wisdom often transcended that of the material world, as well. "I've considered it. But I don't think I want that on my conscience."

"Then that leaves us at something of an impasse."

Quince nodded. "And one we must resolve immediately. I plan to leave for Bath in the morning to see if Mother can help us to identify him."

Sabre looked down at her plate for a moment, pushing peas around with her fork. "One concern I have is that, with all the documents in one place, it is that much easier to destroy the evidence. If he has infiltrated the other houses, why not this one? And if he has an agent here we need to act quickly to secure what evidence we have."

"What do you suggest?"

"We have such a great deal of it that we should parse it out to a number of people for safekeeping. At least Robert and Gideon should be asked to hold enough of it to condemn him. Is there anyone else you trust to hold some as well?"

"It is of no use until we can prove a connection between their code names and real names, so couldn't anyone hold the papers?"

"Perhaps, but I would keep it fairly close if you are able."

"Then an additional packet to my man of business in London, with instruction to secure it in his vault and not open it unless he receives notice from one of us."

Sabre nodded, seeming pleased with the plan. "Shall I compile a suitable packet for each of them?"

The duke stared at her for a moment. Should he be worried that she remained unconcerned about the nature of the papers? The atrocities that they held? Of should he just be relieved that someone he trusted was willing to handle a job he wasn't sure he could accomplish himself? He entertained the thought of letting her take control of the issue and felt himself relax. He even found he didn't care for any more wine.

"Yes, if you wouldn't mind doing that it would be very helpful."

She smiled and gave him a brisk nod. "Would you like for me to select the messengers?"

"As you seem to know the staff better than I do, that would be appreciated."

"Then if you will excuse me, I will get started so that everything will be ready before you leave in the morning as I will need you to seal the cover letters."

"Of course." He rose when she did, as a gentleman should. Then she was gone.

Sabre diligently worked at creating four stacks of papers. She wanted to ensure that each had at least one example of each type of crimes for which Draco and Ursa were accountable. She worked to minimize the evidence against her father except in the stack she designated as being bound for Robert. If anyone were to pass judgment on him, let it be his son. She also tried to minimize any information about Leo himself. If the evidence were to come to light it wouldn't do to embarrass the duchy any more than necessary. However, she noted, his sins were either lighter than that of his companions, or he had been clever enough not to document all of his own perfidy.

Some of the details in the papers were unimaginably gruesome. She couldn't decide if they were more or less breathtakingly horrible because of the cold, detached way in which they were recorded. The complete lack of compassion inherent in the former duke's writing was startling. He documented Draco strangling a young woman with the same tone as he might have a killing frost on the rose garden.

She had become so engrossed in her work that she startled when there was a knock at the panel. Almost calling out, she realized that if it wasn't Quince she shouldn't betray the location of this room. She waited until she heard his voice.

"Sabre? Are you in there?"

"Yes. Do you need me to open the panel?"

Rather than respond he simply opened it and stepped in, closing it behind himself. As there was only the one chair she was sitting in, he sat on the floor next to her with his back to the desk. "Are you doing all right?"

She bit her lip but gave him a determined smile. "Well enough."

He rested his hand on her knee, caressing her through the light muslin. "Thank you for doing this."

"Of course." His simple touch lightened her mood immensely. Perhaps no task was too horrible as long as she had Quince. She leaned down and kissed the top of his head.

He gave her a wan smile. "What was that for?"

"Being here. It's easier when you're here."

His fingers stopped their idle stroking for a moment and he looked up at her curiously. "This does bother you?"

"The only person it wouldn't bother is someone capable of doing such things as are described." She gave a delicate shudder. "It's hard for me to even imagine that we are related to two of them. Conversations between you and your father must have been strange indeed."

He smiled sadly. "We certainly didn't speak the same language. What of you and your father?"

"I know as well as anyone how to handle him. But I never would have suspected..." she made a sweeping motion to include the papers, "this. It would have made me much more circumspect in my dealings with him."

Quince nodded. "I imagine so."

Sabre went back to her work but after a few moments the duke spoke again. "Do you think we should consider sending something to the Prime Minister? Or the Prince Reagent?"

"At this stage? We might just elicit questions we wouldn't want to answer."

Quince frowned but nodded again.

"What are you worried about?"

"These are extraordinarily dangerous men and one of them has directly threatened my mother and sister." More soberly he added, "And I must be careful revealing my attachment to you or you will be in danger as well. Otherwise I would take you to Bath with me."

Sabre felt her heart warm at his suggestion that he would take her with him. It had hurt when he had said *'I plan to leave for Bath,'* making it clear with his tone and words that she wasn't to go. Her fear was that he didn't want to introduce his mistress to his mother. But it was because he was trying to protect her. Silly man. "Well, he already thinks he knows your intentions towards me. If he is there, he will only be vastly entertained to see that you have landed me. And," she said, preparing to deliver her *coup de grâce*, "if he *is* there, I am the only one who can recognize him on sight. And he doesn't know that. What a tremendous strategic advantage you're wasting."

He stared at her for a moment, then took her hand and kissed it. "Sabre, would you like to go to Bath with me?"

"Why yes, Quince, I would."

His expression turned somber in the flickering candlelight. "Promise me that you won't get hurt."

"If I thought we had control over that I would make you promise me the same."

"Well, I suppose there is that." He sighed. "Would you agree to have supper with me? I had planned a special meal for what might be our last evening together."

"You thought to salve leaving me with a fancy meal?"

"Indeed. You were to be swept away with the romance and grandeur of it. Actually, I've asked them to set the table in our sitting room again. Certainly you can't say no to that."

"Yes, Quince, I would love to sup with you."

Sabre was once again surprised at Quince's ability to set aside his worries and enjoy the moment. At first she resisted the idea of simply enjoying herself. But they were in an immensely better position, strategically, than they had been before. In the parlance of her old game War, they occupied their own hill now, and were fortified with troops and artillery. Certainly she could take a few hours to focus on her beloved. And he was correct, everything could go horribly wrong on the morrow and this could be their last evening together. What if another attempt was made on Quince's life? Since she was traveling with him she was equally at risk. Any such attempt could kill one or both of them.

If ever there was a time to simply appreciate being with the man she loved, it was now.

She looked at him across the candlelit table and wondered at the love she felt for him. Today he wasn't the dapper and perfectly turned out duke, but the casual country gentleman that had become her favorite version of him. His eyes sparkled as he told her amusing anecdotes from the various *ton* events he had attended over the years. Everything about him drew her. His wit, his gentleness, his confidence in his own authority. She would never regret this, she knew. She would never regret being with him any way she could be. Reputation and Society be damned. She might never again socialize at a ball, but he would tell her stories about it that would make her feel like she had been there. And certainly Jack and George would never desert her. She hoped.

He stood and held out his hand to her. "Would you care to repair to the balcony?"

She nodded and took his hand. The warmth of his touch was both comforting and thrilling. He led her to the balustrade and trapped her between the railing and himself. She could feel the heat of him against her back as she looked out at the stars.

"Do you have a favorite star?" he asked, his voice low and intimate.

She laughed. "Not particularly."

"All right, then which one do you think is the prettiest?"

She looked out at the blanket of stars. "Hmm. That one," she said, pointing. "The brightest star in Lynx."

"You mean this one?" He reached past her pointing hand and made a plucking motion. When he brought his hand back he presented a ring to her.

Even in the dim light she could see that it was an outrageously lovely ring. A large light-colored stone surrounded by smaller stones. She wasn't sure what it meant. It could mean everything. It could mean nothing. "Thank you," she said, making sure to infuse her voice with delight. But she wasn't feeling delight, it was something more like panic as her mind warred over whether it was a gift to a beloved mistress...or something more.

"You aren't very good at hints, are you?"

She refused to permit her hopes to rise. Refused. But she could feel a bubble of hope already. "What do you mean?"

He sighed and moved so that he was standing next to her. He still held onto the ring. "What is your middle name?"

Now she was confused. "What?"

"What is your middle name?" he repeated patiently.

"Tündér."

"I'm sorry, it's what?"

"Tündér. It was one of my grandmother's names." When he raised a brow at her she said, "It's Hungarian. It means fairy."

He chuckled, apparently amused. "Of course it does." She wasn't sure whether or not to be offended.

Then he gently took her left hand in his and sank to one knee. She felt her heart start to race, her breathing quicken.

"Sabrina Tündér Bittlesworth, would you do me the great honor of being my wife? My duchess?"

She felt lightheaded and her throat was choked with impending tears of joy. She wasn't sure she could speak.

"It's customary to give an answer," Quince prompted.

"Yes," she whispered. He slipped the ring onto her finger with a smile and then rose to kiss her.

302

Forty-One

Quince awoke with something tickling his nose. Sabre was sleeping with her back pressed against him. He smoothed her hair and then let his hand wander over her shoulder to the dip of her waist and on to the flare of her hip. His beautiful, beautiful fiancée. He should make it official by talking to Robert. But then again they had already negotiated. If he wasn't mistaken he should get two of Charlie's best carriage horses, as well. Of course, that was if he took her as his mistress. As a wife there was most likely a dowry. Hopefully it would be enough to give her some spending money. One of his greatest fears for their marriage was not being able to provide for her in the style she was accustomed to. Although she seemed more than capable of making do when necessary, what he had seen of her wardrobe indicated a wealth that he did not currently possess.

She stirred in her sleep, rolling over to snuggle against him. He wasn't sure if she was truly awake until she kissed his chest and gave a contented sigh.

He kissed her temple. "Good morning, love."

Her lips turned up in a smile although her eyes were still closed. "Good morning, love."

"Will you be ready to travel today?"

"Of course."

He trailed a finger over the silken skin on her arm. "Would you mind…"

She opened her eyes and gave him a saucy smile. "Probably not."

He chuckled. "I was going to ask if you would draft letters for me to sign, but perhaps your idea is more interesting."

She sat up. "I would be happy to. What time is it? Should we do that now?"

"You realize you're rather exhaustingly industrious, don't you?"

She poked him in the ribs. "And we're lucky I am if you can't even be bothered to draft your own letters."

He caught her hand to keep her from poking at him again and raised her fingers to his lips for a kiss. He frowned briefly. "If we want to leave today it would be best to leave the writing to you."

She teased, "Do you sit waiting for your Muse to whisper in your ear?"

"No. I…" Quince paused. It was difficult to talk about. "I've never written or read very well. It's odd. I'm much better off hearing information than reading it. Sad, because I happen to adore poetry."

Her brows drew down. "But you left me a note once. It seemed to be in a fine hand."

He smiled briefly. "I didn't want to wake you for fear that you would insist on going with me. But what you could have dashed off in mere seconds took me almost five minutes."

She frowned. "Oh. That's why you have Gideon oversee your accounts, isn't it?"

"Part of the reason. He's also brilliant at it. Why struggle with something for hours that he can do ten times as well in mere moments?"

"Is that fair to him, though?"

"Beg pardon?"

"I've stayed with them. Gideon works endlessly. Are you sure he has time to oversee your accounts?"

Quince frowned. "He's never complained about it."

Sabre sighed. "Yes, your grace."

"That is becoming horribly effective. If you think I'm being ridiculous what do you suggest I do?"

"Obviously I will need to work toward taking over the role from Gideon. You need do very little other than support your wife's authority over the estates and accounts."

He squeezed her hand. "Thank you, Sabrina."

That made her beam at him again. "I will most likely enjoy it."

"Undoubtedly."

"But this morning we have letters to write, packets to prepare, and trunks to pack. That means you need to get up."

"Exhaustingly industrious," he repeated.

"Your insults will find no purchase on me. Arise before I decide to do something dire."

It had been some time since Sabre had experienced butterflies, but apparently the thought of meeting Quince's mother made her nervous. As soon as the carriage had rolled to a stop she had felt tightness in her chest and jumpiness in her belly. Quince was understandably distracted by his need to check on his family, but he did take a moment to squeeze her hand as he helped her down from the carriage. She gave him a smile that she hoped was as bright and supportive as she meant it to be.

The front door opened before they had gained the top step and a butler bowed them into the foyer. Almost immediately a boy raced out from the hallway.

"Quince!"

The duke caught the lad up in a hug. "Hullo, Thomas."

"Hullo, Quince. I told them it was you, but they didn't believe me."

Sabre saw movement in the hallway and a woman and young man emerged. There was indeed no denying that this was Quincy Telford's mother. Their hair was almost precisely the same shade. The shape of the face, the arch of their eyebrows. She even moved in a similar way.

The look she gave her son was one of pure adoration. "Quincy! You weren't expected. What a lovely surprise." She kissed his cheek.

If Quincy looked exactly like his mother, then the young man next to her must look more like their father. He was broader of face with a more saturnine countenance. The duke extended a hand to him. "Jeremy."

"Quince," he said, shaking hands with his brother, "so good to see you." His voice was surprisingly melodious, especially for his age. Her younger brother Justin struggled to keep his voice from cracking at inopportune times.

Then the duke was looking at her and holding out his hand for her to step forward. Once she had, he said, "Mother, I would like for you to meet Miss Sabrina Bittlesworth, my fiancée. Sabre, my mother, the Duchess of Beloin."

Sabre curtsied. "Your grace."

Quince stifled a snort and his mother looked at him curiously for a moment before turning her attention back to Sabre. "It's lovely to meet you, dear. These are my other sons, Jeremy and Thomas."

Both of them bowed and Sabre curtsied again in return.

"Quince," his mother said, "I'm sure the boys would love to show you the model of Bath they have been building."

Jeremy rolled his eyes, clearly indicating that he was far too mature to have found model building interesting. But Thomas lit up with enthusiasm and started pulling on Quince's hand. "Oh yes! You should see it! Jeremy has done all the fine bits, but I'll show you the parts I did."

Within seconds Sabre was alone in the foyer with the duchess.

"We can have a nice coze," the older woman said, threading her arm through Sabre's and leading her down the hallway at a leisurely pace. "How was your journey? Did you come from London?"

Sabre wasn't sure if the duchess was just being idly friendly or hoping to elicit some desired information. Perhaps both. "The weather was lovely for our drive, although it is hard to leave London this time of year. So many social obligations."

The duchess sighed and patted Sabre's arm. "Is your mother in residence then? I should call on her for congratulations."

"She... She isn't receiving callers just now." Having spent so much time with Quince, Sabre was able to see the subtle signs of the duchess's withdrawal.

"Of course. I don't go to London often at any rate."

Sabre stopped and turned to the duchess, taking both of her hands. "Please, your grace, don't think it is you." She looked up and down the hallway, and then leaned in to whisper conspiratorially. "Would you like to hear a secret?"

The duchess seemed amused, with a furrowed brow and curious smile. She nodded.

Still whispering Sabre said, "My family doesn't know I'm engaged yet."

"But..."The duchess, realizing she was using a normal tone also dropped her voice to a whisper. "But then you aren't really engaged."

Sabre arched her brow. "My father has fled to the continent pending legal issues and my older brother knows that if he tries to deny me this that I will run him through. There are no other formalities to consider."

The duchess burst out with a delighted laugh.

"However," Sabre said, "I do think that my mother would take the news best directly from me. Even though she has been expecting it."

"I think you and I shall get along splendidly. And I will wait until you tell me I can call on your mother."

"Thank you. I just... I knew that you had been a bit isolated here and didn't want you think..."

"That was very kind of you, dearest," the duchess said, continuing to lead her down the hallway. They entered a lovely and intimate parlor. The house wasn't particularly large, but had a comfort and grace to be envied. "Perhaps a spot of tea?"

"Thank you, that would be wonderful."

Sabre sat and continued to look around the room. It was filled with art, soft fabrics, and furniture that one could sink into. The colors were muted and blended together in a gentle palette. Not at all a typical modern English parlor. It reminded her of the subtle grandeur she had once seen at a castle she had visited.

The duchess smiled. "This is where our family hides away from the world when we can."

"I like it," Sabre said. "Very much."

"Tell me about yourself, Miss Bittlesworth."

"What would you like to know?"

The duchess thanked the young woman who brought in their tea and then began to pour. "Oh, I don't know. What are your hobbies and interests? What is your family like?"

Sabre accepted her cup. "You probably deserve a more candid answer than the one I would give most of the *ton*."

"I might appreciate that, yes."

"Quince and I came to know each other over our shared love of fencing."

"Oh! That's an unusual sport for a lady. Bravo to you, dear!"

"Thank you."

"Do you practice it or only admire the sport?"

"I practice it. Although of late I have not been spending the time on it as I should."

"No? What have you been doing instead?"

Sabre realized the trap she had accidentally designed for herself and thought quickly to keep from admitting that Quince had been her primary diversion. "Traveling. My brother was indulgent enough to take me on his Tour with him and we spent eight months on the continent."

"How unusual. Was it just the two of you?"

"My mother went as well." Sabre laughed as she recalled, "Charlie, my brother, said she was all that stood between me and conquering at least one small nation on our travels."

The duchess laughed again. "Quince told you just what to say to entertain me, didn't he?"

"No, but he did say that he thought we would find an accord."

"Indeed! I wish that I'd had half your confidence and experience at your age."

Sabre frowned. "It couldn't have been easy, being married to the duke."

The duchess paused. "No, of course not. But we shan't dwell on it."

"Quince tells me that you hold a salon."

"Yes, each week. It will be tomorrow night."

"How fortuitous! He also told me that you dislike Gideon Wolfe, something I must approve of. Although I find that Gideon is growing on me."

The duchess scowled. "Probably for the best, since I find Quincy to be immovable on the subject of his friend."

"Gideon happens to have married my best friend. As Jack is also stubborn on the subject of her husband, it does seem that my best course of action is to make do."

"I wish you the best of luck on that, dear, as I find him to be odiously overbearing. Is that how you met Quincy, then, through your friends?"

"Strangely, no. They had planned to introduce us at their ball but we met at my brother's house before that."

"Then I suppose it was meant to be."

"You believe in fate?"

The duchess's fingers worried the corner of the throw pillow next to her. "Not necessarily. But as I've aged I've begun to wonder. There is often more afoot in the world than I can account for."

The boys came tumbling in at that point. Thomas had to tell his mother every detail of what Quince had asked about the model and how it had been answered. The duchess was finally able to distract him with tea and biscuits. Jeremy asked polite questions such as one expected at a tea, to which Sabre gave her more usual answers. The duke was quiet but seemed to be enjoying the intimate family scene. It reminded Sabre of spending time with the Walters. Jack's family had been her model of what a close, loving family looked like.

As their light repast wound to a close and the duchess set to ensuring that her guests were housed, Sabre was reminded that she would be spending the nights here without Quince's company. This would need to be a short engagement, she thought. Being constantly separated from him for propriety would shortly become tiresome.

Forty-Two

Quince waved away his valet. It wasn't like this was a formal London ball, just his mother's salon of bluestockings from the region. Sabre had convinced him that they shouldn't talk to his mother about Draco's identity yet, lest it should make her nervous and tip their hand if he should be there tonight. His fiancée remained convinced that she could recognize him. And Quince himself was convinced that he would recognize the voice again.

"Aren't you ready yet?" his brother asked.

Quince looked over to where Jeremy was sitting in a chair near the window, holding a book he had been reading until he lost patience. The most entertaining part of staying at his mother's house was that she didn't particularly treat him as a duke. While here he roomed with his brother and received very little special treatment, but a lot of familial affection. As much as he enjoyed spending time with his family, he missed being alone with his fiancée. Last night Sabre was in Jessica's room. It had been difficult not to go to her, but he couldn't imagine anything more beastly than making love in his sister's bed. And no matter his intentions he was sure that if he went to her that is exactly what they would end up doing. Of course, he didn't have to imagine more beastly things, he had read about them. Had some of that documentation with him now.

"Perhaps," he replied drily. In some ways his relationship with Jeremy was strained. The young man had grown up as the oldest brother, the man of the house. Having an older brother appear, and a duke no less, after all those years seemed to be a source of some frustration. But he would grant Jeremy that the young man was generally respectful. "You could go down without me, you know."

"Then they would only ask me where you are. Why invite that?"

"Why indeed? Fortunately I find myself ready."

Jeremy set his book aside and rose.

"One thing," Quince said.

Jeremy stopped and waited with an expectant look on his face.

The duke took a deep breath. It was hard to know exactly how much information to trust Jeremy with. But as of the prior week he was Quince's heir. It was possible that Quince owed him all the details. If not now, then later. "There could be unpleasantness this evening. It would mean a great deal to me if you would ensure that mother and Sabre are safe."

Jeremy narrowed his eyes. "What sort of unpleasantness?"

"That's difficult to say. But if a certain person is here, there will be a confrontation. May I rely on you to see to the ladies?"

"Of course."

Quince nodded and walked to the door.

"What sort of name is Sabre, anyway?" Jeremy asked.

The duke chuckled and put an arm over his brother's shoulders. "The name of your soon to be sister-in-law."

When Sabre saw Quince on the stairs she stepped up to him to whisper in his ear as Jeremy moved past her and into the room. "He's here."

The duke looked worried. "If anything should happen, if there is a confrontation, will you ensure that my mother and brothers are safe?"

"Of course." She stood near him for a moment more. He smelled heavenly.

He leaned closer and whispered, his warm breath tickling her ear and neck. "Which one is he?"

"Brown jacket, buff breeches. He's exceptionally unexceptional tonight."

Quince risked a quick kiss on her ear. "I love you. Please be careful this evening."

"You as well," she admonished.

He squeezed her hand and then stepped away to enter the drawing room.

Sabre stayed on the steps for a moment longer. She still wasn't entirely sure what Quince planned to do with Draco.

The evenings of his mother's salons were, by *ton* standards, extraordinarily casual affairs. A few select guests were invited to arrive early and enjoy some drawing room conversation followed by a meal. After that, more guests would arrive and the topic for evening debate would be raised. He had attended her salons twice before. They were interesting, but required a level of interaction with others that he generally didn't prefer.

The evenings were so casual, in fact, that guests weren't even announced at the door. He simply strolled into the drawing room and over to his mother's side.

"Hullo, mum," he said, kissing her hand.

"Hullo, Quince. I would like to introduce you to my gentle-man friend." She turned to the man standing near her and the duke felt a chill go through him at what her words might mean. If Robert were correct and the dragon ascribed his own motiva-tions to Quince's relationship with Sabre, and if this truly were the dragon as Sabre suspected it was… The conclusion sent a flare of anger burning through him so terrible he was sur-prised fire didn't spit from his eyes. His mother continued the introduction with an indulgent smile at her 'gentleman friend'. "Quince, may I introduce Lord Granby, Baron of Glenmar. Lord Granby, my son Quincy Telford, Duke of Beloin."

Glenmar bowed but Quince said sharply. "We've met, mother."

The baron straightened with a look of mild surprise. "Oh, your grace?"

The baron was a man of middling height and unremarkable style. His features, his manner of dress, even his body language, all spoke of being quite ordinary. If Sabre hadn't identified him, hadn't said that Draco was exceptionally unexceptional tonight, then Quince would not have suspected this man of anything.

"Yes," Quince said with a forced smile, "don't you recall? At the Harrington affair. We spoke about gardens."

Quince saw the barest narrowing of the baron's eyes. "Perhaps you've mistaken me for someone else, your grace."

No, it was the same voice. Pitched differently for current company, but the same voice. "Do you think?" Quince asked. "That's unfortunate because I have recently received the most excellent advice on how to get rid of snakes that are in one's garden. If I could find the man I was speaking to that night it would be very important information for him to have."

"Would it indeed?"

The dragon had an enormous amount of control. He barely betrayed himself by a twitch. But Quince knew the man had to be furious. Undoubtedly he had come here to gloat over the control he had gained by threatening the family of a duke. Now Quince was here to throw it all back in his face. It would do well to remember that there was nothing, literally nothing, that this man was not capable of.

Across the room Sabre saw Quince staring down Draco. This couldn't be good, she thought. Starting a conflict with the man when there were so many innocents on the field? And who knew what lackeys Draco had, either in the room or nearby? It was a recipe for collateral disaster. But she wasn't quite sure how to mitigate the damage as of yet. Trying to make the other guests leave when they saw no potential danger would be difficult to say the least.

At this point the best she could do was watch and look for opportunities. If Quince pointed himself at the vanguard then she would need to guard his flank and rear. And his family, as he had asked. With a small sigh she wished they had brought their swords down to supper.

Forty-Three

Quince clutched his wine glass with such tension he was almost afraid of breaking it. The dragon had thus far refused to be baited, and now they sat at the table across from one another. The dining room was cozy compared to most of the ducal properties. The table only seated ten and the fireplace was so close to his back that he was glad it wasn't winter, when a crackling fire would most likely be unpleasantly hot behind him.

It was customary to spend more time speaking to the guests on your right and left than across the table, so he had yet to speak to the dragon since sitting down. Sabre sat to Quince's right, but was currently entertaining the guest to her other side. Jeremy was across the table and to Draco's left. It gave Quince some pause to have his brother so close to the man. Baron Granby.

Now that knowledge of Draco's identity had been revealed it wasn't possible to let him leave this evening without a resolution. Hopefully a resolution that included the baron leaving England and never coming back. Or, better yet, one where the baron died from some tragic accident and was never able to harm anyone else again. Quince wasn't at peace with simply exiling the man since it was clear he would continue to hurt others. It was how the man was made, it was a sickness. But the duke wasn't willing to risk the safety of his family and he had no doubt that turning the baron over to the Crown for punishment would only lead to unpleasant retribution. And try as he might, Quince wasn't comfortable electing to pass judgment and kill the man outright. Or even by proxy, as he knew Robert would see the job done. That only left him with the option of driving the baron away. Convincing the dragon that leaving the duke's loved ones alone was the safest course of action. That for the dragon to do otherwise was to risk his own life.

Now was not a time to wait. Not a time to observe. It was a time to act. Before the dragon could do more harm to his loved ones. A thought that only made him wonder what sort of relationship the baron had with his mother. Quince glanced down the table to where his mother sat at one end. It was another point to her egalitarianism that she had seated her son, the duke, mid-table rather than at the head. How friendly had she been with the dragon? Had the bastard touched her? More? Even contemplating such a thing made his blood boil again. He took a deep breath. Rage, although justified, could be deadly when confronting such a cold and vicious opponent. He took a moment to center himself, absorbing the buzzing voices at the table. Listening to Sabre chatting with her neighbor. Listening to his brother talk with the dragon.

"Lord Granby," Quince called across the table. "Who else have you decided is a mark from the present company? I'm sure you aren't wasting your time here. Or perhaps you are. Intellectuals aren't known for their wealth as a general rule."

Quince saw Jeremy furrow his brow. The baron, however, remained calm. But that calm had now iced over a bit. "I think perhaps you have had too much of that wine, your grace."

"I doubt that I've had quite enough. Driving snakes from one's garden is thirsty work."

"Quincy," his mother's voice came from her end of the table. "What are you doing?"

"Dealing with a pest, mother. Don't worry yourself."

The rest of the company had fallen silent and watched uneasily and the baron finally spoke again. "What are you hoping to gain, your grace?"

"I have nothing to gain," Quince corrected. "I'm only going to point out what you have to lose. I haven't gone digging in your garden, you see. But I did go digging in my own. And the things I have found there, the papers, are shocking."

At last. The dragon's eyes narrowed to slits. His expression changed from bland insouciance to repressed rage. A dark flush stained his cheeks.

"The rest of you may be excused," Quince said, relying on the authority of his station to be granted their compliance. "Baron Granby and I have some things to discuss."

The guests rose. Granby lurched from his seat and snaked an arm around Jeremy's throat, pressing a knife under the boy's chin. "You have made a terrible mistake, little hedgehog."

The duchess screamed, "Jeremy!"

Quince seized an iron poker from the fireplace and leapt on top of the table, knocking over wine glasses and crushing them under his feet, the red liquid spreading out under his boots and staining the tablecloth crimson. He pointed the poker at Draco's head. "If you harm my brother I can guarantee you will not survive this evening. That's ultimately what you want, isn't it Granby? To survive? If so, there is only one way you will be permitted to do that."

The dragon spit towards Quince's boots. "How dare you threaten me? You are weak. Soft. You were a disappointment to your father."

"My father never understood me. And luckily for him, I never understood him either. Had I known what you all were truly capable of then this day of judgment would have come much sooner." He took another step forward, crunching broken glass and china underfoot. "Because believe me when I say that you have been judged. And found guilty. The only way that you will continue your miserable, execrable life is, like all pests, by scuttling into the darkness. By leaving England and never darkening our shores again, either in person or by your influence. Should any harm come to me and mine I will kill you. Should I die, the men, powerful men, who hold documentation of your murder and treason are instructed to take it to the Crown and you can rest assured that your deeds will find you hanged. Certainly you know that Cygnus' son hates you as much as I do and would not hesitate to see you ended."

"Why should I even believe that you have found papers? That there are any papers?"

Quince used his off hand to reach into his vest pocket, withdrawing one piece of paper. "I brought this just for you." He tossed the paper onto Granby's place setting. He could see indecision flicker briefly in the dragon's eyes. It was something of a risk to take the knife from Jeremy's throat since it was the primary leverage that was keeping the damned man uninjured at the moment. But they were all currently at a stalemate. From the corner of his eye Quince saw his mother drawing closer, a silver candlestick clutched in her hands. The last thing he needed was for the dragon to have two of his family at his mercy. He heard a thump and crunch behind him, and then saw another poker extended toward the baron.

"You had best heed the duke's advice," Sabre said. "it were left for me to decide, you would already be dead."

The dragon sneered. "A weak boy and a woman? I don't find myself intimidated."

Quince arched a brow. "Would you prefer that I call in the Home Office agents that are outside? You don't believe I left my mother unprotected after your threats, do you?"

The dragon looked up and Quince could tell that the man was measuring him, calculating how possible it was that agents were outside. And whether Quince was capable of killing him outright if the situation were pushed any further.

Sabre chimed in, almost gloating. "As it was in service to a duke I'm sure Robert sent some of his best men."

"Jeremy," the baron said sharply, "pick up that paper so that I may read it."

Jeremy nodded slightly. He had to lean forward to pick up the paper, making the dragon loosen his grip for a moment. The duchess took that opportunity to strike, bringing the heavy silver candlestick down on the back of his head. Quince jabbed the poker into the dragon's chest, pushing him backward while Jeremy managed to twist away. Quince followed through, continuing to drive the man before him by force alone as he stepped off the table, and slammed the baron into the wall, rending a sharp exclamation of pain from the man. The dragon raised the hand with a knife in it and Quince knocked it from him with the poker as though it had been a stick held by a child, hearing the snap of bone from the strike, then settled the cold, pointed iron under the baron's throat.

Sabre jumped down from the table to herd Jeremy and the duchess behind herself. She still held up the iron poker, even though it seemed Quince had the dragon in hand. She scanned the room again looking for anyone who seemed inclined to help the baron. It was hard for her to believe that he would travel without some sort of reinforcements, but she had yet to see any of the guests or servants lift so much as a finger to aid the man.

Quince spoke again, his voice cold and sharp as a sword. "Have you decided yet? Will it be death now, death by hanging, or a quiet life somewhere that I will never hear of?"

The dragon's eyes blazed with rage. Sabre recognized that, even through his fury, the baron was still calculating. Quince had obviously surprised the dragon with both his strength of purpose and skill. The duke's righteousness was something to behold. But that would only be a minor consideration in whatever tactic the dragon chose next.

Sabre heard a commotion from the front hallway and edged herself in that direction, just in case the dragon's men were finally riding to his rescue. Then she heard a voice rise in irritation.

"I don't bloody care if the Prince himself is in there. Let me pass before I throw you out of the way."

Sabre almost laughed. Gideon. Of course. Apparently receiving a packet of papers had sent the earl into action again.

Quince pressed the poker more firmly into the baron's throat. "You may want to decide soon. My friend is even less forgiving than I am. And remember, if I allow you to live it is under the condition of not bothering any of us ever again. No threats, no revenge. Just the opportunity to live your life somewhere else."

The dragon nodded. Not cowed, precisely, but recognizing his lack of options.

Quince took a step back, keeping the poker leveled at the dragon, and nodded to the window. "I suggest you leave that way before the earl arrives. And find the nearest ship. If we can find you we will rescind our offer."

The dragon managed to open the window one-handed and fled before Gideon, Robert, and Charlie surged into the room.

Forty-Four

June 1815, London

Sabre had argued that a short engagement was best and her fiancé didn't seem inclined to argue. Thus within a few short weeks she was donning her wedding dress, trying not to succumb to butterflies. Robert had granted the use of his bedroom to the bridal party so she would have more room to prepare. Jack was helping her straighten the fabric and smooth down the skirts.

"Let me give you this while your mothers are out of the room," her friend said, pulling a small book from her reticule. It gave Sabre pause to think that she had two mothers now. More intimidating was the fact that they seemed to like each other, leaving her with the impression that there might be cases of two against one in her future.

"What is it?"

"It's your 'something borrowed.' I had to return to Kellington to fetch it. You must promise me that you won't leave it out where someone could take it."

Sabre furrowed her brow and gave her friend a skeptical look. "What on earth is it?"

"Take a quick peek."

She flipped the miniature book open and its purpose was immediately obvious, filled with lewd illustrations. "Oh my!"

Jack waved her hands. "Now put it away before someone sees it."

A third voice joined their conversation. "Even a fellow Haberdasher?"

Sabre turned to find George standing in the doorway. Their friend was just between their own heights, slender to the edge of gaunt, with pale skin and light hair. Sabre was so surprised to see her that she squealed louder than when she had been a child. They all rushed forward and met in the middle of the room, embracing.

Sabre could feel tears squeezing from the corners of her eyes. "Oh, George! I knew you wouldn't disappoint me by missing my wedding!"

"Well, at least you planned one, short a timeframe as it might have been. Unlike our Jackie."

Jack sniffed. "There were extenuating circumstances."

George chuckled. "Yes. I see what comes of my leaving either of you alone."

Sabre heard her mother's voice. "Sabrina is everything-? Oh, George! You're here at last. No wonder I heard shrieking."

As George turned to greet Viscountess Bittlesworth and Duchess Telford, Sabre tucked the little book down in her bodice.

"Good thinking," Jack whispered. "He'll enjoy finding it later."

Sabre turned incredulous eyes on her friend and said in a fierce whisper. "You are so naughty! I never would have expected it."

Jack arched an eyebrow. "Let us remember who married Lord Lucifer."

"Hush!" Sabrina admonished.

The ladies took to rearranging their bouquets so that George would have flowers to carry as an attendant. Sabre thought now that she had her best friends and was marrying the duke, *everything* was perfect.

Quince would have sworn that his cravat had shrunk since he dressed this morning.

"Stop pacing."

The earl's impatient voice pulled him up short. Both Gideon and Jeremy attended him, but currently they were seated on the wooden straight-backed chairs that lined the wall in the vestry.

"What has you worried, Quince?" the earl asked.

"I'm not worried."

Gideon looked over at Jeremy as though for the young man's support.

"You appear worried," Jeremy confirmed.

"Well, weren't you anxious at your wedding?" Quince accused the earl.

Gideon shrugged. "Of course. I hardly knew Jacqueline and you know I'm not one to back out of my commitments. Marriage, eternity with someone I didn't know, was quite intimidating. You, however, know Sabre quite well. I assume you're entering into this rather well informed."

Quince knew, oddly enough, what he really wanted was Sabre. That she would know the right thing to say to keep his anxiety from overtaking him. He wasn't even entirely sure why he *was* so anxious.

"Perhaps today is a bad day to do this," he heard himself saying.

The earl raised a brow. "My job is quite clear, and that is to make sure you are at the altar at the appointed hour. If I have to knock you out to do it, you know I will."

Quince huffed out a breath.

Gideon stood and addressed Jeremy. "Make sure he stays here. I shall return."

After Gideon left Jeremy said, "He won't be gone long, so what is our plan?"

"What?"

"Obviously as your brother my first duty is to you, and you want to leave. I'm thinking perhaps you should don the vicar's robes and escape out the back. If anyone tries to stop you, simply bless them and run on."

Quince grinned. "I had no idea you had a sense of humor."

"You doubt my seriousness?" the marquess asked with a moderately unsettled expression.

The duke paused. Perhaps what he had interpreted as a formerly unnoticed dry wit was actually dullness. Perhaps Jeremy not only had their father's face but more of his personality than Quince had realized as well.

Then Jeremy's lips twitched and he was shortly reduced to helpless laughter. "You should have seen your face."

Quince lightheartedly chucked his brother on the back of the head. "Unruly brat."

Jeremy smoothed his hair back in place, still laughing a bit. "Like I want the earl to hunt me down and thrash me."

The door opened again and Gideon stepped back inside with a bottle and three glasses.

Quince groaned. "Must you act like alcohol solves everything?"

"I'm pragmatic. If it didn't work, I wouldn't do it."

Jeremy jumped up to hold glasses for the earl as he poured.

"Just a bit of wine," Gideon said. "It will help to settle you."

"Good Lord, this is the sacramental wine, isn't it?"

"The vicar was quite happy to part with it for a generous donation."

"You may be going to hell," Quince said, "you know that, don't you?"

"With a name like Lord Lucifer? One suspects. But maybe not if I drink enough sacramental wine." Gideon winked.

"Lord Lucifer?" Jeremy asked.

"Robert likes to nickname his friends," Gideon said. "Which reminds me," he turned to Quince, "while I was out there I suggested to the Bittlesworth brothers that they might need to be on the lookout for a runaway groom."

Quince scowled. "I wouldn't jilt Sabre."

"As I mentioned, you made it my job to ensure that is true. So I have ensured it. Take another drink."

Quince sipped some more of the overly sweet wine. After a few minutes he had to admit that his nerves had calmed a bit.

Gideon pulled out his pocket watch. "It's almost time, if you're ready?"

Quince handed back the wineglass and nodded.

Gideon gave the glasses and bottle to Jeremy. "If you could find the vicar and return these? I want a word with the duke."

The young man nodded, finishing the dregs of wine so he could more easily hold all the glasses without spilling. Once the door closed, Gideon turned to Quince and put his hands on the duke's shoulders.

"You can do this?" the earl asked.

Quince nodded. "I just... You know social occasions make me nervous. And it's my wedding. And what if Sabre changes her mind?"

Gideon chuckled. "Do you seriously believe that could happen?"

"She left me before," Quince pointed out.

"She left so that she wouldn't throttle you for being an idiot. Trust me, she has my sympathies." Gideon sighed. "But I will never forgive myself for not finding out what was bothering you the day of the duel, since it turned out to be blackmail by one of the darkest souls in England. What is bothering you now? Do you have cold feet or is it something more?"

"Just cold feet, I think. But this means that you'll be even more intrusive than usual, doesn't it?"

"Perhaps a bit, although I trust Sabre to keep an eye on you." Gideon's expression became grave. "And trying to help you only repays you in some small way for all the times you fished me out of the gutter so that I could wake up in my own bed."

"What are friends for?" Quince asked.

"Indeed. To the altar, then?"

Quince nodded. "I'm ready."

Jack was able to enjoy Sabre's wedding in a way she hadn't her own. Her friends had chosen a small church outside London and the guest list had been held to less than a hundred. Leagues more attendees than her own wedding, but small for a typical ducal affair. When Sabre entered, beautiful in the white and celestial blue gown she had chosen, Jack had glanced at Quince. The love shining on both of their faces was clear to see.

The entire affair was lovely and Sabre had been surprisingly quiet and sweet. Jack honestly hadn't known her friend had it in her. But it was clear that Quince brought out a tender and loving side that no one else ever had before. That could only be to the good, Jack thought.

Time flew as vows were exchanged and then the exuberant chords of the recessional filled the nave. Once they were in the vestibule, Jack heard a gasp and bump behind her. Turning, she saw George on the ground, petals and flowers scattered around her, her arm clutched to her stomach. Jack dropped her own bouquet and crouched by her friend.

"Georgie? What's wrong?"

George had grown alarmingly pale. "I think I'm going to faint. Get Robert."

Jack looked up at Sabre and the other Haberdasher shook her head in confusion.

Gideon knelt to pick up George. She gasped and held her ribs more tightly. At the change in angle Jack could see blood between George's fingers.

Jack turned to the wedding couple. "Why don't you two head to the wedding breakfast and we'll take care of George."

Sabre stepped forward, "But…"

Jack waved her off. "Don't be silly. It's probably just some sort of cramps. We'll join you when George is feeling better." Jack turned to Quince's brother. "Jeremy, why don't you make sure that the happy couple is settled at the breakfast while we let George rest for a minute?"

Sabre frowned but Jeremy nodded and did a credible job herding the Telfords out the door to the waiting coach. The door to the nave opened again and guests began pouring out. Gideon backed into an alcove of the vestibule, still holding

George in his arms. George grabbed Jack's hand in a shockingly firm grasp.

"Get Robert," her friend commanded. "I need to talk to him. Now."

Jack looked up at her husband. "Stay here. I'll be right back."

She threaded her way through the attendees, politely shaking off those who wanted to express their happiness for the couple. She spied the Bittlesworth brothers standing against one of the walls of the nave, laughing amongst themselves. Not just Robert and Charlie, but Justin as well.

"Robert," she said, pushing her way past the guests who had been leaving. He looked over to her, his expression becoming concerned.

"What's wrong, Jack?"

"It's George. She's hurt and calling for you."

He tensed immediately. "Where is she?"

"Gideon has her out in the vestibule. We need to find somewhere for her to lie down. She's…"

"She's what?"

"She's bleeding and I don't know why."

Robert made a beeline for the doors, slipping through the jostling crowd. Jack and the other Bittlesworth brothers followed in his wake. He located Gideon in the alcove and moved George's hands to inspect her side.

"What have you done, sweeting?" he asked. "I see blood but this fabric isn't rent. When did you get this wound?"

"This morning," George said, sounding frustrated. "I thought it was bound properly, but…" She waved her hand at the offending blood.

"I'll take her," Robert said to Gideon. Jack saw her husband look at to her with a raised eyebrow and had to nod. If George wanted Robert then she didn't have any compelling reason to say no. Gideon gently transferred George's weight into Robert's arms.

"Charlie," Robert said. "Get my carriage. You two," he said, addressing the Harringtons, "and Justin should go to the breakfast and keep Quince and Sabre from noticing so many of us absent." He looked down on George, his expression softening a bit. "She'll be fine. She's tougher than she looks."

It was difficult to leave George in Robert's care, but Jack let Gideon and Justin lead her out to the waiting carriages.

Sabre hugged Jack as soon as she saw her. "Where's George?"

"She resting."

"I've saved places at the table for each of you. Justin!" She hugged her little half-brother. Sabre thought that if she were any more full of good cheer that she might explode from it. She even hugged Gideon. "Quince is over there talking to some lords. I'm sure he would appreciate it if you saved him."

Gideon bowed to her. "Yes, your grace."

Sabre giggled and wrapped her arm around Jack's. "I find that I like your husband better and better."

Jack quirked an eyebrow at her. "How much wine have you had to drink?"

"Champagne. Provided by your husband, I'll have you know. And just a bit?" She held up two fingers barely separated to indicate the teeny tiny bit. Although, perhaps, it was quite a bit more than that.

Jack kissed her temple. "You are a beautiful bride, Sabre."

"Am I?"

"Yes, your grace."

Sabre giggled again. "I've done a terrible thing."

"What's that?"

"I only call Quince 'your grace' when I want to point out what an idiot he's being."

Jack chuckled. "You've ruined your own honorary title."

"I'm afraid so. Did you see Quince at the church?" She sighed happily. "He's so handsome."

"Yes, and right now he's taking on the duty of circulating to the guests by himself."

"I've already done that once, but perhaps a few new people have arrived." Sabre looked around and saw her brother. "Oh! Charlie!"

When she rushed toward him he picked her up and spun her in a hug. With the champagne her head was truly spinning by the time he set her down. "How is my beautiful little bird?"

"Dizzy! Lud, Charlie!"

He laughed. "Silly girl."

"Silly duchess," she corrected. "Where is Robert? I want to rub in the fact that I outrank him now."

He laughed and put his arm around her shoulders. "He'll be here soon, no doubt."

She frowned. "Is he with George? She was calling for him."

Charlie paused for a moment and then said, "Yes, he is. She wasn't feeling well."

"Are they... are they forming a *tendre?*"

Charlie laughed. "I have no idea. But I wouldn't have thought so. At least, not before today."

Sabre nodded. "Exactly. But, I suppose it's possible."

"Does that not meet with your approval, your grace?"

She poked him in the ribs. "You manage to say my honorary with even less respect than I do. But it is not for me to approve or disapprove. George will certainly do as she likes, regardless of my opinion."

"True enough. Don't look now, but I think a man is coming over here to bother you. If you like you can hide behind me. I'll swear I haven't seen you."

Sabre looked up to see that the man approaching them was Quince. She happily stepped forward into his embrace.

"Hullo, love," he murmured into her hair. "I missed you."

She giggled. "I was only across the room."

"Too far away, I assure you." He kissed her briefly on the lips.

"You are scandalous, sir!" she admonished.

"You have no idea what I might be capable of. Shall we sit down to eat? It seems most of the guests are here now."

"Yes, although I was hoping George would be here." Sabre frowned. "Terrible of her to show up for an hour and then disappear."

"I'm sure she'll be along."

George did appear within a quarter hour of the breakfast being served. She sat down in her assigned place a bit delicately. Sabre leaned out to look past Jack and Gideon to her. "Are you feeling better?"

George nodded, a bit pale but seeming in good spirits. Sabre still sensed something amiss, despite her friend's assurances. Something in George's posture, in her eyes. Whatever it was, she would soon worm out the answer. She'd always been able to get to the bottom of things. She always, as she had proved again today, gained what she wanted.

Sabre smiled up at her husband. "Now," she said, "everything is perfect."

Author's Note

Thanks for reading the second book in the Haberdashers series! Don't miss the first glimpse at the third book after this note. *Fates for Apate: Haberdashers Book Three* is about George meeting Casimir. You have no idea who Casimir is, you say? Well, you have to figure that George was off doing *something* while her Haberdasher sisters were busy getting married.

I'm a bit of history nerd, even though I insist that this sort of book is history *fantasy* and plenty of it is just made up. But when I can look up a bit of history to include it gives me a special thrill. What's entertaining to me is that the pieces of history Quince and Sabre wanted to look at were completely different than Jack and Gideon's interests. Remember all that political historical context? Not so much for these guys.

One of the first things that Sabre wanted to know was some place to eat. And I thought it would be neat if I could identify places that she could eat then and we could eat now. Fortunately, in 1815 there was the *Epicure's Almanac* (the first comprehensive list of London eateries) and in 2012 *The Guardian* identified places that were still open. Believe it or not. (I always was a lucky duck)

Check it out at http://www.theguardian.com/travel/2012/aug/20/london-historic-food-drink-bars So we (that means Sabre, Jack, and myself) selected the "George and Vulture" and "Twinings" to feature in the story. Since I've never been to either place, especially in 1815, all details are completely made up. If you go to the G&V looking for a private room they may not have one. But I certainly think it would be fun to look. Report back to me (@cmdrsue) if you find out!

Quince, on the other hand, made sure that I was much clearer on the art and poetry of the day. Although it doesn't figure strongly in the plot I can assure you that he educated me on Romanticism. I think that he most likely exchanged letters with Keats, procured the 1814 copy of Shelley's *Queen Mab*, and collected Friedrich from the beginning. With his love of poetry you can rest assured that he hates, *hates* his reading disability. (He doesn't like to talk about it so I'm not even clear on exactly what the problem is yet. I assume at some point he will tell me.) He also bears a striking resemblance to the Romantic artist Turner, a fact I discovered shortly before this book went to press. It's a little odd to stumble across an almost exact portrait of how you envisioned your character. You can see it at http://en.wikipedia.org/wiki/File:Turner_selfportrait.jpg

They both, of course, had me read about fencing until my eyeballs were ready to fall out. They are concerned that I still don't get it. And it turned out that they had a shared affection for theatre, especially Shakespeare. We'll just say they kept me on my toes.

Oh! And if you love perfumes, you can frequent Floris London, just like Sabre. It's been a perfumery since 1790. Still family managed and you can get a customized fragrance for a terribly reasonable price. They are online at http://www.florislondon.com

Thanks for reading!

About the Author

S ue London began writing short stories about horses and teen sleuths when she was seven years old. After that she traveled to distant worlds, fought with swords and sorcerers, and played with a few undead things. As you might have expected, this means she went into accountancy. Well, maybe that was an odd plot twist, but "that's the difference between real life and fiction – fiction has to make sense."

In her twenties she developed a deep affection for romance, especially enjoying the works of Nora Roberts, Mary Balogh and, most recently, Rose Gordon, Courtney Milan, Lauren Royal, Danelle Harmon, and Diane Farr. You can thank those authors for leading a sci-fi tomboy into writing historical romances set in the Regency period.

Keep up with Sue and the Haberdashers on these websites:
Haberdashers on Twitter: http://twitter.com/haberdashersfic
Haberdashers website: http://haberdashersfic.blogspot.com
Haberdashers Club (email list): http://eepurl.com/Bicsb
Sue on Amazon: http://amazon.com/author/bysuelondon
Sue on Goodreads: http://www.goodreads.com/CmdrSue
Sue on Twitter: http://twitter.com/cmdrsue

For more on Sue you can check out her Sueniverse or be her fan on Facebook. You can also catch up on all her interviews at http://bysuelondon.blogspot.com/p/interviews.html.

If you would like to report issues in this version of *Athena's Ordeal*, or in any books from Graythorn Publishing, please drop us a line at publishing@graythorn.com.

Fates for Apate
(Haberdasher's
Book Three)

"Good greeting, lady of wily mind and wily snares! Not Hermes Hoax-the-wits himself can outdo you..." ~ Hera to Apate

"Everyone sees what you appear to be, few experience what you really are." ~ Niccolò Machiavelli

"Honor is purchased by the deeds we do." ~ Christopher Marlowe

One

*G*eorgiana Lockhart sat quietly, her hands folded primly in her lap. She didn't know why Robert had summoned her to his office but hoped it was because he finally, finally was going to give her a real assignment. The hope of that sang in her blood. Whispered its promises in her ear. But outwardly she remained calm. Ladylike. Not that there was anyone in the office to see how she was behaving. Robert's clerk had shown her in, saying that Robert would be there shortly. But almost a quarter hour had passed and there was no sign of him. She had already looked at all the items on his shelves and walls to confirm for herself that nothing had changed. She was tempted to go through the drawers in his desk, but couldn't come up with a plausible excuse for why she might have been doing so if caught. Just as she was considering giving into the temptation, she heard the door open behind her.

"Good morning, George," Robert said, passing by her and moving around to sit behind his desk.

"Good morning, Robert."

"All of your training reports have been excellent. You have received nothing but praise from your mentors."

George hid her smile. "Thank you, sir."

"What remains for me now is to find something to challenge you."

She remained perfectly still, maintaining a neutral, pleasant expression. Robert stared at her long past discomfort, but she knew that long silences didn't bother Robert in the least. He often used them as a simple way to make others squirm.

George refused to squirm.

After some minutes had ticked by Robert laughed and sat back in his chair. "You've grown up, haven't you, Georgie?"

"I like to think so."

He tapped his finger against his lower lip. "Do you think you're ready for another visit to your Aunt Martha in Scotland?"

At last there was something to smile about. "I adore Aunt Martha."

Robert had invented her rich, controlling aunt as a way to give her time for some of her more intense training. Dear Aunt Martha held the promise of inheritance over the heads of the Lockhart family but required that only her eldest niece attended her. In her overbearing way, rich Aunt Martha would send a carriage with maids to whisk George away. It said something of George's parents that they acquiesced without complaint, provided that a packet of funds was included in the exchange.

Stay tuned for the full first chapter to be posted at http://haberdashersfic.blogspot.com/ in Fall 2013! Or pre-order on Amazon.com.

Made in the USA
Las Vegas, NV
24 June 2021

25393334R00204